# WHAT MIGHT HAVE BEEN

Sharon Francis

ISBN: 978-1-8381173-4-4

Cover design by: Megan Saunders

# CHAPTER ONE

When the object struck Lily straight between the eyes, there was no time for her entire life to flash before her. All she managed to review were the last few hours, but in essence that pretty much summed up the whole thirty-six years anyway.

That morning, she'd left for work with a packed lunch tucked in her handbag. Adam had been walking down his own path at number eight, which meant she saw him before he could see her, and in that brief interlude she had straightened her skirt, tucked her mid-length brown hair behind her ears and pulled in her stomach, ready to pretend she hadn't seen him at all, when their paths inevitably crossed.

'Morning, Lily.'

She spun round as if he had been the last thing on her mind, whereas, in fact, he occupied much of her waking hours and quite a portion of her sleep time too. 'Oh, Adam. Hi. How are you?'

'All the better for seeing you.'

His words brought a tantalising prickle to her skin, but she pretended to ignore his comment, as if it was the sort of thing she heard every day.

'Still have your nose to the grindstone then?' He fell into step beside her. 'I thought most of the country had the day off today.'

'No. Service as usual at the library since it's only New Year's Eve, I'm afraid.' She didn't want to come across as a whinger. 'Day off tomorrow, of course.'

He laughed. 'To nurse the hangover?'

'Me? No. It'll be a quiet night in, watching it all happen on the TV.'

'What? I had you down as a party girl.'

Partying had never been one of her vices and, at her age, she didn't really consider she qualified for "girl" status either. She simply laughed and dared a quick pat to one of his alluring biceps with her woolly gloved hand. 'Oh, Adam. You are funny.'

'I'm going around to…'

The door was thrown open at number seventeen as the pair drew level, as if whoever was inside was in a hurry to get out. The woman almost sprinted down the path to the gate, in time to intercept Adam and Lily. She was scantily clad, in feather-adorned mule slippers and a revealing satin dressing gown, loosely tied around the middle, and she made as if to drop a rubbish bag on the pavement but pulled up short and adjusted her hair when she reached Adam's side. Flirty Flick, Lily's least favourite neighbour.

'Oh, Adam. Fancy seeing you here. Don't mind me.' She straightened her robe, drawing attention to it. 'Are you going to the party tonight?'

Adam was taken aback by the abrupt interruption. 'Oh. Hi, Felicity. Yes, I think so. I was just telling Lily about it.'

Felicity tilted around him. 'Oh, morning, Lily. Didn't see you there.' She tightened the tie at her waist, only to emphasise her cleavage further. 'Anyway, I should get back inside before the whole neighbourhood sees me in my frillies. Hope to see you later, Adam.' Leaning around to include Lily. 'And you, Lily, of course.' With that, she disappeared as hastily as she arrived, inexplicably taking the bag of rubbish back inside with her.

Lily and Adam stared after her for a few moments as the air of calm returned.

'As I was about to say before…' He nodded towards Felicity's house, and briefly raised his eyebrows before walking on. 'I know it's short notice, but I don't suppose you fancy spending the evening with me? I'm going along to the annual shindig at number twelve. It's nothing fancy, a few nibbles, bring a bottle, fireworks at midnight, but it's usually a good laugh. You've probably seen about it on social media.'

'I don't do social media,' she replied absent-mindedly.

This was exactly what she'd been dreaming of for months. It had finally happened. Yes, she would love to spend an evening with him, any evening, let alone one of such significance, but… There was always a "but". Her mind went into overdrive. What if it led to something? What if she was to really, truly fall in love with him? Not the current schoolgirl crush, worship from a distance, fantasising in the bath surrounded by candles and sipping red wine scenario, but proper core deep love. Could she cope when he let her down? Was she strong enough? On second thoughts, perhaps she was reading this wrong. How arrogant was she? Only minutes ago, she had been telling him she would be spending the evening alone, New Year's Eve, alone. Perhaps he had only asked because he felt sorry for her. Well, she was nobody's good deed for the day. She didn't want anybody's pity.

'Listen. Sorry. I didn't mean to make you feel awkward or anything.'

He must have seen the conflicting emotions flicker across her face and made his own interpretation. She was quick to reassure. 'No, it's not that, honestly. No awkwardness at all. I was just working out in my head if I could make it work. What time I'll be home, things I have to get done, that sort of thing. It's not that I don't want to come.'

The radiance of his face had definitely dimmed. 'Well, listen. I'll be going about nine thirty. If you feel like it, come round. If not, that's fine. No biggie.'

It appeared he was disappointed, but her anxieties still hadn't been quelled sufficiently to give an instant agreement. 'Ok. I'll see what I can do.'

His car was parked by the curb, whereas Lily had to continue to the underground station at the end of the road. The car gave a double bleep as he operated the fob. She desperately wanted to reassure him further of there being no bad feelings. 'Thanks again, Adam. Maybe see you later.'

He smiled and held up a hand, then climbed into the driver's seat.

As she walked away, she squeezed her eyes tightly together, silently swearing under her breath, livid with herself. Why had she not said yes? Why, when her dream had been there for the taking, had she not grabbed it with both hands? She was a fool to herself. Nothing new there.

All day at work she had repeated the same internal debate. One minute she was going to the party, of course she was, why wouldn't she? The next minute, there was no way she could go through with it. She wished she wasn't always like this, but it had been the way with her for as long as she could remember and, as usual, having created a completely unnecessary, but nonetheless vicious, inner conflict, the day went completely to pot. Her concentration was off, and she managed to misdirect customers, misfile documents and on numerous occasions found herself in one room or other with no idea what she was there for. She generally enjoyed her work, the quiet, the calm, the routine, but by the time the library closed at six thirty, and she was finally free to escape, it was a welcome release.

The streets and the tube were busy, commuters rubbing shoulders with revellers in costume, already half-cut, and the atmosphere fuelled her optimism to the point she almost felt ready to take a chance on Adam's invitation, to become part of the celebration. She fantasised about knocking on his door, his face when he opened it, his pleasant surprise. Perhaps he would even greet her with a kiss on the cheek before asking her in. They would spend a fantastic evening together and then, who knew?

Exiting onto her street though, every step seemed to knock her flatter. A group of drunk young men elbowing past into the station battered her reserve, and a huddle of teenage girls, waiting at the bus stop, all bare legs and exposed midriffs, while she hugged her voluminous overcoat tighter, knocked her further. They made her feel old and invisible and the fizz of building excitement in her tummy transformed into a familiar dull ache of tension. As she passed Adam's gate, she put her head down and marched on, hoping desperately for the first time ever not to bump into him.

When she slammed the front door against the elements, the argument struck up again and she simply couldn't settle. She got as far as donning her best dress, make-up applied and one hand on the door handle, but, even as she jangled keys into a sparkly clutch bag, her resolve was failing fast. She held the door open and Tabitha, her cat, appeared from the front yard, rubbing against Lily's legs, as if she hadn't seen her in days, tail pointing to the sky.

'Come on, Tabs. Where have you been?' Lily re-latched the door and sidestepped her pet into the kitchen. 'You must be a block of ice out in that cold.'

All the cat was interested in was the dish of tuna in her allocated corner, but Lily didn't mind that. It might be cupboard love, but at least it was reliable.

'You ought to stay in tonight. There's going to be fireworks, you know.'

Tabitha ignored her.

'You know what happened last year. Goodness knows where you'll end up if you get spooked again. Mr Ahmed has moved and taken your favourite shed with him.'

Lily remembered how fraught she had been for the short time her four-legged friend had been missing. 'Perhaps I should stay in with you. Keep you company.' Even as she said it, she knew she was manufacturing an excuse not to go out.

The cat brushed past into the lounge, suggesting she would be agreeable to attention, hopped onto the sofa and stared through narrow, come-to-bed eyes.

What should she do? Face her fears and run round to Adam's sharpish, before he went without her, or curl up in front of a chick flick with a hot chocolate, feeling sorry for herself? She checked her watch. It was highly possible Adam had left already. Lily looked from the cat to the door and back again, then, with a sigh, kicked off her heels. Home was where the heart was, and when all was said and done, nothing good would have come of her getting fancy ideas about Adam and parties and romance. It never had, and it never would. Her own stupid neurosis would see to that and there didn't appear to be a thing she could do about it. Heaven knows, she'd spent a lifetime trying.

A few minutes before midnight, Lily came to on the sofa to find the film had ended and her disloyal moggy was escaping through the cat flap, which was supposed to have been locked. The screen showed scenes of crowds, celebrating the end of one year and onset of another, laughing and waving, kissing and cuddling, and she felt completely alone. There was no one for her to embrace as the clock struck twelve.

'Where's that stupid cat going?'

She unlatched the door and stepped into the garden, in time to see Tabitha tearing over the fence. Lily stopped at the gate and tutted. She wasn't going chasing round at this hour.

At that moment, fireworks began further down the road, loud bangs accompanied by appreciative shouts, but at such an angle she didn't get the benefit of seeing the lights. That must be number twelve. Where she could have been.

The young family next door was busy in their own garden, the mother trying to herd their excited children in the covered porch, as the father lit a magic fountain, as far away from the house as he could manage. Lily smiled at the wows emitted by the kids.

The party down the road was loud. It sounded like they were having fun. She wondered if Adam was still there, if he had found someone to keep him company, as she had let him down, or if, heaven forbid, Flirty Flick had got her claws into him.

'More, Daddy. More.'

The boy next door jumped up and down, clapping his hands in delight. The dad was busy fiddling with something at the fence.

Lily gripped the gatepost, absorbing the happy sounds, the flashes of coloured lights coming and going on the skyline, the acrid smell of smoke on the frosty air, and breathed deeply. She wondered if this brand-new year could possibly bring anything good for her. Please. It was long overdue.

Turning to go back into the house, a flash of orange caught her attention as she faced the garden next door, and she saw a lit Catherine wheel, which the father must have been attaching to the post, spinning at lightning speed. One minute it was whirling and jerking in a hypnotising dance, the next it was flying through the air, directly at her. There was no time to move out of the way, no time to shout even, as its trajectory sent it straight at the centre of her forehead. She felt her mouth form a surprised "oh", immediately before the missile hit, and then nothing, not even a bump, as she slumped to the floor.

# CHAPTER TWO

'She's here. It's alright, I've got her.'

Lily was curled in a foetal position around a mop and bucket at the bottom of a storage cupboard.

'Oh, my Lord! I thought I'd seen everything.'

The Texan drawl woke her from a deep sleep.

'Here, come along out of there.'

An arm was hooked under her shoulders, and she gradually came upright, legs either side of the pail, feet hanging out on to the tiled floor of a room, laid out as a small kitchen and dining area. She had the most bizarre feeling, like she'd been through a fast spin in a washing machine. A woman in a smart uniform was crouched down, holding both hands to keep her vertical, which was quite a task as Lily's vision seemed incapable of staying steady and her body strained to follow its path.

'Lily Armitage, what in the Sam Hill are you doing in there?'

Lily wished she knew, but her mind was a blank. 'I… I don't know.'

'Well, may I suggest you let go of your new friend here.' The woman dragged the cleaning utensils out of Lily's way with one hand, still holding on to her with the other. 'Then perhaps we can get some leverage…'

The woman grunted with the effort, but there was no movement. 'Lily, honey, do you think you can stand?'

'I'm not sure. Do I have any legs?'

'That's a no then.' She leaned back towards a door behind her, in the far corner of the room. 'Blessing? Blessing, can you come in here for a moment?'

As they waited, Lily's vision began to clear, and she blinked at the stranger still holding onto her hands. 'Do I know you?' Then, before the woman could answer, 'I don't think I know you.'

'No, my dear. I know who you are, but this is the first time we've met. I'm Grace, by the way, and with a little help I'll endeavour to get you out of your current predicament and explain what's going on. You'll feel a lot more like yourself when you're not in a closet.'

Lily smiled. 'My granny was called Grace. She was lovely.' Her thought processes were fractured. 'But you have nicer hair.'

'Why, thank you, I think.' Under her breath. 'Where is she?' Another figure appeared in the doorway. 'Oh, here, Blessing, grab yourself an end, will you?'

Together, the pair manhandled Lily into the room and onto a plastic chair, then stood back, satisfied the arms would at least prevent her falling out the sides.

'How in the world did she end up in the staff room cupboard?' Blessing was a large, black woman, wearing a suit that matched Grace's in design, if not in style. Her clipped cockney accent, however, was a complete contrast.

'I wouldn't even like to hazard a guess, and I don't think Lily knows either. Anyhoo, it's time we got this moving along.' Grace turned to a nearby table and poured a glass of water from a jug. 'Here.' She handed the tall glass to Lily. 'Drink this down, young lady. It'll do you the power of good.'

Lily was too dazed to argue and accepted the refreshment. As soon as she began to drink, an enormous thirst came over her, and she downed the entire contents without stopping, the cold liquid gradually reviving her, then reached out to clunk the empty vessel back on the table. 'Thank you. I needed that.'

'Good girl. We'll soon have you back in the land of the living, where you belong.'

Lily laughed a small laugh, which ended abruptly as the words came into focus, a deep frown replacing her smile. 'Isn't that where I am now?'

'You're not anywhere right now.'

Lily chewed on a thumb nail, unable to piece her thoughts together.

In spite of her bulk, Blessing knelt in front of Lily, so they were at the same level. 'Lily.' She smiled, as she waited patiently for Lily to make eye contact. 'What's your last memory, babe? Do you remember anything at all?'

Lily squeezed her eyes together in concentration. 'My name is Lily Armitage and I live at five Laburnum Terrace, and I work at the library.' She perked up, proud to be able to supply the information. 'Oh, and I might be thirty-six.'

Blessing's smile widened. 'Well done. Now then, there's good news and bad news and I'm going to start with the bad, so you've got something to look forward to. Alright?'

Lily nodded.

'Right. Well. It turns out you were standing on your front lawn watching the world go by on New Year's Eve and got zapped between the eyes with a Catherine Wheel.'

The words jogged Lily's memory and her hand flew to a spot on her forehead, her eyes wide. 'Am I alright? Did it hurt me?'

Blessing's head tipped to one side, and she gave a little shrug. 'You only went and popped your clogs, babe.'

'What?' Lily's horrified expression deepened.

'Yeah, but it's alright. That's the bad news. The good news is you've only temporarily popped your clogs. Right now, you're in Limbo, but in two shakes of a lamb's tail we're going to have you back in your body in Laburnum Terrace and all's well that ends well.'

'I don't understand.' The words made a sort of sense, but the concept didn't. 'Limbo?'

'Yeah, Limbo. The Location and Intervention of Misdirected Beings Office. But that don't matter. All you need to know is we've got the situation under control.' She turned to Grace with a smile. 'It's alright, Grace. I've got this.'

Grace's shoulders jerked back at being so dismissed. 'I see. Well, in that case I'll be moving along.' She tossed her hair and flounced out of the room.

Blessing pulled up another chair and sat facing Lily. 'Between you and me, stuff like this crops up all the time. Little accidents happen and before you know it, poof, the person on the receiving end pops out of their body. It's like, they see it coming and jump before they're pushed, sort of thing.'

'This is so weird.' Lily shook her head in disbelief. 'I've never heard of anything like this before.'

'Course not. When you get back, you won't remember much. It would cause all sorts of problems if people knew all the ins and outs of Limbo. It would give 'em licence to behave like complete nutcases if they thought people like me would dive in to save 'em every time they did something dangerous. No, we're a secret emergency service, always busy on the front line, but never seen.'

'But where are we? Where is Limbo? What is this place?'

Blessing's face worked as she tried to form a response. 'Limbo's everywhere and nowhere. It's an in between place, where people who, for some reason, don't make a smooth transition from the earthly plane to the heavenly one pause. It's our job to help those people along the way in one direction or another. We're just glorified cabin crew really.'

'But how do you know who's going to arrive and where they need to go next?'

'Here, are you after a job?' Blessing laughed and tapped Lily's knee. 'It's a complicated system, babe, but it's easy when you know how. You, for instance. We got an alert to say you were on your way and a message explaining what had happened, and then we do the necessary. Which, in your case, is to send you straight back. Funny thing is, we were waiting for you in Arrivals, but there was no sign of you, so we had to make enquiries. Sure enough, you'd left your body, but for some reason, you ended up in the staff room cupboard instead of the space we'd prepared for you. Goodness knows what that was all about.'

Lily needed clarity. 'I see. So, what you're saying is, I'm going to go back to my body, and it'll be as if this never happened. Nothing will have changed.'

'Nothing much'll have changed. We run on a different timescale here, so although you've been here a little while, nobody there'll even know what's happened yet. You'll have a bump on your head the size of a tangerine, but otherwise normal service will continue.' Blessing pushed herself up from the chair and poured another glass of water. 'Now, my advice is, get this down you. Rapid transitions dry you right out and you'll have a big enough headache from the Catherine Wheel without adding dehydration into the mix.'

She did as she was told, watching as Blessing pulled a small tablet computer from her pocket and tapped at it with a stylus. Lily's functions were slowly returning to normal, her thought processes sharpening. She noticed a tension in her chest, which was probably understandable considering the strange situation she found herself in. But she also noticed that rather than relax at the thought of going back, the tension intensified, her breathing became shorter, shallower, whereas the thought of never going back held a strange appeal.

'I suppose I have to go, do I?'

'Sorry, babe. What was that?' Blessing dragged her gaze from the tiny screen.

Saying the words aloud made Lily realise how strong her feelings were and she repeated them louder, more confidently. 'I said, I suppose I have to go, do I? I don't suppose I could give it a miss?'

Blessing's glossy black curls bounced as her head twisted to one side, her eyes narrowed. 'How d'you mean?'

Lily chewed her cheek before replying. 'Assuming that if it wasn't possible for me to go back to my body, I'd be going to heaven instead, then I think I'd rather do that. I haven't exactly enjoyed my time on earth.' She shook her head at the memory. 'In fact, every single day of my life has been a struggle. The world petrifies me. I wake up scared; I walk down the road scared; most of the time at work I'm scared and even when I go to bed at night I'm scared. I don't want to do it anymore.'

Blessing's brow furrowed. 'Are you having me on?'

'No, I'm not. I'm sorry, but I really don't want to go.'

Blessing opened her mouth wide and yelled. 'Grace. Can you come in here, please?'

Within seconds, Grace's figure appeared in the doorway. Her tone was self-satisfied, her smile smug. 'Did you need me after all, Blessing, dear?'

'She says she don't want to go.'

Grace took a step forward. 'Run that by me again.'

Blessing was studying Lily's face like an insect under a microscope. 'Lily says she don't want to go.'

'She doesn't want to go?'

'To her body. She don't want to go. Apparently, she'd rather not. Because life is too scary.' Blessing jerked her head to face Grace. 'Can we do that?'

They continued to discuss the matter as if Lily wasn't there. 'I'm darned if I know. Seems to me an issue like this is way above our pay grade.'

'Then what do we do? Why don't you try talking to her?'

'Me?' Grace stepped forward slowly as if she were considering her style of approach, then straightened up, making herself as tall as possible. 'Lily. You listen to me, honey. You are supposed to go back to your body, so I suggest you pull yourself together and do just that.'

'You can't make me.' Lily swung her head from Grace to Blessing. 'She can't, can she?'

'No. I don't think so.' Blessing looked to Grace for confirmation.

Grace looked Lily up and down. 'I reckon between us we could get her strapped in and send her back, but...' She shook her head. 'It sure wouldn't sit easy with me. I'm pretty certain that sort of manhandling would be outside our authority.'

'So, what do we do with her?'

'I don't think we have any choice. I think we've got to refer this up the line.'

Blessing's eyes were wide. 'You mean... upstairs?'

'I mean upstairs.' Grace turned to Lily one last time. 'You're absolutely sure about this?'

Lily gave a tentative nod.

'Then I'd better make the call.' Grace straightened the knotted scarf of her uniform and marched out of the room.

Blessing stayed silent, eyeing Lily like a creature from another planet. Lily bit her lips together, unable to think of anything to say. She realised she was creating havoc, but her whole future was on the line, and she wasn't about to change her mind.

Grace returned within minutes and stood in the doorway, hands on hips. 'Right then, little lady. Let's move this along.'

'He's going to see her, then?' Blessing found her feet first.

Grace nodded and pulled a wheelchair into view. 'He's going to see her.'

'You're taking her up the escalator in that?'

'Nope, he's in the new studio in the east wing.' Grace helped Lily out of one seat and into another with a huff. 'Let's get this nonsense over and done with. I'll see you in a while, Blessing.'

Blessing hovered by the door, wringing her hands. 'See you later, Grace. Good luck, Lily.'

Grace whisked Lily into a broad carpeted hallway, keeping up a rapid pace to the end, where she turned left into a corridor, then stopped outside a set of doors. She rapped on one briskly, and waited for a response.

In the ensuing seconds, Lily felt her tension grow. Who knew what was on the other side? Who knew what she was about to face? What sort of person had the authority to make such a momentous decision about her future?

'Come.'

Grace tipped her head to one side as she met Lily's terrified gaze. 'Here we go.'

She backed through the doors and rotated the wheelchair to face a middle-aged man. He was sitting at one end of an L-shaped, mustard leather sofa, with one ankle rested on his opposite knee, a clipboard in his lap and a pen tucked behind one ear. Jumping to his feet, he held out a hand to Lily.

'You must be Lily Armitage.'

Lily stared at him but didn't move.

Grace tapped her on the shoulder. 'Come along, Lily. This man's here to help you. Say hello to the Spiritual Ombudsman.'

# CHAPTER THREE

Grace made her exit almost immediately, leaving Lily at the mercy of the man with the clipboard.

'I'm going to have a coffee. Would you like one?' He moved to a table at the back of the room, which held a selection of jugs, jars and cups. 'I could probably run to a tea, if that's your poison.'

She studied his every move. She didn't know exactly what she had expected but he certainly wasn't it. He was so... ordinary. There was no officiousness about him. In fact, he seemed quite approachable. Yet, he would be the person who decided her future, or lack of it, as the case may be.

He raised one eyebrow, waiting for a reply.

'Do you have decaf?'

He pulled his chin back in surprise. 'Decaf? Really?'

At her nod, he moved some of the jars around then held one aloft. 'Apparently we do.' He set about making the drink, intermittently glancing at her over his shoulder. 'Could never see the point in the stuff myself. You either want a coffee or you don't, but it takes all sorts, I suppose.'

'Caffeine's not good for you,' she explained. 'It's bad for your blood pressure, stops you sleeping and heightens anxiety, and I have problems with all of those things already without drinking stuff that make them worse.'

He carried the cups around the sofa, handed one to Lily and sat back down in his original seat. 'Ah, well. Each to their own.' Pursing his lips, he referred to notes on his tablet. 'Now then, Lily. You're a bit of an oddity.'

'Am I?' She couldn't decide whether to be offended or not.

'Yes, you are. In all my years, I've never had anyone request *not* to go back to their body. I've had a fair number the other way round, who thought they had unfinished business and weren't ready to move on, but not one who was in a hurry to leave it behind. What's that all about?'

Hugging her mug with both hands, she tried to find words to describe her situation. 'To be honest, it's always been a struggle. I don't know, I suppose I'm just not cut out for life. It's so unpredictable and... threatening, and... exhausting, to be frank. No.' She waved the image away with one hand. 'I can't deal with any more of it.'

The ombudsman pulled the pen from behind his ear and made some notes. 'Unpredictable.' He repeated. 'Threatening, and exhausting, was it?'

She nodded.

'Are we talking specifically about your life? Or life in general?'

'Both, I guess.'

He tapped his lips with one finger, in contemplation. 'Ok, unpredictable I'll grant you. I've observed a lot of humanity and if there's one thing there's no shortage of, it's curve balls, that's for sure.'

Lily was relieved he seemed to be taking her comments seriously.

'Exhausting? Hmm.' The tapping resumed. 'I suppose in certain circumstances it can be: walking five miles every day to the nearest water supply in Mozambique; eighteen-hour shifts, six days a week, in a textile factory in India; herding llamas in all weathers in the Andes. Thirty-eight hours a week in an overstaffed English library, complete with comfort breaks, not so much.'

'Overstaffed?' she interjected. Ok, so it wasn't the most challenging job in the world, but there was always plenty to do.

'Yes, by at least one and a half members of staff. It's not essential to read the blurb on every single book before refiling them, you know, and the fire escape at the rear is a fire escape, not a smoking den.'

She was certainly offended now. 'That's not what…'

'And, threatening? I don't see what you're basing that on. Are we talking violence, domestic abuse, coercive control?'

His response was rather disconcerting. After a promising start, he was completely missing her point. 'No, you're not getting it.'

'Are you bullied at work? Or is it financial? Are you getting scary letters from the bank manager? Afraid you're going to lose everything and end up living on the streets?'

'No, no, no.' Lily shook her head with vigour. 'Nothing like that. It's not that at all. It's not one single thing, it's more an amalgamation of everything. It builds up, you know?'

He narrowed his eyes. 'No, not really. I think you'll have to spell it out for me.'

Lily downed her coffee in one, wincing as the hot liquid burned her throat on the way down. With no alternative resting place, she perched the empty cup on the sofa next to her, freeing her hands to add emphasis to her words. 'Look. I've spent three decades on that planet, and every day was a trial. Every day I had to make decisions. Decisions about all sorts of things. Massive things. Where to study. What to do for a living. Where to live. Who to spend time with. Who not to spend time with. Who to trust. Who not to trust. A constant internal debate about the right thing to do. That's what's exhausting. And, as for threatening, every time I made one of those decisions, it hung over my head like a mallet, just waiting to knock me flat.' She gripped her head in her hands, before throwing them wide. 'I've got to the point I can barely decide whether it's a good idea to get out of bed or not. In fact, some days it takes me all day to even make the decision, by which time it's too late anyway.'

The ombudsman peered at her askance. 'Whether to get out of bed or not is not a big decision.'

'It is to me! And it's generally followed by whether or not I should leave the house, whether or not I should speak to the neighbours, and whether I should take the tube or the bus. It's very wearing. And threatening, as I said before.'

He scribbled a number of notes, pausing at intervals to chew the end of the pen.

She waited for him to finish, an uncomfortable churning in her stomach in anticipation of his verdict, until she could no longer stand the tension. 'Well? What are you thinking? Can I go straight to heaven, or not?'

He removed the pen from his lips, but the frown remained on his brow. 'I see the point you're trying to make. I appreciate there are issues, rather large issues at that. Weighing it up, there are a lot of marks in your favour.'

The huge sense of relief rejuvenated her, and she shot out of the wheelchair to the seat next to him and grabbed his hand. 'Thank you, thank you, thank you.'

Her mind flooded with images of what heaven could be like, how everything would be arranged, how she would never have to worry about anything again, but he slammed on the brakes. 'Don't thank me yet. You put up a good argument, I'll grant you, but there's one important fact which remains.'

'What's that?'

He shrugged. 'You haven't completed the tasks you were put on earth to do, and until you do, I'm afraid you're going nowhere.'

# CHAPTER FOUR

'Tasks? What tasks?' Lily was dumbfounded. 'Nobody told me about any tasks.'

The ombudsman raised an eyebrow. 'Life doesn't come with a manual, you know.' The blatant confusion on Lily's face softened his manner. 'Look, everyone has a role to play. There's a point to each and every human. Nobody's there merely for decoration.'

Lily waited for him to expand. She couldn't for the life of her imagine what tasks she, a simple library assistant, should have completed, which were important enough to prevent her moving on to her rightful slot in the afterlife.

'In fact, the average person has a whole range of jobs they need to do, at various levels of importance, centred around either themselves or others. Of course, individuals rarely realise the impact their actions have on those around them, but something minor to one person, can change the entire life of someone else.'

'Ok, but I've been in work ever since I left school.'

'I'm not talking about paid jobs.' He rested his head on his fingertips for a few moments, then rose to his feet, Lily presumed to aid his concentration.

He paced up and down as he explained. 'When a person is born, they have a plan already laid out for them, a framework. There's a lot of fluidity built in to allow for free will, as you said yourself, every day decisions are taken, which can have a profound effect on that framework, but there are also certain fixed points built in.'

Lily nodded. 'I've never given it a massive amount of thought, but I guess I always assumed not everything could be random. There had to be some sort of order.'

'Right.' He pointed at her as if she had made an important discovery, before continuing to pace. 'Well, although there's a lot of dross, programmed within that framework is a network of interactions and events relating to a higher purpose.'

She frowned. 'You mean like destiny?'

'Very good, you're catching on.'

'But, if those things are programmed in, how could I have not completed them when I should have? Surely I would have had to.'

'It all comes down to the free will element I mentioned. "Wiggle Room" as we call it in the business.' He settled himself back on to the sofa. 'For example, say the fixed event was a man being hit on the head by a flying object.'

Lily rubbed the spot on her forehead where the Catherine Wheel had struck. 'That's a little close to home.'

'Ok. Then let's say a man being flattened by a steam roller instead. The man is a stranger to you, but your actions cause him to be in the right place at the right time. I don't know, perhaps clumsy old you drops your shopping at his feet, and he pauses to help.'

'Charming.'

The ombudsman dismissed her comment with a wave. 'Illustrative purposes. Anyway, the fixed event is him being flattened. That has to happen. You dropping the shopping is merely a means to an end. The thing is, because of free will, a million things could intervene. You could cross over to the other pavement or stop to do a bit of window shopping or purchase a bag with stronger handles, thereby negating your own part in his demise.'

'Right.'

'Now, to ensure the fixed event takes place, a whole network of actions is prepared, involving a huge number of different individuals placed along the man's route, should the need arise, but only a small number of them actually come into effect.' He spread his hands wide, as if his explanation should answer all of her questions.

Lily mulled it over for a few moments. 'So, you're saying, I can't go straight to the afterlife because I didn't cause a man to be squashed by a steam roller?'

The ombudsman's shoulders collapsed as he exhaled a great puff of air. 'No, no, no. The steam roller was purely an example.' He waved his hands as if wiping away his previous explanation. 'When you were born, you had already been allocated your quota of potential future tasks, weighted from trivial to consequential interventions. No one completes all of them because of the Wiggle Room element, and that's ok. It's a bit like the driving test criteria, you know? You're allowed a certain amount of minor faults, but no majors.'

'Oh, I see. Yes, I think I've got it now.'

'Good. Now, of course, because you've arrived here early, a relatively high number of infringements is understandable, purely because you haven't been alive long enough to get them done, but that shouldn't interfere with the world order, because of the network of interactions I mentioned, which adjust to take up the slack.'

Lily nodded. 'Ok. So, if I'm alright on that front, what is it that's stopping me from moving on?'

The ombudsman referred to his tablet. 'Hmmm. It's the major infringements that have the impact. Occasions when your contribution was paramount to the completion of certain events, and where those events haven't occurred as and when they should, because of your actions, or, should I say, inaction. Usually when that happens, the framework is rejigged to give you a chance to put things right further down the line.' He threw her a sideways glance. 'I've seen better stats.'

Her heart sank. 'I've been on earth for thirty-six years. I must have achieved quite a lot, probably about half a life's worth, maybe just under. So, I've missed the odd mission. Is there no leeway? Can it not be overlooked, this once?'

He rapidly swiped from one page to another on his screen. 'I really don't think so. The data…' He shook his head in thought.

'Right.' She wasn't ready to give up hope yet. 'Surely there must be something that can be done. I mean, if it's pretty close. Exactly what percentage of tasks have I completed so far?'

'Aah, well.' His face morphed into a grimace.

'What? What is it?'

'I'm afraid, as a percentage, that would be zilch.'

# CHAPTER FIVE

Lily snatched the tablet from the ombudsman's hands and stared at the confusing information it displayed. 'What? You're telling me that in three-and-a-half decades I've failed to complete any important tasks whatsoever?'

'So it would seem. I must say, statistics like these - it's quite the shocker.'

'But, but, but…' Shocked was not the word. The concept that her entire life had pretty much amounted to nothing had hit Lily harder than the Catherine wheel. 'You're saying my life was worthless. I was a complete waste of time.'

'Now, hang on. I never said any such thing.' The ombudsman reclaimed the computer and referred to it. 'You did lots of small things, here and there, you just didn't do anything significant.'

She forced a laugh. 'Oh, that makes all the difference. I wasn't a waste of time, I was simply insignificant. That's exactly what a person wants to hear on her deathbed.'

There was a pause before he answered. 'To be fair, you're not actually on your deathbed. Technically, you're already dead.'

Lily scrabbled in her pocket for a tissue and dabbed at moist eyes. 'You're not helping.'

He didn't seem to know how to handle a weeping woman, keeping his focus firmly on the screen, avoiding eye contact with her. 'I'm sorry. I don't know what to say.'

She shrugged. 'What is there to say? I'm a complete failure.'

He patted her hand awkwardly. 'Not a complete… failure.' Realising the implication of his words, he petered off.

For some time, the only sound was Lily's quiet sniffs, as she struggled to come to terms with her shortcomings and with facing another stint back on earth. It seemed so unfair.

The ombudsman filled the void. 'I really haven't ever seen stats like this. You occasionally get a few blips here and there, but nothing this extreme.'

A thought suddenly occurred to her. 'I suppose the figures are right, are they? There couldn't be a mistake?'

He pursed his lips, frowning. 'No. I don't think so. There have never been any mistakes before.'

The glimmer of hope energised her. 'But you've never seen stats like this before either. It might be an error.'

He looked askance at her, but she was not to be put off, and continued, 'It might. It wouldn't do any harm to check, would it? To be sure?'

'I suppose…'

She sat up straight and shoved the soggy tissue back into her pocket. 'Great. How do we do this? Do you have to call an engineer or something?'

'Gosh, I don't know. I've never had cause to find out. Let me think.' Leaning forward he rested his chin on one hand, pinching the tip between finger and thumb. 'I know. I'll look up some of the more significant tasks you should have completed, and you tell me whether you did them or not. If we can find even one which doesn't match the record, we'll know there's an issue. Does that sound fair?'

'Absolutely. I'll bet I've done lots more than that thing says I have.' She rubbed her hands together. 'Go on, fire away.'

'Hold your horses. It'll take me a minute.'

As he fiddled with the controls, Lily's legs jiggled, her mind whirred with activity, fists curled tight. *Please let me have done something worthwhile. Please.*

'Right. We'll start with something simple, something in the recent past, so you don't have to rack your brains. Sometimes these things are so vague, you may not even remember what you did or didn't do at the time. Here we are.'

She gripped the edge of the sofa with both hands, determined to prove her point. 'Ok. I'm ready.'

'Do you know a Mr Ahmed? He used to live in the house behind your own garden.'

This was a promising start. 'Yes. Yes, I know Mr Ahmed, at least, I used to. He moved away in the spring. There was a hole in the back of his shed and my cat would hide out there when she was scared. Once, poor Tabs was missing for a day and a half, after she was spooked by fireworks. It turned out she'd got into his shed and knocked over a sack, blocking the way out. She'd made quite a mess, but he was really nice about it.'

The ombudsman grunted an acknowledgement. 'And did you invite him round for tea, to say thank you?'

She frowned. 'No, I didn't. Funnily enough, it was something I thought about, in fact, I can't remember why I didn't in the end. I think I was afraid it might be awkward as we didn't know each other well, and he's an old man so we would have had nothing in common. I hate it when you run out of things to say and it all becomes, you know, embarrassing. I bought him a box of chocolates.'

'Aah, never mind. It was worth a shot. Let's look at another one.'

'What? Are you telling me that asking Mr Ahmed around was a major event? Surely not. I mean, how could something so trivial be classed as important?'

'Cause and effect. As I said before, just because something seems trivial to you, it may be a major thing to someone else.' He pressed buttons and read the resulting page. 'Yes, Mr Ahmed's only remaining friend in the area had died shortly before, and he was extremely lonely. He needed someone to talk to, to help him over the sticky patch, but he didn't feel anyone cared. As a result, he sold the house and now he's in sheltered accommodation on the other side of the country.'

Lily's hand flew to her chest. 'I didn't realise.' She paused. 'At least he's in a safe place, surrounded by company, I suppose.'

The ombudsman looked down his nose at her attempt to offset the guilt. 'Yes, but it's a shame, because if he'd held on a few months, a particular elderly widow was going to move in to a flat on the corner.' He sniffed. 'They would have made a delightful couple in their twilight years.'

Lily inhaled sharply as the ramifications of what the ombudsman said sunk in. Had she really come between a lonely old man and the love of his life? There had to be some redeeming element to her behaviour. 'I gave him chocolates.'

Pursing his lips, the ombudsman studied the text on the tablet, muttering quietly. 'Yes, chocolates for the diabetic Mr Ahmed.' Then, louder. 'Here's another one. I wonder if you'll remember this.'

She was somewhat subdued by the first example, but gritted her teeth, ready for the next. It was bound to be more positive. 'Go on.'

'Six years ago, you held discussions about starting a literacy project for disadvantaged adults with your colleague at the library. Kiki, was it?'

Lily's heart sank. 'Move on. It would have meant doing presentations to the council for funding, which simply isn't me. I don't do public speaking, it petrifies me. It was a good idea though.'

'It certainly was.' He read to the bottom of the page. 'Yes, Kiki proceeded without you. She's done a lot of good. Of course, the reach would have been further if she'd had support, but…'

'Yes, yes. I said move on.' Proving she had done something useful during her life was harder than she'd anticipated.

'Perhaps we should look at something where the consequences are more connected to your own life.' The ombudsman drummed the chair with his fingers as he scrolled through.

Lily waited. He seemed to be taking an age to find a relevant point, and a pause in his drumming made her glance up. He was studying her out of the corner of his eye, but as soon as he saw her looking, instantly reverted his gaze to the screen.

'What?'

He pretended to be unaware of being caught out. 'Hmm? What?'

'Why were you looking at me? What is it?'

'Who, me?'

'Yes, you. I saw you. What were you looking at?'

His shoulders collapsed, knowing he was busted. 'Oh, ok. I was checking for a wedding ring, that's all.'

She shot forward in the seat. 'Good grief! Am I supposed to be married?'

'Um, well.' He bit his lips together before he answered, buying time. 'You're not divorced, I suppose?'

'No, I'm not divorced.' Collapsing back, she threw her arms wide. 'I'm supposed to be married.' She shook her head. 'I have completely stuffed up my life, haven't I?'

The fact it was meant as a rhetorical question bypassed the ombudsman. 'Well, I wouldn't say that. He wouldn't have been the greatest catch. I mean, he wasn't your soulmate or anything, but you might have gone the distance. You certainly would have licked him into shape, that's for sure.'

Lily buried her head in her hands. 'Oh, Lord.'

He dropped the tablet into his lap. ‘I was afraid you might take it like that. I probably shouldn’t have mentioned it. I could have looked the information up myself, but I didn’t want to lose my place in your history.’

She looked up, keeping her hands as they were, in case they were required again. ‘Who was he? When should I have met him, or married him?’

‘Ooh. Hang on. Mmm, Darren Chantilly. He went to the university you should have gone to. You would have met him during Fresher’s Week at Scrabble Club but wouldn’t have got together until the third year at a Christmas party at your best friend’s accommodation.’

‘I would have had a best friend?’ Her head collapsed back into the waiting hands.

‘There, there. On the upside, you would have been Mrs Lily Chantilly.’ He chuckled. ‘Dodged a bullet there, if you ask me.’

Realising his humour was doing nothing to cheer her, he tried another tack. ‘How come you didn’t go to university? You had the grades. You had the offers.’

She slumped back into the cushions and sniffed, allowing her hands to drop. ‘I was afraid. I couldn’t be sure it was the right university, or the right course. I didn’t think I would make friends and didn’t want to be alone.’

He reached across and patted her hand. ‘And yet, you’re more alone now than you’ve ever been.’ He frowned. ‘Being afraid seems to be quite the theme with you, doesn’t it?’

She nodded. ‘I’ve always been afraid. I can’t remember a time when I haven’t been completely petrified of my world falling apart.’

‘Can’t you? People aren’t generally born with fear. It’s something which develops through experience.’

She cast her mind back, to early adulthood, to school and all she pulled up were memories full of the fear of doing something stupid and doubt about her own judgement. And yet there must have been a time when this wasn't the case. Somewhere in the recesses of her mind she recalled doing cartwheels across the playground, singing silly songs she had made up to her friends, reading stories she had written aloud to the class. There had been a time when she really thought she belonged in the world and the world was there for her benefit. 'Actually…'

'Yes?'

She shook her head, trying to order the pictures forming. 'There was something, I just can't quite put my finger on it.'

The ombudsman studied her face. 'Try to recall. I mean, it won't help the situation now, you still won't have done the tasks you should have, but it might be of immense help after we send you back, if you were to overcome that fear or get it into perspective.'

Lily screwed up her eyes, desperate to remember. 'It's there, but I can't quite grab it, somewhere around the end of junior school and the beginning of senior. Oh, I wish I could remember.'

He looked at his watch, clicking his tongue in thought. 'Look, I'm not supposed to do this, but I've had some new equipment delivered and I'm dying to try it out.'

'What? What equipment?'

His face lit up with a grin. 'Virtual Reality. In the past, if we wanted to review someone's history it's all been computer data or video screens, but, well, we've got to keep up with the times, haven't we?'

'I'm not sure I understand.'

He rolled his eyes, obviously expecting her to keep up. 'We can use the VR to look back at your past and, if we play our cards right, locate the exact scene where things changed, the exact moment when you went from happy-go-lucky child to fearful young lady. Quite fascinating.'

Lily's stomach gurgled. The idea of revisiting such a scene made her uncomfortable. 'Do you really think that's a good idea?'

The ombudsman was already on his feet, reaching for the first of several small boxes stacked in the corner of the room. 'Of course it is.' He pulled out a headset and waved it at her. 'What could possibly go wrong?'

# CHAPTER SIX

It took only minutes for the ombudsman to unpack headsets from the boxes and set up the equipment. A laptop stood on the table, alongside the coffee making paraphernalia, and he tapped at the keyboard while issuing Lily with instructions. Although she was paying close attention, the prospect of reviewing her own life kept getting in the way, and his words flowed over her head.

He sat on the sofa, face glowing with excitement, and waved his goggles at her. 'This should be awesome.'

She watched him pull them over his head, still unsure about the process.

'It's totally wireless, so you can move around if you want to,' he continued. 'But do be careful. I don't want any accidents. You're already going to have a massive lump on your head from the firework, when you go back, but it would be difficult to explain away a broken leg. Probably best to simply sit back and enjoy.'

She wasn't sure there would be anything enjoyable about re-experiencing her own childhood. An uncomfortable tension remained at her core, and it wasn't easing. In fact, if anything, it was worsening by the minute.

'And its voice activated, so it should be easy to operate. Are you ready?' He didn't wait for a reply. 'I've set it to somewhere during your eleventh year. Let's go.'

He instructed the machine to switch on, then fell quiet, an inane grin on his face.

Afraid she was missing out, Lily quickly pulled the goggles into place. A blurred picture came into focus, and she saw a youthful version of herself skipping down the road, hand in hand with a friend. She took a sharp intake of breath and a wave of nostalgia washed over her. 'Susie?'

She had forgotten about her old friend. For years they had been joined at the hip, their likes and dislikes aligned. They had shared experiences, whispered secrets to each other and laughed constantly at jokes only they understood. Susie had been the best friend Lily ever had, before or since.

'Wow!' The ombudsman was clearly impressed. 'Look at the picture quality. Clear as day, isn't it?'

Lily reached out to touch her pal's arm, but her outstretched fingers passed straight through the girl's body. 'I can't touch her.'

'No, you can't. You must remember, we're observers only. We can't interact with the subjects or change anything, but we can move around them to get the best viewpoints.' He rubbed his hands together. 'Oh, this is so exciting.'

She wasn't sure she could agree wholeheartedly, but the sight of Susie's smiling face certainly intrigued her.

The ombudsman, receiving no reply from Lily, raised his voice and instructed the computer. 'Play.'

*LILY ARMITAGE – AGED TEN AND A HALF*

*Lily and Susie turned the corner at the end of the road, into the playpark they often frequented on the way home after lessons. Schoolbags were abandoned wherever they landed, as the girls dived around the swings, slide and fort, burning off the pent-up energy from an afternoon in the classroom, but as usual ended up on their favourite, the monkey bars. Susie hung by her knees at one end and Lily at the other, facing each other, conversing as easily as if they were sitting down to tea. Lily was giggling.*

*'Is it Ben Turner?'*

*'No.' Susie gave an adamant shake of her head, the movement causing her body to swing forward and back gently.*

*'I know. It's Jason Kennedy.'*

*'Ughh, no! He's got dandruff.'*

*Lily pulled herself up with her arms and allowed her feet to unhook, then turned so she was dangling by her hands, facing her friend's legs. 'I don't know then. Is it Jeremy Archibald?'*

*'No, he's going out with Sara Bellamy.'*

*'I give up then. Who are you going to ask to go to the Easter disco with you?'*

*Susie manoeuvred and dropped down to the ground. 'Troy Bank-Owens.'*

*Lily let go and landed heavily on her feet then rolled on the floor laughing. 'Troy Bank-Owens talks like this,' she adopted an American twang. 'Hey, Susie, how you doin'?'*

*Rather than be offended, Susie joined in, strutting around her prostrate friend. 'Hey, Lily. I sure like yer hair.' She stopped and wrenched a wrinkled sock up to her knee, returning to her normal voice. 'I know. I don't mind. I think it's funny.'*

*Lily got to her feet and, as one, the two girls walked to retrieve their bags.*

*'I thought it might be Jake Arbutt.'*

*Susie pulled the bag onto her back and twisted to knock Lily with it. 'No way. Jake Arbutt eats bogies. I saw him in science.'*

***

The footage paused and, after waiting a few moments for it to continue, Lily pushed the headset up so she could see the room. The scene had brought back a raft of warm feelings. How many times had she and Susie met like that, discussing the hot topics, sharing confidences? Whether it had been a good or bad day, it was something they dealt with together.

'I'm going to move it on. You're clearly still full of the joys of spring at that age. Let's jump a couple of years.' The ombudsman instructed the computer accordingly, without removing the goggles or waiting for Lily's response. 'Ah, this is more like it. What are you here? Thirteen? Gosh, that was never a good look.'

Lily re-covered her eyes and immediately saw the difference. It was bad.

*LILY ARMITAGE – AGED TWELVE AND TEN MONTHS*

*Lily was hunched on a bench at the edge of a playing field, elbows on the faded knees of her jeans, staring at nothing in particular, an orange woolly hat pulled down over her ears. Her expression was as empty as the field and, when she got to her feet, the effort it took showed in a deep scowl. As she walked away, one muddied trainer scudded on a rough patch of ground, and in temper she kicked out at it, ramming fists into the pockets of her voluminous overcoat, before dragging herself onto the path.*

***

'Right. We've clearly gone too far forward. Whatever happened was before this. Any ideas yet?' The ombudsman's voice was business-like, eager to get on with the job in hand.

Lily watched the retreating form of her younger self with a solid weight in her gut. It was all coming back.

'It was before this, weeks though, rather than months, I think. I can't be sure…'

'Are you picking up clues? The season perhaps?'

Lily shook her head. 'No. It's the hat. There's something about the hat.'

'Righty-oh. I'll skip back a few days at a time. You shout if you think we're getting close.'

The image hopped, skipped and jumped back through the previous days to the one they had visited in the field, one downcast, miserable Lily replaced by another and another. All at once, a particular scene flicked a switch in her head, but by the time her body was able to react they had moved back even further. Rather than an instruction to pause, all Lily managed was a long, drawn-out moan, as the significance of that day came back in all its original horror.

The ombudsman paused the footage. 'Jolly good. I take it We've struck gold.

# CHAPTER SEVEN

*LILY ARMITAGE – AGED TWELVE AND NINE MONTHS*

*At the breakfast table, Lily could barely sit still.*

*'I'm so proud of you, sweetie. I can't wait to see you on stage. Have you decided what you're wearing?' Lily's mother, Marion, rested back against the sink unit as she wiped dishes and stacked them on the worktop.*

*Lily replied through a mouth full of milky cereal and spoon. 'I've got to wear my school uniform.'*

*'Uniform?' Marion was horrified. 'Well, I call that mean. This is your chance to shine. You need to be looking your best. Uniform, indeed.'*

*Lily was used to having to keep her mother's feet firmly on the ground. 'It's only a spelling bee, mum, not a fashion show. Everybody'll be wearing the uniform of the school they're representing, not just me. I don't mind.'*

*'All the same...' Marion turned back to the sink to take up another pan. 'A girl wants to make a good show, on stage, in front of hundreds of people. They'll all be looking at you, you know?'*

*Lily would have preferred not to have been reminded of that particular aspect of proceedings. It was quite an accolade to have got through to the spelling bee finals, but something she never aspired to. To begin with it had just been a bit of fun, but it had grown and grown. She had always loved words, reading them, writing them, even simply rolling peculiar sounding ones round her tongue for fun, but now her passion had become something more, something which made her stand out in an environment where it was sometimes difficult to do so, at least, in a good way.*

*Since the beginning of the school year there had been a change to the way her fellow pupils interacted, friendship groups were becoming cliques and that meant a constant changing of boundaries: those inside protecting their status and those outside pushed away. It made Lily uncomfortable, and she wasn't sure where her place was. The competition, and preparation for it, had been a welcome and fun addition to her schedule.*

*'Are you sure you couldn't wear the dress we bought you for Maggie's wedding last year? It's such a lovely outfit, all sparkly and wow.' Marion was staring into a space over Lily's shoulder, somewhere between the Welsh dresser and the faded print of Judy Garland.*

*Lily clattered her spoon into the empty dish. It was time to make an escape, before her mother dragged her into one of her flights of fancy. 'Definitely not. It's got to be uniform. Besides, that was two years ago, and the dress doesn't fit anymore.'*

*Marion's shoulders dropped. 'Oh, what a shame.' She set to vigorously polishing the bottom of a frying pan, then paused mid-wipe. 'What about a new hairdo? Just to make you feel a bit special. Shall I see if I can book you in after school? For a little confidence boost.'*

*When Marion got an idea into her head, she was like a dog with a particularly juicy bone and Lily knew she was going to have to submit to some sort of pampering before the day was out. In addition to which, a couple of girls had come into school over the recent weeks sporting trendy new styles, which had gone down a storm. Perhaps it would be good to have a trim. 'Well, maybe…'*

*Marion clapped in delight, almost dropping the pan in the process. 'Fantastic. Leave it to me. I'll have it all sorted by the time you get back this afternoon. Oh, it'll be great. Yes, and maybe a little touch of lippy too.'*

*Lily jumped off her stool and pulled on a jacket, before she could be talked into a full makeover. 'Alright, but I won't have long so it'll have to be as soon as I get back.'*

*'Don't worry, you can trust me.'*

*Lily rolled her eyes but decided she would let it pass and get to school early enough to catch up with Susie before lessons.*

*Lily and Susie walked to school together less often these days. Their classes were rarely together, and it made sense for Susie to get together with girls from her own form on certain days, and on others she'd leave home before Lily got there, but Lily didn't mind. It was a pleasant surprise today to see Susie at the end of her path, presumably waiting for her.*

*'Hello.' Lily went in for a hug.*

*Susie happened to be turning toward the road at that moment and Lily ended up hugging her rucksack instead. 'Let's go.'*

*They fell into step. Neither of them seemed to have much to say and Lily frowned as she walked. There never used to be awkward moments between them, they had always been so in tune, always desperate to share the latest gossip.*

*The only thing on Lily's mind was the conversation she had just had with her mother. Actually, that was something Susie might be interested in. She was all about beauty and fashion these days. 'Mum's booking me in for a haircut this afternoon before the bee. What do you think I should have done?'*

*Susie threw her a glance but kept walking. 'I don't know.'*

*Lily, the shorter by several centimetres now, almost had to jog to keep up. Although her friend always liked to be on time, there was something not quite right about her haste this morning. She was concerned there may be problems at home, as Susie's home life could be as unpredictable as her own, but she didn't want to be nosey. Sometimes you just didn't want to talk about things. However, when the school building came into view and Susie still hadn't spoken, Lily felt compelled to.*

*'Suse, is everything alright? You're not yourself today?'*

*'I'm fine.' Susie muttered, without meeting Lily's eye. Then, a few paces further on, she stopped and turned to face her. 'Do you have to do this stupid bee thing tonight?'*

*Lily was taken aback. 'Well, yes. I've said I'll do it so I've got to now. Why?'*

*Susie ignored the question. 'Couldn't you say you were sick or something?'*

*'But why would I do that? I've been practising for weeks, and I might even win. It would be pretty stupid to back out now.'*

*'Well, you'll look pretty stupid if you don't.'*

*Lily didn't know what to say and stood staring at her friend.*

*'Marie says the bee is the lamest thing the school has ever done and anybody who has anything to do with it is lame too.' Susie looked everywhere to avoid looking Lily in the eye, but, as the silence lengthened, her tone softened. 'Look, you know what Marie's like. She won't have you hanging with us if you do stuff that's not cool.'*

*'I'm surprised you want to hang with her if she's like that.'*

*'Everybody wants to hang with Marie.'*

*'I don't.'*

*'Well, you might get your wish then.' There was a sulk to Susie's tone. 'Look, we've been friends a long time and I thought I should warn you. But it's up to you if you do it or not.'*

*Lily thought hard, staring into a puddle by the roadside. Somehow it felt like her friendship was on the line, but she couldn't see a way out of the commitment she had made to the bee and her teammates. Besides, her mother would go spare if she walked away from her moment of fame. 'I think I've got to do it.' She kicked a stone on the edge of the pavement. 'We'll be alright though, won't we? It doesn't matter what Marie says.' She already knew the answer.*

*'It's up to you.' Susie straightened her backpack and marched away. 'See you later.'*

*Lily stayed there, staring after her, until a group of other children forced her to move forward, out of their way. She'd had words with Susie before, all friendships had their moments, but this felt important, it felt like it mattered. But so did the spelling bee. She knew what her mum would say, the other girls were only jealous, because she was cleverer than them, and she shouldn't let them spoil her fun, but being clever wasn't such a big deal these days. What was she to do?*

*Her stomach gurgled and clenched as she walked through the school gates, and she picked up speed, walking with a new purpose. If it carried on like this, she wouldn't have to pretend to be ill to avoid the evening's event.*

***

'I think I can see where this is going.' The ombudsman interrupted Lily's train of thought, pausing the footage mid-scene. 'You pulled out of the bee, didn't you? And now you think, if you'd gone ahead with it, you would have had more confidence in the future.'

Lily's skin was pale and clammy. Although only observing events of her past, her body had reacted as if it was living it all again and this time, she knew exactly what was to come. 'No. No, that wasn't what happened at all. If only it was.'

'You mean, it gets worse? Did something happen at school?'

'Oh, yes, it gets worse. At school, at home, at the bee.' She shook the images from her head. 'There's something I should explain. My mum… She had issues. She *has* issues, but back then we didn't know, I mean, it wasn't properly diagnosed. All I knew, in those days, was not to upset her, to try and keep her calm, or things could escalate in an instant.' Lily's lips were dry, and she ran her tongue across them to stop them sticking together. 'Man, did they get worse.'

The ombudsman's face was full of concern. 'I see. Right, well, let's see this through and then we can decide what to do next. Should we watch the whole day or is there a specific time we should move to?'

'No, we can skip the rest of the school day. There were a few jibes and stuff, but nothing major. The important bit begins when I got home, around three thirtyish or four, maybe.'

He instructed the computer to skip forward and waited for the image to come into focus. 'Hell's bells!'

'Oh, yes. I'd forgotten, I got an early pass that day, so I could go home and get ready, and it had already started.'

'Oh, my, yes. This I've got to see.'

# CHAPTER EIGHT

*LILY ARMITAGE – AGED TWELVE AND NINE MONTHS*
*THE HAIRCUT*

*Young Lily was sitting on a stool in her kitchen, a striped tea towel tucked around her neck. Her mother applied scissors to Lily's hair, referring to a picture in a magazine, spread open on the table.*

*'I may not be an expert, but I know a good hairstyle when I see it and I saw this today and knew immediately it would suit you down to the ground.'*

*'I don't know though, Mum. Perhaps I should wait until they can fit me in at the salon.' Although Lily spoke the words aloud, she knew her mother wouldn't listen. From the moment she had walked in the door the die had been cast. Her mother had been waiting there, scissors in hand, a wide smile on her face and a steely look in her eye, and when Marion was determined, nothing would stand in her way.*

*'Tsh! Stuff and nonsense. My girl will not get on that stage tonight with a great mop of hair on her head. She will be modern and chic and...' She searched the air for the right term. 'Sophisticated.' Crouching down, she hugged Lily from behind, pressing a warm, pink cheek to Lily's own. 'Sweetie, you'll look fabulous.'*

*Lily clenched and unclenched her fists. She wished her stepdad, Ray, would come home. He would put a stop to this immediately, but Lily simply didn't know how, without throwing her mother into a fit of hysteria. 'Maybe, just trim the fringe, so it's not in my eyes. That'll do. I should really be doing some last-minute practice anyway.'*

*'No, no, no. Cinderella shall go to the ball, and if she can't have an amazing dress, she can at least have amazing hair. Now, sit still.'*

*Lily closed her eyes tight, wincing with every snip. The day was going from bad to worse. As the morning wore on, she had pretty much convinced herself everything would be alright. If the bee was so "lame", Marie and her posse probably wouldn't bother showing up, so no problem, although she had been hoping Susie would be there for moral support. Secondly, if Lily did well, it would all be forgotten by the end of the week, so all she had to do was not stuff it up completely, because failure remained a talking point far longer than success. Now, though, her worries were growing by the second and there wasn't a thing she could do about it. Please, please, come home, Ray.*

*It was almost as if he'd heard her thoughts, as the scrape of his key in the front door, cut through her mother's happy humming.*

*He strolled into the kitchen, launching his car keys at a bowl on the dresser, and stopped. 'What's going on here then?' His voice was calm, but Lily detected an underlying tension.*

*'I'm making Lily beautiful for the show.' Marion stepped aside so he could see.*

*At the same time, it meant Lily could now see his face.*

*His mouth dropped open. 'Shit, Marion, what have you done?'*

*'Language, Ray.' She pointed at Lily with a comb. 'Young ears.'*

*'But, Marion…' He strode towards them and purposefully removed both the comb and scissors from Marion's hands. 'Look at the state of it.'*

*Marion laughed, with an air of desperate optimism and squeezed Lily's shoulder. 'Like he knows anything about modern trends.'*

*Lily's gaze had slipped from Ray's horrified expression to the mountain of brown locks on the linoleum. Her hands flew to her neckline, where she expected to find the bottom of her bob, but there was nothing there. Eyes wide, she let out a sound, half sob, half scream, and dived for the bathroom and the mirrored tiles above the sink.*

*'Now look what you've done, Ray.' Marion scampered after Lily 'She was perfectly happy until you walked in. Why can't you leave well alone?'*

*'But, Marion, what were you thinking?'*

*Marion ignored him, her head appearing next to Lily's in the reflection in the bathroom. Lily was transfixed with the horror of it, uneven layers, spiky tufts and the complete absence of a fringe, but her mother's face was alight with manic pride. 'You see? It's choppy, you know, edgy, not all flat and boring. I just need to tidy up a couple of places and it'll be perfect. Don't you think?'*

*Lily lacked the air in her lungs to reply and dragged in a breath to facilitate a response. 'No, Mum. It's not perfect. I'm sorry, but it really isn't.'*

*'You don't like it?' Marion's bottom lip trembled. 'Well, let me try again. I'm sure I can turn it around.'*

*'No. No.' Lily felt panic building inside her, and she had to get away. She pushed past her mother, back into the kitchen. 'Ray, what am I going to do? I can't go out like this. I can't be seen...'*

*Marion followed. 'Now, there's no need to be melodramatic...'*

*'Melodramatic?' Ray roared, making both Marion and Lily flinch, so unused were they to him losing his temper. 'You've ruined it.'*

*At his words, Lily broke down in tears. Clearly, it was every bit as bad as she'd thought. 'I can't go to the bee. You'll have to tell them, I can't go.'*

*'What? Not be in the show? But you've got to. It's your big chance.' Marion joined the wailing and started to wrench at her own hair, until it came out in small clumps. 'I've ruined my baby's big chance. I'm a terrible, terrible mother. I'll never forgive myself.'*

*Ray grabbed her. 'Stop that, Marion. Stop it. Calm down.' He took hold of both her hands and breathed deeply. We all need to calm down. Let's not overreact. Lily, go to your bedroom while I deal with your mother.'*

*Lily was quick to retreat, sitting on the bed, listening to the ongoing situation with her parents through the door.*

*'She must go, Ray. She absolutely must. I won't hear of her not going.'*

*'Where are your pills, Marion? I think you should take one to make you feel better.'*

*'I don't want...' Her mother's voice was shrill.*

*'I know you don't, but just one would be helpful. Here you are, get that down you... Is it gone?'*

*'Yes.'*

*Lily could imagine Marion sticking her tongue out for him to check.*

*'Good girl. Now, you have a little lie down, while I go and see to Lily. Can you do that?'*

*'But I'm not tired.'*

*'You will be in a minute. Go on, put your head down for five minutes, then we'll have a nice cup of tea.'*

*Lily heard her mother's bedroom door close, and the voices became muffled. She waited for Ray to come back, though she had no idea how her hair could be made right. Surely nothing could be done.*

*He tapped on her door before entering, then sat on the bed next to her, examining her head as if it were a road map. 'Why did you let her do it?'*

*'I don't know.' Lily could barely speak. 'She kept on and I didn't know how to say no without a row.'*

*He ruffled the top of her head. 'On this occasion, I think a row would have been the better outcome. Listen, I'm going to give my cousin, Jenny, a ring. She's a hairdresser. Maybe she can do something to tidy this up.'*

*'Thanks.'*

*'In the meantime, have a shower, get ready to go and we'll make a decision about what to do once we've seen her. Ok?'*

*'Will Mum be ok?'*

*'You know your mum.' He tried to laugh, but it petered out before it could get going. 'She always comes out sunny side up in the end. She won't make it tonight though. I've given her a pill and they knock her for six for a good few hours.'*

*Lily nodded and, as Ray walked to the phone in the hallway, she made for the shower.*

*Jenny wasn't at the salon that day, which was just as well. It meant Ray could deliver Lily to Jenny's doorstep, without her having to face the interested glances of other customers.*

*Jenny was professional and helpful, but there was only so much she could do with the aftermath of Marion's escapade. She sat Lily on an office chair and slowly swung it full circle to assess the damage. 'I'm not sure what look your mum was going for, but I don't think this can be it.'*

*Lily sat in shame-faced silence, hoping against hope Jenny could perform some sort of miracle.*

*'Well, I can tidy it up, but unless you want to really make a statement with a shaved head, I'm limited. You don't want a shaved head, do you?' Jenny's tone was momentarily optimistic.*

*Lily shook her head vehemently. She wasn't that brave.*

*'Right. Thought not.' Jenny reached for the scissors and began to work, standing back intermittently to ascertain progress, usually accompanied by a tut or a sigh.*

*Eventually she stepped away and reached for a mirror. 'This is the best I can do. What do you think?'*

*Lily dissolved into tears. Yes, it was a marked improvement on her mother's attempt, but the thought of having to face her schoolmates, or, in fact, anyone looking like this was devastating.*

*Jenny pulled Lily into her chest for a hug, while Ray watched from afar. 'I know, love, but remember a haircut is temporary. A couple of months and it'll be a different story. We'll have more to work with. Then, we could really make a difference.'*

*'Months?' The volume of Lily's sobs increased.*

*Ray mopped his brow with a handkerchief. 'What are we going to do, Jen? She's supposed to be on stage tonight. It's a pretty big deal.'*

*'I can't do it, Ray. I'll be a laughing stock,' Lily gulped. 'But Mr Willis will go spare if I don't. I don't know which is worse.'*

*Jenny frowned at Ray in confusion, and he mouthed. 'Headmaster.'*

*'Oh,' she mouthed back.*

*'Well, Lily, at the end of the day, it's down to you. What do you want to do?' Ray tried to be practical.*

*'I don't know. I did want to do it, but now…' She waved both hands around her head.*

*Jenny nibbled at a nail as she continued to observe Lily on the stool. 'You're going to have to face everybody at some point though, you realise that? If not tonight, then tomorrow at school, or next week. You can't put it off until it's grown back, they'll have your mum and Ray up in court if you hide away for that long.' She allowed her hand to drop and smiled softly. 'You strike me as a brave girl, and I'm sure there's something we could do.' Her fingers were wiggling as she concentrated. 'I've got it. A hat!'*

*As Jenny ran from the room, Lily looked to Ray. 'A hat?'*

*He shrugged, but before he could answer, Jenny was back with an armful of colourful fabrics. She pulled out a navy-blue cap, then discarded it. 'Too boyish.' Next was a lavender sun hat, complete with floppy brim and flowery ribbon. 'Too…everything. Ooh, what about this?' She held up a cerise beret, with an air of achievement.*

*Lily was dubious, but allowed Jenny to place it on her head, and adjust it this way and that.*

*'Hang on.' Jenny disappeared from the room, returning with a plastic box of odds and ends and set to work.*

*Lily's hair was arranged around the hat; hairspray liberally applied, and a multitude of grips pushed into place, before Jenny allowed her to see the result. It was the miracle Lily had been looking for. In fact, the face in the mirror looked not only well-groomed, but stylish, like everything about it was intentional.*

*She turned to her stepfather in awe. 'What do you think?'*

*His smile was genuine. 'You look a picture, Lils. You really do.'*

*'You can't see the bald bits or the sticky up bits at all, can you?' She twisted her head at all kinds of angles to check for gaps.*

*'No. It's fantastic.' He slipped an arm round Jenny's shoulders, and the pair admired Lily's transformation. 'Thanks, Jen. You're a marvel.'*

*She shrugged. 'Don't mention it. It's a temporary fix, but, you know, it'll take the edge off. It'll do for tonight, anyway.'*

*A thought suddenly occurred to Lily. 'But do you think they'll let me keep it on?'*

*Ray's chin lifted. 'You leave that to me. I'll have a word when we get there.'*

*In a second Lily was out of the chair, her arms around his chest. 'Thanks, Ray.' She turned her head to face Jenny. 'And you, Jenny. I don't know what I would have done without you.'*

*Jenny's head tipped to one side, as she smiled. 'You're welcome, my lovely. You knock 'em dead tonight. Right?'*

*Lily gave a determined nod. 'Right.'*

***

The ombudsman paused the footage and pushed his headset up to the top of his head, creating an upstanding brush of salt and pepper hair, behind it. 'What a nightmare.' He whistled a sigh. 'No wonder you were traumatised, but surely there were some positives you could take from the situation? Look how Ray stood up for you. Look how Jenny came to your rescue. There are a lot of good people in the world and your mum didn't mean to … I mean, it was well intentioned.'

Lily spied the ombudsman from beneath her goggles. 'Oh, please,' she muttered. 'You ain't seen nothing yet. The best, or the worst, depending how you look at it, is yet to come.'

'That wasn't it?'

'Uh, uh.' She shook her head. 'Another couple of hours of young Lily's life and all will become clear.'

He grimaced. 'Oh, dear. I guess we'd better get on with it then.'

# CHAPTER NINE

*LILY ARMITAGE – AGED TWELVE AND NINE MONTHS*
*THE BEE*

*By the time Lily and Ray had raced across town to the school hall, the event was well underway. Most of the audience were in the auditorium, seated in tiered rows, looking down at the main stage, while others milled around the foyer with cups of tea, chatting. The contestants were seated in their school groups, at right angles on the perimeter of the stage. As Lily and Ray crossed the foyer, the headmaster stepped out to usher Lily on.*

*'Here's our star of the show. I was beginning to worry. Let's get you in with the others.'*

*Ray patted Lily's arm. 'You pop to the loo, love, while I speak to Mr Willis.'*

*She was happy to oblige. Her head was spinning and time in the relative calm of a private cubicle would allow her to pull herself together, but a couple of minutes were all she could spare. When she re-emerged, Mr Willis was hovering, ready to whisk her away.*

*'Right then, Lily. Off you go. I'll have a quick word with Miss Tanner as soon as she's free. I'm sure she'll be understanding under the circumstances.'*

*Reassured, Lily skipped across the stage, where her teammates were waiting, a girl from the year below, patting the seat saved for her.*

*As Lily slipped into the chair, the girl leaned over. 'I like your hat,' she whispered. 'My sister's got one like that.'*

*More of Lily's reservations melted away. She knew the girl's sister, by reputation, and she was one of the trendiest, most admired girls in the upper school. Perhaps it would all turn out right, after all.*

*Lily watched the evening unfold with growing confidence. Miss Tanner kept them in check, straightening ties, buttoning jackets and whispering encouragement. Her teammates excelled in their own particular battles, the generous training schedule allowing them to shine over their opponents, and every word they were given to spell, Lily quickly recited in her own head, warming up. She was on form. She could do this.*

*Her moment arrived. She straightened in her seat, waiting to be called and then, as she heard her name, stood up, took a deep breath and shuffled out from the end of the line. At that moment, Miss Tanner whipped the hat from Lily's head and gave her a small shove towards the podiums at centre stage. Lily's hand flew to the uneven tufts in horror, and she heard her teammates gasp. The entire audience was staring straight at her, waiting for her to take her place, gawping at her strange appearance. A low murmur travelled around the hall.*

*Lily's first instinct was to run away, but that would mean running down and out, past the hall full of people, which would have been mortifying in itself and, even in this moment of terror, she recognised that that would provide an even greater source of entertainment for the classroom for the coming weeks than a bad haircut. She bit her lip and took her place, avoiding eye contact with the other three opponents lined up next to her, and the competition began.*

*The compere was enjoying his role and introduced each contestant with flair, before presenting them with their first challenge, a relatively simple warm up word, to get the flow going.*

*Lily was last in the line, and as the man, something to do with the council as far as she could remember, read out her details, she lifted her eyes to the crowd, blood pounding in her ears. The audience were mostly strangers, parents from other schools, and didn't know her from Adam. As far as they were concerned, she might always look like this, some sort of anarchist, who rebelled against conventional hairstyles. Besides, by tomorrow they would have forgotten all about her. The pounding slowed a little. But, dotted between them were parents of children she knew, who she recognised from the school gates in years gone by. Some were staring blankly at the front, waiting for something to happen; others were fiddling in bags or with leaflets, obviously there under the duress of parental responsibility, going through the motions; others were looking at her, leaning in close to each other, whispering, and she could guess what their topic of conversation was. Her heart speeded back up.*

*The compere spoke her name and she turned to face him and, in doing so her eyes swept past Susie in the front row, in the midst of a group of giggling girls, including the dreaded Marie, and Lily would swear her heart actually momentarily stopped.*

*'Lily. Your word is "scarecrow".'*

*It was an easy word, no problem, except she heard a titter from her teammates, and her concentration lapsed, her mouth so dry, her lips stuck to her teeth.*

*'Sorry, could you say it again, please?'*

*The man frowned. '"Scarecrow". Do you need a definition?'*

*'No, thank you.' She shook her head and reeled off the letters.*

*There was a short burst of applause, and the second round began, quicker now all the introductions had been done, and it soon came round to Lily again.*

*'Your word is "Unkempt".'*

*There was another, louder titter, but she was determined to rise above it. She gave her answer and the competition, and her ordeal, continued.*

*'Your word is "Coiffure".'*

*Every time it was Lily's turn she squirmed as the words seemed more and more ironic, and the laughter spread, beyond the highly literate team at her side, to the wider audience.*

*'Your word is "Bristles"'*

*Her stomach churned. She was trapped on stage and there was no escape which didn't involve even more shame. Although she tried not to look at the laughing faces, every time she glanced up another would catch her eye and another flood of embarrassment would wash over her.*

*'Your word is "Unsightly". Your word is "Grotesque". Your word is "Hideous". Your word is "Humiliation".'*

*Her whole life right now was humiliation. Would it never end?*

*A couple of her opponents dropped out.*

*'Your word is "Aberration". Your word is "Alopecia".*

*The compere had got to the point of huffing every time he selected Lily's next challenge, embarrassed by the onslaught of inappropriate words, which only seemed to add to the enjoyment of the majority of the room.*

*Lily was becoming numb to it. Everyone was laughing at her, and there was not a thing she could do about it, except let it play out, head as high as she could possibly hold it, though her heart was in her boots.*

*The one remaining opponent made a mistake, gave a wrong answer, and the spotlight was on Lily. If she got the next one right, she was the winner, and she was determined to win. It was the only chance to regain any level of self-respect.*

*'Your word is "Cymotrichous".' The host gave an audible sigh of relief at the normalcy, and yet difficulty, of the word, sure this could cause no hilarity.*

*Lily's throat constricted. She had no idea. It was time she got a break. She couldn't let it fall apart at this late stage. It needed to be finished. 'Can you give me the definition, please?'*

*For the first time during the evening, a tense silence fell across the room as people waited for the outcome. The host referred to his card. Clearly the word was new to him too. There was a pause, and he bit his lips before responding. 'It means "having wavy hair".'*

*Once more, sniggers broke out behind her, in front of her and at various points around the room. How she didn't burst into tears, Lily would never know, but she ignored the sounds, jutted out her chin and dug deep for the correct letters.*

*When she was named as the winner, the place exploded with applause, and cheers from Lily's teammates. She accepted congratulations, automatically shook the hand which took hers and returned to her seat. A few speeches and a handful of minutes more and it would be over.*

*At the earliest opportunity, having spoken to no one, she marched down the couple of steps to floor level, past the audience, now on their feet meeting and greeting those around them, out through the foyer to the car park, only stopping when she reached Ray's car, convinced that at any moment the panic would finally overtake her and she would collapse on the pavement.*

*A stream of people passed her, heading home, a few shouting congratulations as they went, but she concentrated on breathing in and out, her eyes on her shoes, silently praying for Ray to be quick. A knot of teenage girls sashayed past, pausing a few feet away, whispering and nudging each other, until Lily was unable to ignore them any longer. There was Susie, biting her lips and avoiding Lily's eye, but in the centre of the scrum stood Marie, holding court, her face a mask of undisguised disdain.*

*'Freak,' she muttered and thrust her chin in Lily's direction. 'Let's get out of here.'*

*As one, the group moved on. Susie didn't even look back. Lily's face burned with shame.*

*Finally, Ray appeared, pushing and shoving through the crowds to get to the front, striding to the car. He unlocked the door and climbed in, Lily settling into the passenger seat at the same time. Silence stretched.*

*Ray put the key into the ignition, then paused. 'Lily, I am so sorry. Miss Tanner didn't get the message.'*

*She gripped her knees with such force her fingernails bit into the skin, cutting through the numbness. 'Not as sorry as I am.'*

*'Is there anything…'*

*'Please can we go home?' Her voice broke. 'I just want to go home.'*

# CHAPTER TEN

Lily was aware the ombudsman had paused the footage and, in the lull which followed, could hear him speaking, but she couldn't make out his words over ringing in her ears. She forced the headset over her head so she could see his lips move, in the hope that would help, but her vision was blurred, and, although he remained seated in his corner of the sofa, his image seemed to be moving away from her. It was an uncomfortable sensation, but when she tried to cry out, she realised there was no air in her lungs to facilitate sound, and all she managed was a croak.

Mid-sentence, the ombudsman lifted his goggles to peer at her. 'Sorry. What was that?'

Her hands clutched her chest, mouth opening and closing like a fish, her face slowly turning puce.

'Lily?' He threw the headset to the floor and jumped up, leaning over her. 'Lily? Whatever's the matter?'

She couldn't have replied had she had an answer to offer, but a quick appraisal of the situation on his part was all it took.

'Lily. You need to breathe.' He shook her shoulders and repeated louder. 'Breathe.' When she didn't respond, he sat back on his haunches and pulled in a breath through pursed lips, waving his hand in a rolling inward motion, as if a demonstration would be sufficient to kick-start her into action.

She watched, eyes widening as panic set in.

The ombudsman got to his feet and marched to a panel on the wall next to the door and pushed a button. 'Can I have some help in here, please?' He released the button, took one more glance at Lily's red face and pressed it again. 'Quickly.'

Possibly because of the tension in her body, Lily slowly slid from her perch on the sofa onto the carpeted floor. The ombudsman grasped a handful of hair on the top of his head as he considered what to do, then he strode round to the refreshment table, snatched up a pitcher of iced water and launched the contents at her face.

Ice slipped inside her top and Lily gasped a lungful of air, coughing and spluttering in shock. As she did so, the door flew open, and a huffing Blessing stumbled into the room.

'What's going on?'

The ombudsman, now confident he was master of the situation, glanced around calmly. 'Ah, Blessing. There you are. It's alright. Everything's under control. Lily had a little panic attack, that's all.'

Blessing stared at Lily, lying in a heap against the sofa, dripping from head to toe, still gasping. 'Blimey. Look at the state of you. What brought all this on?'

It wasn't clear who Blessing's question was directed at, but Lily couldn't muster a response, so the ombudsman stepped in. 'It turns out Lily's childhood was more "horror" than "family saga".' He tapped his chin in thought, muttering to himself. 'Perhaps we should give some thought to a rating system for people's histories before letting them watch in future.'

Blessing tiptoed across the room to Lily, avoiding the pools of water, soaking into the carpet. 'Come on. You can't be staying down there, my lovely, you'll catch your death, if you'll excuse the pun.'

Chuckling, Blessing grabbed Lily's arm, pulling her to her feet, while glancing over her shoulder at the ombudsman. 'I'll take this one to the ladies and find her some spare clobber. You'll be needing maintenance in here with a mop, if you ask me.'

'Thank you, Blessing. You take care of Lily and I'll take care of housekeeping.'

Lily was glad to lean on Blessing's hefty form as they passed along the corridors to the bathroom.

Once there, Blessing settled her onto a bench and turned around. 'Two ticks,' she called.

Lily sighed long and hard. Her lungs still smarted from the coughing, but it was nothing to how her heart felt, bruised and battered. The scenes of her childhood trauma were as vivid as if they'd happened yesterday and yet, until a few minutes ago, the memory had been buried so deep she couldn't have recalled a moment of it. No doubt, it had been hidden away on purpose, padlocked by her own brain, so she didn't have to deal with the shame and hurt and anger of it all. Now it had come back to her, it certainly made sense of certain things. No wonder she hated public speaking. No wonder she didn't like being the centre of attention. No wonder she didn't trust people. She had been let down that day in a million different ways.

Blessing bustled back into the room, a sweatshirt tucked under her arm and a pair of baggy tracksuit bottoms held in front of her. 'Goodness knows where these came from, but they should do the job.' She held them up to Lily. 'Twice over, I'd say. Never mind. It's not a fashion show. Just put these on and we'll get your own clothes dry in a jiffy, ready for you to go home.'

Lily did as she was told, shrugging out of her sopping outfit and handing it to Blessing. It was so unfair. Not only had she had to endure that appalling event as a girl, but it had gone on to affect every part of her life since, would affect the rest of her life as well, and her death, as it turned out. Talk about adding insult to injury.

'Cheer up, babe. It might never happen.' Blessing applied a towel to Lily's hair.

'It already has.' Optimism was not an option.

Blessing briefly lifted the towel so she could look into Lily's face. 'Well, then. In that case, it's over and done with, so no need to fret.'

Lily shrugged and submitted to being rubbed dry, her hair rearranged to some order.

'Everything looks better with a smile on your face.' Blessing was persistent. 'Go on, try it.'

'Oh, Blessing. You've a very sunny view of things, haven't you?'

'Course I have. You only get one life, you know. You got to make the best of it, or what's it all for? Too precious to waste, that's for sure.'

Lily observed her reflection in the mirror, tucking a stray lock of damp hair behind one ear, as Blessing tidied away. She'd had thirty-six years of life, but if she separated out the bits which felt worthwhile, they would probably fit into less than a third of that time, and those bits were so far into the past she could barely remember them. Did she really have to go back to earth and do another thirty-six years? Maybe more? If only that day had never happened, the spelling bee cancelled or if her mother had stayed on her meds or lost her scissors. Or if Lily had pretended to be ill and hidden away until it was all over, like Susie wanted her to. It would have turned out differently. It would have been better. It all changed because of one bad choice.

She drew her focus in from the straggly hair and the faded sweatshirt to make eye contact with herself. Everything had hinged on that one poor decision, but it didn't have to anymore. Starting now, she could make a change, and she would. She would walk back to the ombudsman and tell him straight. It simply wasn't fair. The system wasn't fair, and it was time the system changed. She would not go back to her life. She would go on to the other place, a calm, restful, peaceful and happy place, because the outcome should be about more than one solitary lapse in judgement.

'Ready to go, babe?' Blessing was holding the door open wide.

‘Do you know, I think I am.’

There was a more positive tone to Lily’s voice which made Blessing stop, her head tipping to one side in delight. ‘That’s my girl.’

# CHAPTER ELEVEN

The ombudsman was sitting on the sofa fiddling with his tablet computer when Lily and Blessing returned, and he glanced up, waving his hand at a pile of towels laying on the floor. 'Avoid the area there, please. They'll bring a dehumidifier in when we're finished, but for now we'll have to work around it.'

Blessing hovered in the doorway. 'Will you still be needing me? Or shall I get back?'

'Hang on, if you would, Blessing. Another five minutes and we'll be ready to send Lily on her way. Just a brief summing up to do and then we're done.'

Lily was pretty sure it would take more than a few minutes to say what she had to say, and she wasn't about to be dismissed so easily. 'I don't think so.'

He scratched his forehead, still focused on the screen. 'Yes. We've seen what caused your anxiety, and quite understandable it was too, but now you need to gather up what you've learned, hunker down and put it to good use. Mistakes were made, but people rallied to help you through and, well, you did come through it and out the other side. No harm done.'

'No harm done?' Lily's voice rose considerably, forcing the ombudsman to look up, and Blessing to cough uncomfortably from the doorway. 'No harm done? You have got to be kidding me.'

‘I don’t think there’s any need to take that kind of tone ....’

‘I beg to differ. I think there’s every need.’

‘Now...’

Watching her past life as a witness rather than participant gave Lily a strange mix of emotions, all at once feeling victimised, but also a peculiar empowerment. As an adult, she was now able to stand up for right, in a way her young self hadn’t. ‘No, you listen to me. How can you possibly say no harm was done? The whole of the rest of my life has been affected by what happened that day, every opportunity, every challenge, every decision, tarnished. So, I’m sorry, but I’d say a great deal of harm was done. I should have gone to university. I should have had friends. I should be married.’

‘Now, I never said that. I said you could have *been* married, not that you still would be.’

‘That is hardly the point, is it?’

He clasped his hands together in this lap. ‘Well...’

‘No. Don’t you “well” me.’ Her hands were on her hips, legs straight, shoulders thrust back, daring him to deny her speech. ‘I arrived here today, quite against my will, after living a half-life because of what happened when I wasn’t even a teenager, only for you to tell me, I can’t go on to the next place and rest in peace but have to go back and serve another life sentence. And why? Because, surprise surprise, I was so traumatised by what I went through, I couldn’t carry on as if nothing had happened. If that’s fair, I’m a monkey’s uncle.’

Blessing coughed from the doorway. 'Shall I pop back in a bit?’

‘No, Blessing. Stay where you are.’ The ombudsman’s gaze never flinched from Lily’s. ‘Everyone has problems in their lives.’

‘Of course they do. I’m not denying that.’

‘Then I’m missing your point.’

Lily breathed deeply, holding on to her temper by a thread. ‘My point is, that my whole life, and death, should not hang on one single decision. That simply isn’t fair. You only get twenty years for murder, for crying out loud, but I've already done twenty years for that one decision, and you want me to go back and do twenty more. And it wasn't even me who did something bad. I was the victim. I was a child, and I was vulnerable.' She threw her hands out into a wide question. 'Talk about kicking someone when they're already down.'

The ombudsman seemed to be struggling for a reply. 'Huh.' He dropped his tablet onto the cushions, stood up and walked around in a circle, flexing his shoulders and stretching his fingers as he went. After a circuit and a half, he paused, looking back at Lily. 'So, you're suggesting, if you'd backed out of the bee the whole course of your life would have been different.'

'Yes, obviously. My self-esteem, my faith in other people, my whole outlook, would have been completely different.' She was adamant.

He pursed his lips in thought, tapping his chin with one finger. 'I can't see it myself, but we have to play fair. The whole point of my job is to ensure rules are followed and people are treated fairly.'

'Then it's a no brainer. It's clear that wasn't the case.'

He tipped his head to one side, like a bird studying a worm. 'So, if I could prove to you that even if you'd taken a different course of action that day, the fundamentals of your life would still have remained the same, would you say it was fair then?'

'I'd like to see you try.' As far as she was concerned, there was no way he could possibly win the argument.

'Yes, but would you go back to your body without any further nonsense?'

'It won't happen.'

'But would you?'

She shook her head in frustration. 'Yes. Yes, alright. If you could prove such a thing, then yes, I would go back. It would mean it was all my own fault, wouldn't it, so, yes.'

He immediately bent down to pick up their discarded headsets and threw one to Lily to catch, then glanced over his shoulder. 'Ok,

Blessing. Off you trot. Have a cup of tea or whatever it is you do when you're on a break. I'd say we'll be finished here in about half an hour, give or take.'

Blessing winked at Lily. 'See you later, babe.' Then disappeared out into the corridor.

Lily was unimpressed. She couldn't see how revisiting her past again was going to make any difference, but the ombudsman was busy fiddling with the settings on the earpiece of his equipment.

'Ah. There we are.' He pointed to a switch. 'Just flick that little button down.'

She followed his instruction but was none the wiser.

'Now,' he said. 'If you'll put them back on, we should soon get to the bottom of this.'

'I don't see how.'

There was a certain smugness to his air. 'Because, my dear Lily, we are now on simulation mode. You want to know what would have happened if you'd not gone to the bee? Let's find out.'

# CHAPTER TWELVE

*LILY ARMITAGE – AGED TWELVE AND NINE MONTHS*
*TAKE TWO*

*The image in the mirror at Jenny's house was certainly an improvement, but the thud of Lily's heart still told her there was no way she could face the crowds in the school hall. Ray watched expectantly, his face rigid with a hopeful smile.*

*'No. I'm sorry. I can't do it.'*

*His chest sunk down as he expelled the air from his lungs. 'Are you sure, love? Your mum will be so disappointed for you.'*

*'I can't help that, but if I get on that stage looking like this, I'll never live it down.' She shook her head. 'Please don't make me.'*

*He wrapped comforting arms around her. 'It's not for me to make you do anything, is it? Don't worry. I'll phone the school and explain.' After a few moments he pushed her away, holding her shoulders at arm's length. 'You know you're going to have to face the music tomorrow though, don't you?'*

*Tears leaked from the corners of her eyes and rolled towards her chin. 'Do I have to? If you explain, won't they let me stay home until it looks better?'*

*'I shouldn't think so, but maybe they'll let you stick with the hat for a few days, or perhaps they'll have another suggestion. Why*

*don't we find out?' He backed away and called down the corridor to his cousin. 'Jenny, do you mind if I use your phone.'*

*Jenny had clearly been waiting right outside, as she instantly reappeared. 'Course you can. On the stand, by the front door.'*

*Ray passed Jenny into the hall, Lily following, to hover in the doorway. It was a sorry tale he relayed to the headmaster, when the secretary finally tracked him down, and Ray's brow furrowed as he absorbed the response.*

*'Yes. Thank you, Mr Willis. I'll tell her.' He replaced the handset.*

*Lily's fists clenched as she waited for the verdict.*

*Ray was slow to speak. 'Mr Willis is disappointed about tonight, but he understands, so you're not in any trouble for backing out.'*

*'Good.' That was a relief.*

*'But he says you do have to attend school as usual. If it was something that could be repaired in a couple of days then he would have agreed to you taking some time out, but as it stands, it's going to take a while for your hair to grow back and you can't afford to miss that much.' He wiped a hand across his brow, but it didn't remove the frown there. 'About the hat idea.'*

*'Yes?' Lily was hopeful.*

*'That's a no go, I'm afraid. If they let you wear one, they'd have to let everyone, and rules are rules. In fact, he reckoned wearing a hat would probably draw more attention to you which, of course, you don't want.'*

*Lily's body was shaking, and Jenny stepped up behind and placed an arm around her shoulders for support.*

*'He says he knows it'll be hard for you, but it's got to be done, but he'll brief all your teachers in advance, and they'll be extra vigilant to make sure you don't get any hassle.'*

*'They'll only be in the classroom though, won't they? What about when I'm in the playground or outside?'*

*'I'm sorry, Lils. You're going to have to take it on the chin.'*

*Lily sobbed into her sleeve. 'I don't want to.'*

*'I know you don't, but in a couple of weeks it'll be the holidays, and by the time you go back you'll look completely different. You can do a couple of weeks, can't you?'*

*Jenny squeezed Lily's shoulders. 'Course she can. Course you can, Lily. Brave girl like you.'*

*'It doesn't sound like I've got any choice, does it?'*

*Ray stepped forward and squeezed her shoulders. 'Sorry, Lils, but no, I don't think you do.'*

***

The scene froze, then speeded up, moving through the hours to the following day. Lily watched her young self, going through the motions of going to bed, tossing and turning throughout the night and, eventually, getting up and ready to go to school. There was still no sign of her mother, but Ray must have held off from going to work, to drive her to the school gates, which meant she had avoided the crowded pavements and the pushing and shoving and catcalling which often went with it, but it also meant she was suddenly there, in the deep end, stepping out of the car into the midst of the rabble. At that point, the footage paused again.

'There you are then, Lily. As requested, no spelling bee. Are you happy to view the results?' The ombudsman's voice broke through her concentration.

'Umm…' Seeing herself from this angle, she had a feeling it wasn't going to end well for her. Perhaps she should have given the deal more thought.

'Yes? No? The clock's ticking.'

She detected an element of smugness about his tone but couldn't come up with an alternative solution under such pressure. 'I think so. Yes, ok. Go on then.'

There was a sound like he was rubbing his hands together with glee. 'Right, then. Let's go.'

The images began to move once again.

*LILY ARMITAGE – AGED TWELVE AND NINE MONTHS TAKE TWO*

*Lily climbed out of the car, but hovered in the crook of the door, gazing at the sea of children flowing around her. Ray was trying to be patient, but the growing line of traffic building behind the car was making him edgy.*

*'I've got to go, Lily. I'm sorry, love, but you're going to have to get going.'*

*'Yeah, alright.' She stepped away and slammed the door but didn't step up onto the pavement.*

*He leaned into the passenger seat and shouted through the open window. 'You'll be fine. Just hold your head up and any trouble you go to the teacher straight away. Right?'*

*'Yes, ok.' She still didn't move and felt the rush of air against her legs as the car rolled away. Taking two deep breaths, she straightened her spine, held her head high and looked right ahead, determined to ignore everyone around her. It was going to be hard, but she could do this.*

*Within seconds shocked retorts and bursts of laughter broke through her consciousness and, without turning her head, she knew people were staring, nudging each other, whispering, as the news of her changed appearance spread like a virus. She speeded up, marching past them all to the lockers, where she unlocked the door and stuck her head in, away from prying eyes*

*She was aware of clusters of teenagers passing her in one direction, then back, trying to see what all the fuss was about, but she pretended to be busy, packing and unpacking her backpack, buying time before she would have to emerge. A voice spoke up from the other side of the open door. It was Susie.*

*'You didn't do the bee then?'*

*Lily's heart sped up. It was one thing to have to deal with the mob, but quite another when it came to someone she actually knew. 'No. I didn't do it in the end.'*

*'I didn't mean to... Yesterday, I was only trying to help, you know?'*

*Susie's tone was normal, like she hadn't heard the whispers yet, and Lily didn't want to have to face her. She stayed where she was, tucked away in her locker. 'Yeah, I know.'*

*There was a pause. 'Well, you don't need to be off with me then. Are you avoiding me? You didn't wait for me to walk in with you.'*

*Lily didn't point out the fact that Susie often didn't wait for her. Realising she was merely delaying the inevitable, she took a deep breath, mustered courage and emerged from the locker.*

*Susie inhaled sharply. 'Hell, Lily...'*

*Before she could say anything further, another voice joined the conversation. Marie. 'Shit, Armitage. Look at the state of you.'*

*Lily bit her lip.*

*'Had a fight with a lawn mower?'*

*Lily clenched and unclenched her hands. She had thought she was ready for this, but she so wasn't. No words came.*

*Marie sniggered. 'I guess it must have got your tongue too.' She pushed Lily's head against the loose locker door and stalked away, muttering. 'Freak.'*

*Susie lingered a moment longer, as if she wanted to say something else, but Marie got in first. 'You coming, Suse? I wouldn't hang around here, you might catch something.'*

*There was an awkward pause, as neither Susie nor Lily knew what to say. Finally, Susie gave up. 'Yeah, I'm coming.' She walked away without looking back.*

***

'Ouch. That would have stung.' The ombudsman's voice broke through as the images on the screen stalled.

Unable to see his face, Lily tried to gauge his tone, but failed. 'Do you find this entertaining?'

'No. Not in the slightest.' He seemed offended by the question. 'I find it rather sad actually. If you remember, we're only watching this because you had a point you wished to prove. Personally, I've seen enough – I don't imagine for a moment this outcome is any rosier than the original. Teenagers are a brutal lot; the pack 'll take down a wounded animal in seconds without batting an eyelid. But for evidential reasons we need to revisit the other scene, you know, you in the park a few weeks further on, to see if it's changed.'

As he spoke, he was fast forwarding the footage, jumping through days at a time, until he reached the correct spot. 'Yes, there you are. Same day, same time, same outfit and demeanour.'

Lily thought she heard him shudder.

'I think it's rather conclusive – different choice, same outcome. Do you agree?'

She ripped off the headset and flung it onto the seat between them, and the ombudsman, probably sensing the impact, pushed his up onto the top of his head so he could look at her.

'I do, but…' Lily huffed loudly.

'What?' He frowned. 'You're clearly not satisfied. Come on. Right to reply and all that.'

Lily shook her head. 'Look, the simulation showed exactly what you expected it to, but in retrospect, the outcome didn't change because the overall situation didn't change. I still stand by my original comments: I'm being penalised for one error of judgement, but the error wasn't whether or not I turned up at the bee. I realise now it was earlier. I should never have let Mum loose with the scissors. If you hadn't been rushing me when Blessing brought me back from the loo I'd have realised, but now I suppose I've missed the boat.'

'Rushing you? I don't think there was any rushing… Hmm.' He scratched his head. 'Well, I can't have that. If you felt rushed, then I have no choice but to review the issue further.'

Lily's eyebrows shot up. It seemed she might have bought herself some time, and possibly another chance. 'I definitely felt rushed,' she confirmed.

'Right, then. Do you want me to run a simulation where you refuse to have your hair cut? Would that clear this up?'

Adrenalin simmered in her stomach. The bee hadn't been at fault, it was all down to the diabolical hairstyle. She felt sure this would turn out in her favour. How could it not? 'Yes, I think it would.'

'Alright then. Let's do it.'

# CHAPTER THIRTEEN

*LILY ARMITAGE – AGED TWELVE AND NINE MONTHS*
*TAKE THREE*

*As the front door banged shut, Lily turned to face the kitchen, only to find her mother six feet away, brandishing a large pair of scissors. She backed up as far as her rucksack would allow.*

*'What are you doing?' She kept her tone light, though she had a sneaking suspicion she already knew and didn't like it one bit.*

*The light in Marion's eyes showed a child on Santa's knee level of excitement. 'You won't believe me if I tell you. Ooh, this is going to be great. Go on, guess.' Her feet danced a contained jig on the spot.*

*Lily carefully unhooked her arms from the straps of her bag and lowered it to the floor, buying time. 'I don't know. Having tea with the Queen?'*

*'Silly sausage. No. Go on, try again.'*

*'You'd better tell me,' she said. 'You know I'm no good at guessing.'*

*'Well.' Marion took a deep breath and slowed her speech. 'I phoned the salon and they were fully booked until next week, but don't worry. I went into town and picked up some magazines and I've found the perfect style for you.'*

*'That's alright. I don't mind waiting until next week.' Lily tried to skirt around her mother into the hall.*

*'No, no, no, no, no.' Marion spread her arms, preventing Lily from getting past. 'It has to be done for tonight. Your big night, after all, let's not forget. So, I've done some research and I'm quite sure I can do it for you, right now.'*

*That's what Lily had been afraid of. Past experience told her that Marion considered herself an expert in pretty much anything after reading a couple of articles or watching a show on TV. This had been proved to Lily's cost on a number of occasions, such as the time she had requested a unicorn birthday cake when she was six, and was presented with a shocking pink monstrosity, complete with marshmallow teeth and a wonky ice-cream cone horn. Or the fancy dress outfit for World Book Day, which was supposed to be a lavish tiered princess affair, but ended up as Cinderella before the upgrade, thanks to unfinished hems, detached ruffles and the absence of any actual dress shape.*

*'No, that's alright, Mum. I'd rather stay as I am, and I've got so much practising to do before tonight, I should go and get on with it.'*

*'Absolutely not. My baby wanted a haircut and a haircut she will have. It won't take long.'*

*Lily recognised the determination in her mother's voice and realised a line was about to be crossed, but the alternative was unimaginable. 'No, Mum. I must get on, really.'*

*'But I've gone to so much trouble. Getting the magazines, reading all day, planning…'*

*'I know. Thank you. I really am grateful, but I don't have time. There's homework to do and words to look up and…' Lily took a tentative step away, one eye on the clock, checking to see if Ray was likely to appear any time soon. She needed the moral support, and he always seemed to know how to calm her mother down.*

*'I forbid it.'*

*Too late. Marion was about to blow.*

*'You said you wanted a haircut. If you didn't have time, why didn't you say so? I've been here, there, all over the place and now you're saying no. I forbid it, do you hear me? Sit in that chair and let me make you beautiful.'*

*'No, Mum, I can't.'*

*'Sit!'*

*Marion's voice was a shriek and Lily cowered away. This was going to be bad, but she couldn't give in. Not this time. 'No, Mum. Sorry, but no.' She saw a gap between her mother and the hallway and went for it, planning an escape to the bathroom. She would lock the door, put her fingers in her ears and wait it out until Ray got back.*

*Marion picked up a glass and launched it at the wall above Lily's head, screaming as loud as her lungs would allow. Lily shrunk back, sticky fruit juice spattering her face and hair. Clearly there was no going forward. She would have to go back, out the way she'd come in.*

*Lily flung open the door and ran down the path to the pavement. As far as she could remember, her mother had never allowed one of her episodes to continue outside their own home, they'd always stayed contained within those four walls, so all she needed was to find somewhere to hide out until it was over. As the garden gate swung closed behind her, she glanced back, to see a mug flying towards her. The china bounced off the low wall, smashed pieces flying in all directions, one small slither catching Lily on the ankle. She bent down to grab the damaged skin and, as she did, another missile flew over her head.*

*Her mother raced down the step to the path, yelling all the way, only stopping halfway to the gate. Lily didn't know what to do, where to go. One of their neighbours, old Mrs MacDougall, had appeared in the road, alerted by the kerfuffle, while others twitched curtains to watch, but not partake in the scene. The old lady was not put off by the ruckus and stepped forward.*

*'Young Lily, come along this away. Into my garden.' Her Irish lilt was a boon to Lily's ears, and she scurried past most willingly. 'Now, then, Marion. What's all this to do? Sure, it's not for the street to hear now, is it?'*

*But Marion's ire knew no end and she continued to scream, the only outlet for her anger now she had run out of missiles. Lily watched, cowering behind Mrs MacDougall's Hydrangea bush.*

*'Come on, now,' Mrs MacDougall continued. 'Take yourself a wee deep breath. Your man'll be along in a while and sure, you don't want him seeing you in this state.'*

*Marion's head of steam was reducing, and she fell to her knees, grabbing clumps of grass in her hands as if she wanted to squeeze the life out of them, her face contorted by anger.*

*Mrs MacDougall talked quietly and calmly, ignoring the growing huddles of onlookers and, slowly, Marion's yells reduced in power and frequency, until all that remained was a deep, heartfelt sobbing.*

*'There now, isn't that better? There can be nothing worth that kind of show now. That's it, settle down.'*

*A car turned into the avenue and pulled up a short way away and Lily realised it was Ray, earlier than she ever could have hoped. It seemed to take him only a moment to get the lay of the land and Lily saw his lips compress as he bolstered himself to do whatever was necessary.*

*'Everything alright?' He spoke to Mrs MacDougall, but his gaze ranged over the scene, Marion prostrate in the front garden, their matronly neighbour's reassuring tone, Lily peering from behind the bush, nosey parkers craning for a good view.*

*'Just a wee upset, that's all. Nothing to set the world on fire.' Mrs MacDougall leaned back and raised her voice. 'Nothing to see here. Go home the lot of yous.'*

*One or two onlookers, embarrassed to be caught out, instantly dispersed, others pretended to be otherwise occupied, trimming bushes, adjusting bins, but holding their ground.*

*'The wee girl's across the way there. I'll take her in and give her a biscuit while you give Marion a hand. Sure, she'll be right as rain in a minute.'*

*Ray threw another glance in Lily's direction and nodded. 'Thanks. I'll come and fetch her in a while.' He pushed open the gate and crouched down to Marion, talking quietly and steadily as if she were a spooked mare.*

*Mrs MacDougall strolled back to her own garden and up the path. 'Come on then, Lily. Let's me and you have a sit down inside.'*

*Lily watched her pass but didn't move. 'I'll come in a minute. Is that alright?'*

*'As you like, but there's no point hanging around there in the damp. The kettle'll be on and I'll leave the door on the latch.'*

*Lily turned back to Ray and Marion, where they were huddled low in their yard, biting her lip. Perhaps she should have just let her mother have her way. The results surely couldn't have been any worse than this.*

*She straightened up, ready to go inside, when a group of people caught her eye on the other side of the fence, openly standing on the pavement, staring. It was Susie and Marie and their cronies, giggling and whispering, and although she knew Susie would recognise her parents, Lily hoped the others would remain unaware. At that moment, one of them looked over her shoulder and caught sight of Lily and nudged Marie to get her attention.*

*Marie's face screwed up with disdain, her lip curled. She met Lily's eyes and muttered. 'Freak.'*

*Lily could find no words, so Marie turned away to her pals. 'At least now we know where she gets it from.'*

*The group strutted away and Lily, desperate to hold back the tears, let herself into Mrs MacDougall's house.*

# CHAPTER FOURTEEN

As the footage ended all became quiet, until the ombudsman's voice broke through. 'That's that then. Mission accomplished. No haircut. Now you need to make a decision, to bee or not to bee.' He laughed at his own joke. 'Do you get it? To bee or not to... Oh, never mind.'

Lily's silence made it clear she didn't appreciate his humour.

'Seriously, where do you want to go from here? Do you want young Lily to go to the event or not? There's a fork in the road and you need to tell me which direction you want to go.'

She huffed loudly. 'I don't actually think it will make a blind bit of difference.'

'Huh?' He pulled off his headset. 'Why would that be?'

Lily removed her equipment also and looked at him, her shoulders slumped in defeat. 'It doesn't matter what I do. If I go to the bee, it'll be a disaster and if I don't it'll be a disaster. Marie will see to that. I'd forgotten how awful she was. She made my life a complete misery, for years, and I think she would have found a way to do that no matter what I did. I can't bear to watch any more of this. I've clearly lost the argument. Can you look and see what happens and just tell me?'

'Hang on, I don't need to watch it all. I'll flick to the field scene on the tablet and check for results from both possible simulations.' He tapped buttons and swiped the screen left, then right and back again. 'You're absolutely right. There you are, in both scenarios, sat on the bench, unkempt and unwashed, in that awful hat. I figured if your hair was intact, at least the hat would have gone, but no, it's still there.' He shook his head in bewilderment.

'The hat made me feel invisible. I was trying to hide away from the world.' Having previously blocked this part of history from her memory, she was now able to see herself with a fresh perspective, a new understanding.

'And yet there you are, large as life, in all your grungy glory, for the whole world to see. A different attitude might have made things less distressing for you, may have helped you to snap out of it a bit sooner?'

'Snap out of it?' The sharpness of Lily's response sent the ombudsman's eyebrows flying up his forehead. 'What do you mean, snap out of it? Were you not watching the same thing as me? I was being bullied. I was dealing with a mother with horrible mental health issues, and I was on my own. I was a child for goodness' sake. Snap out of it, indeed.'

'Alright. Simmer down. I was only saying things as I saw them, and attitude has a great deal to do with resilience. It's not the events in our lives which create the perception of crisis, it's our reactions to those events.'

'What the heck is that supposed to mean?'

He huffed before trying to explain. 'Lily, that period of your life was always going to be challenging. There wasn't a secret tunnel which would allow you to bypass those obstacles, you had to work through them and out the other side. They're a part of your framework, which is made up of millions of different pathway choices, not just one and, if you don't mind my saying so, you overlooked a lot of positives which could have been taken from the situation, because you were concentrating on the negatives.'

Lily sucked in her cheeks. 'My mother had thrown a tantrum in front of everyone and his dog, and you think I should have been concentrating on the positives. Well, excuse me, for not having the insight to look beyond the embarrassment and shame and fear and…and… and humiliation. Tell you what. I'll try now, shall I? Oh, look, it was supposed to rain all day, but the sun came out for the ten minutes my mum was throwing a paddy.' She threw her hands out in a shrug. 'Would you know it? Suddenly I feel far better about things. Why didn't I try this before? Silly me.'

'Yes, alright. Point taken. I'm sorry, but, well, I've got to send you back in a short while and I'd like to think I could help you turn things around a little, so you were better prepared for the next stage of your life. I'd like it to be a more positive experience for you, that's all.'

'Huh, I can't see that happening.' She picked at the stitching on the edge of the sofa cushion.

'I won't point out what a negative comment that was.' He snorted and tapped his fingers on his knees in thought. 'A lot of people actually come back from these near-death experiences with a whole new outlook. I'm sure you'll have heard stories. You know the ones, "I almost died on an escalator and now I climb Everest every weekend", sort of thing. Play your cards right, you could be one of them.'

'Never have I ever wanted to climb Everest.'

'I didn't mean literally. In your case it could be "I was afraid to step outside my front door, but now I live life to the full". Wouldn't that be fantastic?'

Lily tipped her head to one side. 'I guess so, but it would take a miracle, and I can't say I've witnessed many of those.'

'To be honest, Lily, right now, I don't think you'd recognise one if it jumped up and bit you on the nose.' He waved a hand to move the conversation on. 'Well, miracles are outside of my remit, but you never know, a tweak here, a life lesson there, we might be able to do something. The question is, are you willing to try?

There's no obligation. You can simply go straight back if you'd rather.'

'I've nothing to lose really, have I?' She shrugged. 'Go on, then.'

The ombudsman smiled. 'Do you know, that was very nearly a positive comment? You're coming along in leaps and bounds already.' He checked his watch. 'We don't have an abundance of time, but let's see what we can manage. Lily Armitage, I am determined to turn your life around.'

# CHAPTER FIFTEEN

'Right then, first things first.' The ombudsman pulled a stylus from the side of his tablet and began to make notes on the screen. 'I think what I'd like to do is do a quick review of what we've already seen. Then we can visit some key points in your history, places where an alternative decision would have set you on a different thread of your framework. We can discuss why you made the choices you did, and then look at what would have happened had you not gone that way. How does that sound?'

Lily's eyes narrowed. 'It still sounds like you're trying to make everything my fault, rather than blaming circumstance, or the crap deal I was dealt early on.' She shook her head. 'I'm sorry, but I'm not letting this go.'

'Lily, as I've already told you, everyone has problems. It's how you choose to deal with said problems which affects your future, not those problems themselves.'

She pretended to stifle a yawn. 'Yeah, yeah. It's not about dodging the raindrops; it's about learning to dance in the rain. But look, not everybody had Marie blinking Willkie in their lives. It blows my mind to think what my life could have been like if she hadn't been in it. She destroyed me.'

'No, she didn't. She caused you no end of aggravation, granted, but at the end of the day, she was a teenager like you, who had to find her own way through the adolescent minefield.' He frowned. 'Though I'll admit she did seem to have it in for you.'

'She was never "like me",' Lily argued. 'I'd never have behaved the way she did.'

'Remember the saying, "walk a mile in another man's shoes"? You and Marie had very different backgrounds and influences. Although your mother had issues, on the whole she was supportive of you, and Ray was there for you too. I suspect Marie didn't have that. I suspect she used offence as a defence, to deflect unwanted attention from herself. Why she chose you as the victim, goodness knows, but she did, and I can understand your bitterness, to a certain extent.'

'I bet she hasn't lived the sort of life I have. I bet she came out of school all rosy and never looked back. I bet she's married, with the perfect family, and a career, with loads of money and a big posh house somewhere out in the country and ...'

The ombudsman interrupted. 'Lily, this isn't helpful. Regardless of who or what she is now, the point is, she's nothing to you. She has no influence on your life now. She can't hurt you anymore. Move on.'

Lily bit back the torrent of words rushing to escape her lips and frowned, chastised, but still angry.

'If this is going to work, we need to go into it with an open mind, as a learning experience, not an opportunity to cast blame. It's your future we're concerned with now and your past is only of value if it teaches us something. Right?'

'Hmm,' she agreed with bad grace.

'Otherwise, I might as well call Blessing back now and not bother.'

'Yes, alright. A learning experience. Ok.' Lily hadn't yet given up hope of proving her point and finding a way to go directly to the hereafter, so it seemed worth sticking with him, even if she wasn't fully on board with his methods.

'Good. Now.' He pointed at her headset. 'Put those back on. I want to show you a couple of things from the real version of your life which you missed first time round. It'll only take a minute, then we'll get to the real nitty gritty.'

She obeyed his instructions. The images rushed by at a dizzying rate of knots, as the ombudsman located the scenes required, and stopped on the morning of the bee, when Lily had walked to school with Susie and been warned not to take part. In the still, Susie had stalked away, and young Lily was staring at the floor.

'Now, then, I'm going to click forward in thirty second blocks and I want you to tell me what you see to the right of the front entrance.'

Lily concentrated on the entrance, ignoring her own figure and the crowds behind, but suddenly they were inside the building, and she was none the wiser. She shrugged in confusion. 'I didn't see anything. What was it?''

'Let's go back.' He jumped back to the outside. 'There.'

'What? I don't see anything.'

'Really. You don't see anything?' Lily could tell from his voice that he'd turned towards her. 'I'll give you a clue. About four foot six tall, young girl with brown hair in pigtails.'

'What, you mean Harriet? Harriet Hemming?'

'Well done. Give the girl a fish. Now, look how you react.'

In slow motion, young Lily walked straight past as Harriet tried to greet her with a smile, even stepping forward to get her attention, but young Lily was oblivious.

'Yes? So? I had a lot on my mind right then.'

'So you did, so you did,' the ombudsman agreed, but as he spoke the film was already flying forward. 'Now, here.' It stopped again, this time at the end of the bee, as young Lily stalked through the foyer, to escape into the car park. 'By the refreshments table.'

Lily was confused. 'It's Harriet again. What's your point? I don't get it.'

'No, I know you don't, and you didn't then either. Harriet desperately wanted to be your friend, but you were too busy moping about Marie and the disloyal Susie, who was equally as bad as Marie, if you ask me, not standing up for her best friend in her time of need. Your teenage years could have been a whole other experience if only you'd allowed Harriet in.' He went in for a close-up of the girl's sad face. 'And so could hers.'

'But I didn't know…'

'Of course you didn't. No one knows these things in advance. You've got to be constantly on the alert for opportunities around you and grab them with both hands. Quite often they come to nothing, or very little, but on the odd occasion they're a stepping-stone to something life changing.' He pulled the camera angle back. 'Like a best friend for life.'

'Harriet Hemming would have been my best friend?'

'The most loyal, supportive and loving friend anyone could want, and she was there for the taking, if only you'd lifted your eyes from the floor to notice.' His tone was gentle. 'Do you see my point now? Why it's so important to look for the positive aspects of everything?'

Lily couldn't quite take it in. 'Harriet Hemming?'

'Yes, Harriet Hemming. Anyway, time's cracking on and we need to move forward so we can squeeze in as much as we can. Are you ready?'

'I guess so. What are we going to see next?'

'Aah, well.' There was a great deal of relish to his tone. 'Next, Lily Armitage, this is your life, or at least, what it could have been.'

# CHAPTER SIXTEEN

'What do you remember from your fifteenth year? How did you spend the summer holidays?'

Lily felt this was some sort of test, one she didn't want to fail, so she dug deep. 'The summer when I was fifteen.' She tapped her chin with a finger as she thought. 'Not a lot. I was going into my final year at school, exams were coming up and I had masses of reading to do, so I think I spent the break doing that. It's not like I had many other options. We never did exotic family trips abroad or anything like that.'

'No summer job then?' The ombudsman glanced at her askance, poorly disguised humour in his eyes.

'No. I didn't have a job until I left sixth form, but would getting on the employment treadmill sooner really have been better for me?' She frowned. 'I can't see it myself.'

'Hmm, we've already talked about your tunnel vision, haven't we? Anyway, thinking about that summer, if you had to score it out of ten, where would you have placed yourself on the happiness scale? In fact, let's call it the Best Life scale, come on, marks out of ten.'

She could tell his excitement was mounting, but she was yet to see the reason, and looking back to that summer wasn't going to improve things one iota. It had been a miserable period of her adolescence, still at the mercies of Marie and estranged from Susie. Schoolwork had been the only thing which distracted her from her loneliness, the constant tension at school and the growing paranoia of her mother. It was then she'd developed her love of books, colourful worlds away from the grey one she resided in in reality. 'I don't know. Not high. Four, maybe? No more than five.'

'Right, well, let's ramp that up, shall we? Ok. We can't watch the entire six or seven weeks for obvious reasons, but we're going to enter just prior to the end of term, when your friend Harriet makes you a proposition.'

'Harriet Hemming?'

'Yes, keep up. Harriet Hemming. In this version you didn't ignore her after the bee, you accepted her friendship and your relationship has gone from strength to strength, leading to this scene, and I'm very glad to say the hat has gone. Come on, chop-chop! You need to focus.'

*ALTERNATIVE LILY ARMITAGE - AGED FIFTEEN*

*Lily was alone in a corner of the study space outside the school library, her head leaning against a bulging rucksack as she bit into a sandwich, while reading a hefty textbook, open on the table in front of her.*

*'I thought I'd find you here. Chaucer?' Harriet leaned over to read the heading on the book, before unpacking her own lunchbox.*

*'Yes.' Lily groaned. 'Why, why, why, did we have to have this on the reading list? It's not even proper English.'*

*'Never mind that. It'll wait until September. I've got amazing news.'*

*Lily needed no prompting. She slammed the book shut and pushed it into her bag. 'What news?'*

*'My Aunt Sandra, well she's not really my aunt, she's my mum's best friend from school, or college, or she used to work with her, or...'*

*'Your Aunt Sandra?' Lily knew from experience Harriet sometimes needed a nudge to keep her on point.*

*Yes, sorry, she came round last night for a cup of tea.' Harriet made speech marks with her fingers around the "cup of tea", 'which means they downed a bottle of Lambrusco in front of the tele and thought I wouldn't notice when they got all giggly. Anyway, she's got a contract at a holiday park on the seafront, organising entertainment for the kids, and she's looking for people to help out.'*

*Lily bit into her sandwich, still waiting for the exciting news.*

*'She said her budget is rubbish and if you pay peanuts all you get are monkeys so me and you can have first refusal of a job, if we want.' Harriet's eyes were wide with excitement.*

*'You realise that would suggest we're monkeys?' Lily was less than impressed. 'Besides, why would we want to spend the summer surrounded by screaming kids?'*

*'Lily, you're such a numpty. There are lots of reasons.'*

*She raised an eyebrow. 'Go on, then. Name them.'*

*Harriet huffed. 'Cash, obviously; work experience to put on our college applications, and it'll be fun.' She shrugged.*

*They all seemed good reasons.*

*'And, honestly, me and my mum went to the park last summer to use the pool and it was full of the hottest boys. It was like I'd died and gone to heaven, except my mum was there.'*

*Lily let out a shriek of laughter. 'Should have known. Harriet, you've got a one-track mind.'*

*'Have not.' She pretended to be offended but couldn't keep it up for long. 'Alright, maybe I have, but why not? Go on, Lily. Say yes. Mum says I can if you can, 'cause we can keep an eye on each other. Please, please, please.'*

*Lily took a moment to think it over. It sounded scary, a job, with a load of strangers, doing goodness knows what, but her friend's agonised expression as she waited, pressed for an answer. She laughed. 'Alright. Maybe. I'll ask Mum and Ray, but I don't think they'll mind. Anything to get me out of the house.'*

*'Yes.' Harriet launched herself at Lily and the pair disappeared in a scrum of arms and legs as the bench they sat on tipped up and deposited them on the floor.*

***

The ombudsman paused the scene, his voice recalling Lily to the present.

'Here's your choice, Lily. You can a) take the job and spend the summer frolicking with your friend, gaining precious life experience, or b) use your parents as an excuse and stay at home, in your bedroom, on your own.'

'Frolicking?' She chuckled at his phrasing. 'I can't help thinking you're pushing me in a certain direction.'

'No, no. No bias from me whatsoever. What's it to be?'

'Yeah, right. No bias at all.' It was obvious she was supposed to go for it, jump into the unknown to experience something new, but at the same time, that was the summer she had developed her love of reading, which influenced her choice of A-level study, which led to the job at the library, and if she hadn't spent the entire time with her head in a book, perhaps the whole future would change. Then where would she be?

'Come on, come on. Sometime this millennia. Excitement or boredom?'

'I'm sorry, but I'd have to say no. Staying at home it is.'

'What? You have got to be kidding.'

She heard the sofa sigh as the ombudsman sat back heavily in his seat. Clearly, she was frustrating him, but he didn't understand. 'But if I do it, it could change everything, forever, and I don't think I could handle that.'

He spoke slowly, but succinctly. ‘Lily, nothing we watch today will actually change anything. When you go back to your body, you will be in exactly the same place, at exactly the same time, in exactly the same position. This is merely giving you the opportunity to see what life could have been like.’

‘But what if it’s awful?’

‘None of it is real. It’s a TV show, nothing more. It can’t hurt you, but it can teach you something.’ He paused. ‘The one thing you’ve never been afraid of is learning. You read books all the time to learn things. This time you’ll be watching instead, that’s all.’

‘I suppose that’s true.’ She was tempted, but her gut fizzed with unspent adrenalin, holding her back.

‘I’ll be with you every step of the way.’

It was now or never. Step into the unknown or stay put, and never know what could have been.

‘Go on, Lily. You can do it.’ His voice was little more than a whisper.

She grabbed her knees and squeezed tight. ‘Ok. Let’s do this.’

‘Good girl. You won’t regret it. This could have been your alternative summer.’

# CHAPTER SEVENTEEN

*LILY ARMITAGE - AGED FIFTEEN*

*Lily and Harriet were following Aunt Sandra around the holiday park as fast as their legs would allow, but even so she had to pause at points for them to catch up.*

*'I've pretty much got free rein. The owner needs an entertainment programme, guests expect it these days. If you go abroad, it's a part and parcel of the package, but he doesn't really want to pay for it. I mean, why would he? He's got away with it this long, but people want more nowadays, if they're going to keep coming back. With that in mind, I'm drawing up a schedule of events to keep a wide range of kiddiewinks occupied, but at minimum outlay.'*

*Sandra halted and the girls concertinaed into her back. She pointed at a wide green space. 'We have access to one of the tennis courts for three sessions a week, two mornings and one afternoon. We can cordon off a third of the playing field, from the fence around the courts to where that tree is. We'll have to use cones or bunting. Cones, I think, we don't want it looking like a crime scene.' She stopped to write notes on a jotter she was carrying for the purpose. 'Do you know the rules for rounders and cricket and so forth?'*

*Both girls looked at each other and shrugged simultaneously.*

*'Never mind,' Sandra continued. 'We'll come up with a simplified version. Nothing too complicated. It's best to keep it simple and busy, so no one is tempted to wander off. Some kids have such short attention spans these days. Oh, and see the cabin on the corner there?'*

*She gestured to a large shed, painted blue, in the distance and the girls nodded.*

*'That's where the surfer dudes hang out. They store their equipment there and offer all sorts of lessons and experiences, so please, please give it a wide berth. To the type of kids that come here on holiday, these teenage lads come across as super trendy and I don't want our attendees abandoning our play sessions for body boarding instead. We'll be struggling to make a decent income as it is, without them stealing our clients. Besides, they've got a bit of reputation with the girls, if you know what I mean, and I don't want to have to answer to your mothers either. Now, let's get back inside.'*

*Harriet nudged Lily, smirking and winking, in case the elbow in the ribs wasn't sufficient to make her point. Lily tried to ignore her. She was quite happy for her friend to embark on a mission to pep up her love life, but personally, her life was complicated enough already.*

*The tour continued down pathways and side gates until they returned to the large hall where they had started.*

*'This doubles as a function room. They have all sorts of parties and stuff at the weekends, but it's ours Monday to Friday. We don't need it on Saturdays and Sundays anyway because they're changeover days: families going home and new families coming in; lots of cleaning going on, much too complicated, so you'll have the weekends off.' She smiled as if this was a real bonus.*

*'We'll have regular indoor events. I'm thinking dance classes to wear the little tykes out; arts and crafts, though not too much of that because of the need for equipment, and the mess, etc. And on*

*the odd occasion we can't use the outside space, we'll move the whole caboodle in here. Fingers crossed that doesn't happen too often or goodness knows how we'll manage. Can either of you do face painting?'*

*'Lily's good at drawing.' Harriet was quick to intercede.*

*Sandra glanced at Lily. 'Great. I'll put you in charge of that then. Don't worry. I'll come up with a plan and run it by you daily, so you're not thrown in at the deep end.'*

*Lily's stomach gurgled at the idea of being in charge of anything.*

*'Hopefully, we'll have a fantastic summer and will spend most of it in the great outdoors.' Sandra crossed the fingers on both hands and waved them vigorously. 'Right. Any questions?'*

*The only question Lily had was whether it was too late to back out, but a quick look at Harriet's face, alight with excitement, soon closed that down.*

*'Good. In that case, what I'd like you to do is to start next Friday. You've finished school by then, haven't you?'*

*Harriet confirmed school was out from Wednesday.*

*'Ideal. You can meet the others and we'll spend the day going through the schedules, making sure you know what you're doing. Super.'*

*The girls traipsed out, but as soon as the door closed and they were in the open, Harriet threw her arms around Lily.*

*'We are going to have such fun.'*

*'If you say so.'*

*'I do. I know we'll be nervous to start with, but then it'll be fantastic.' She grabbed Lily's elbow and directed her around the back of the hall. 'Let's go the long way to the bus stop.'*

*Lily followed, her mind elsewhere. 'But what if we can't do it? What if the children don't like us? Or won't listen to us?'*

*'Why wouldn't they? Look, we're doing this together and we'll be fine. Think of all that fresh air and getting paid to play games and ...'*

*As the pair rounded the corner a slightly older boy jogged by carrying a surfboard under one arm, shoulder length wet hair stuck to his forehead and neck, a trickle of water running down his bare chest, his wetsuit having been pulled down to the waist. Harriet stopped short and he glanced over his shoulder to wink and nod at them, whether as an apology for almost crashing into them or as a thank you for them giving way to him, was unclear.*

*With an open mouth, Harriet followed his progress as far as she could see and then pulled Lily into her side. 'Did you see that?' She shook her head and continued on. 'I told you, didn't I? Absolute heaven.'*

***

The images faded into a blur as the ombudsman changed scene. Lily could hear him humming a happy tune as he did so, obviously taking enjoyment from his job.

'I'm glad you're having fun.' She interrupted him.

The humming stopped. 'Well, aren't you? A jolly little scene of teenagers doing what teenagers do?'

'No,' she erupted. 'I can see exactly where this is going and I don't like it one bit.'

'What?'

Her vision went dark, and she assumed he had switched the equipment off, so removed the headset to find him glaring at her. She waved her hand at the place where young Lily and Harriet and the mysterious boy's image would have been. 'That… that boy. He's trouble if I ever I saw it. Either he's going to play me and Harriet off against each other, or he's going to dump me, or break my heart or something along those lines. I don't know why you would want to show me that. I've seen enough disappointment and humiliation for one lifetime, without you giving me even more to think about.'

‘And why would you assume anything of the sort? He looks a perfectly reasonable kind of young man to me.’ The ombudsman’s brow was low over his eyes.

‘There speaks a man who’s never been dumped, or two timed or wasted his time mooning over a guy who was never going to be interested in him in a million years.’ She rolled her eyes.

‘You have me there.’ The ombudsman sneered. ‘However, you’re assuming this has anything to do with that young man. There is in fact a much bigger life lesson to be had during that period and, actually, that young man is nothing but window dressing. Clearly he caught your eye though.’

Lily blushed. ‘No… Well, yes… Ok, so I got the wrong end of the stick, but that’s just indicative of the life I’ve lived. I can’t help that.’

‘What, you’ve lived a life of ogling innocent young men, minding their own business, and thinking the worst of them?’

‘I… You… Oh!’ She huffed, unable to think of a response which didn’t dig a deeper hole for herself. ‘Get on with it, will you?’

The ombudsman sucked in his cheeks to stop a smirk taking over his entire face. ‘Fine. Let’s see what’s next.’

# CHAPTER EIGHTEEN

*ALTERNATIVE LILY ARMITAGE - AGED FIFTEEN*

*Harriet had not slept the night before their induction out of pure excitement. Lily had not slept out of fear and, if it wasn't for the sake of not ruining things for her friend, would have pleaded sickness to get out of going. Three days in, she had to admit, it was more fun than she could ever have imagined.*

*So far, the sun had shone to order, and their young clients had arrived eager to be entertained, eyes wide at the countryside and beaches at every turn, most of them more used to the greyscape of inner city living. One or two were more challenging, but Sandra had a skill for spotting troublemakers a mile off and getting them onside, one way or another. The bulk of each day was spent laughing, as they hurtled round after footballs, tennis balls, frisbees or whatever the missile of the day happened to be. Lily's confidence had grown already, having dealt with minor emergencies, in the form of grazed knees, twisted ankles and, at one point, even fisticuffs between twins who proved more competitive than anyone could have anticipated.*

*At the end of their shifts, or indeed any opportunity Harriet spotted during intervals, Lily was dragged toward the infamous cabin, gradually getting closer each day, in the hope of making the acquaintance of the surfer crowd. They'd seen the guy they'd run into before, who Harriet had dubbed "Adonis", on a couple of occasions, surrounded by equally buff beach types and once he'd made eye contact, winked and growled, 'ladies' as he passed them, a posse of young would-be surfers in his wake. Harriet had almost choked on her tuna mayo sandwich in the excitement of being acknowledged. Lily was less impressed and would have preferred to eat her lunch in the safe confines of the storage-cupboard-come-staffroom.*

*In the second week things changed. Harriet and Lily's friendship group had expanded to incorporate a couple of other girls from Sandra's team, and this had bolstered their courage to the extent that they planned to actually walk directly past the front entrance of the cabin. To Lily, it felt unnecessarily daring. She was quite happy to approach the territory, to bask in its perceived glory somewhat, but this was to put themselves in the way of being noticed, of being approached, and possibly even invited in. It made Lily uncomfortable. It made the rest of the group giggly with what could be.*

*They crossed a grassy bank to join the path a hundred metres before the cabin, so it would look as if they were innocently passing by with no ulterior motive, except Lily feared the fact they'd swapped their tracksuits for skinny jeans, dolly shoes and handbags, was a bit of a giveaway. There had been much primping and nudging en route, but as they turned the corner and the cabin came into view, shoulders were straightened, hair flicked back and conversation died away. They were just four teenage girls taking a stroll at the seaside in their lunchbreak – nothing to see here.*

*A seating area had been set up along the front of the cabin under a veranda, comprising brightly coloured canvas camping chairs and upturned crates, littered with drinks cans. Wetsuits were hung from a makeshift rail at roof level at one end, dripping onto wooden decking or onto the grass as the odd gust of breeze sent them swinging, and garish towels were slung over handrails. A radio inside the shack played the latest tracks, but it was overpowered by the chatter and laughter from the residents, sitting around.*

*Adonis was there, in an old khaki chair, low to the floor, his feet crossed up on the handrail. He looked incredibly cool. Another boy, lounging against a post alongside him, spotted the girls at the same time they saw him and must have said something to the others, as another stepped forward to lean over the rail and ogle the new arrivals unhindered.*

*'Coming for a surf lesson while you're on holiday, girls?' He muttered something under his breath to his buddy before continuing louder. 'I'd be happy to teach you a thing or two.'*

*The mere fact of being acknowledged set Lily and Harriet's new friends giggling. Lily would have simply put her head down and kept walking, making sure she returned a different way, but Harriet seemed to find a new level of bravado from somewhere.*

*'No, thanks. We're not on holiday, we work here. We haven't got time to ponce about all day paddling and catching crabs with you.' She halted, her actions belying her words.*

*'Ooooh. Chester, mate, she obviously knows you. Catching crabs.' The boy's friends found her response highly amusing.*

*Rather than react to their goading, he slammed his palm against his heart. 'Ah, girl, you're killing me. Surfing's a way of life.' He leaned over the rail towards her, holding eye contact. 'Believe me. Try it once and you'll never look back. Come inside and I'll give you a one-to-one demo, no charge.'*

*Lily didn't like the tone the conversation was taking and hung back from the others.*

*'I really don't think you've got anything to show me that I'd be interested in. One surfboard is much like another, as far as I can make out.'*

*His eyebrows raised. He seemed to be enjoying the challenge, egged on by the catcalls of his mates. 'Come on. Everyone knows, it's not the board, it's what you do with it.' He shrugged, turned to a stack of boards and, selecting one, lay it on the grass. 'Though, looking at you, you've probably never been on a board in your life. Wouldn't know one way up from another.' His gesture invited her to prove him wrong.*

*Lily could feel her temperature rising. She didn't want to be here. 'Come on. We should get going. We've only got thirty minutes.'*

*Harriet glanced back, but the temptation to prove herself was more alluring. She thrust her handbag into Lily's arms. 'Here, hold this. It won't take a minute.'*

*'She's coming for you, Chester.' His friends were enjoying the banter.*

*He moved around to meet her. 'You're not coming near my board with those shoes on. You've got to treat this baby with kid gloves.'*

*Unperturbed, she kicked her pumps into the grass and mounted the board barefoot.*

*'You see. You've got it all wrong.' He climbed on behind and put his arms around her to change her stance, pushing one leg forward with his knee. 'It's all about balance.'*

*'She glanced over her shoulder at him, accepting his support. 'Like this?'*

*'Here, let me show you.'*

*He began talking her through the basics of how to handle a board and his friends, spurred on by his seeming success, jumped up. 'Any of you girls want a lesson?'*

*All but Lily stepped forward and were claimed by one of the lads and led to the nearest space. Lily's heart thudded uncomfortably. Innocent though this may be, she didn't want to get involved.*

*Adonis rose from his seat. 'What about you? We can't leave you out.'*

*She didn't know what to say without going against her own discomfort or sounding a prude. 'I really should get back.'*

*'That's a shame. I'd be happy to show you.'*

*His beauty and presence were wearing her down. He really was a good-looking guy. 'I...'*

*Another figure stepped out from the corner, hidden by the dangling wetsuits until now, and placed a possessive hand around Adonis's shoulder. Marie Wilkie. 'Don't bother, Jason. She's not interested. Anyway, I thought you were going to show me how to get up from horizontal in one move.'*

*He glanced at the hand on his shoulder, then back to Lily. 'You sure?'*

*The sight of her nemesis here, of all places, hit Lily hard and, if her resolve had been weakening before, it was now stronger than ever. 'Sure.'*

*He took Marie by the hand, still looking at Lily. 'Another time, maybe.'*

*Marie smirked at Lily and silently mouthed. 'Freak.'*

*Lily turned on her heel to head back to the staff room. She should never have let Harriet talk her into this. In future, she would stick to her guns and eat her sandwiches in peace.*

***

Lily took advantage of a lull in the footage to vent her frustrations. 'Didn't I tell you it would end in tears?'

The ombudsman was undeterred. 'As far as I can see, nobody's crying and, besides, it hasn't ended yet.'

With that, the images began to move once again.

*ALTERNATIVE LILY ARMITAGE - AGED FIFTEEN*

*Harriet leaned against the doorframe, fiddling with the handle of her handbag. 'Are you sure you won't come, Lils? It's not the same without you.'*

*Lily avoided eye contact, deliberately flattening a textbook on the table in front of her. 'No, I've too much to do. It's all very well having a job, but I've still got to fit in my prep for next term.'*

*'They were all asking about you, when you were going to come and join in. Honestly, Lily, it's such good fun. You'd love it if you gave it half a chance.'*

*This was a daily occurrence, Harriet desperately entreating her friend to come, while Lily did everything she could to avoid it.*

*Lily sighed. 'A, they don't even know me, so I don't see how they could be asking after me, and B.' She held her book in the air to illustrate her point.*

*'Ok.' Harriet backed out of the room. 'If you're sure. See you later then.'*

*Lily didn't bother responding, knowing as soon as her friend had left, her mind would be filled with other things. She knew she was being a killjoy, but she simply wasn't ready for all this boy stuff, especially those boys and even more especially with Marie blinking Wilkie in the mix. She had enough of her at school.*

*Sandra lumbered in and stacked a box in the corner, then stood up straight, rubbing her back. 'I didn't think anybody used the staff room. Not heading out with the others today?'*

*Lily stayed focused on reading, hoping to avoid conversation. 'Some of us have got homework to do.'*

*Sandra leaned over the table and lifted the book to read the cover, before dropping it back. 'Ugh, rather you than me. I'm guessing the rest are down at the cabin, completely ignoring my advice?'*

*Lily shrugged. She didn't want to get anyone in trouble.*

*Sandra studied her through narrowed eyes. 'Thought so.' She wandered towards the door and paused. 'Not your cup of tea, eh?'*

*Lily shook her head but didn't answer. She couldn't even begin to explain how she was feeling about the situation she found herself in.*

*Sandra smiled. 'Don't blame you either. Plenty of time for that sort of nonsense. Clever girl like you doesn't want distractions.' She made to leave but turned in the doorway. 'You've a lot of potential, Lily. I've been watching you with the little ones, and you really seem to have a connection with them. I could see you as a teacher one of these days.'*

*'I don't think...' Lily was more than ready to refute her abilities.*

*'Stop with the modesty and take praise where it's due. I've been glad to have you on my team, and it doesn't hurt to be told your worth once in a while.'*

*The door swung shut behind her and Lily was left alone. Her cheeks felt warm from the unexpected compliment. It wasn't something she was used to, but it felt good, nonetheless. She pushed the book away and reached for her sandwich. Her appetite had suddenly returned.*

# CHAPTER NINETEEN

*ALTERNATIVE LILY ARMITAGE - AGED FIFTEEN*

*As September approached, the weather took a dive and Lily began counting down the days to the end of the season and the return to school. They played chicken with the raindrops whenever possible, twenty damp, but well-exercised children being far easier to handle than twenty dry, stir-crazy ones. However, for the last four days, the storms came in good and proper and there was no let-up in the downpours and Sandra found her indoor provisions close to exhausted. It didn't help that the clientele this week were the most challenging yet. She was fretting during the early morning set-up routine.*

*'It took me an hour to get the paint off the skirting boards last night, but I can't see any other option but to get the easels out this afternoon. You can only make charades last so long and, to be honest, I don't think Brandon's got the attention span for it. We can't have him kicking off like yesterday, I thought he was going to give someone a black-eye with his windmill dancing.'*

*'That wasn't dancing,' Lily interrupted. 'He was being Wonder Woman. The day before he was Batman. He's quite keen on superheroes.'*

*'Whatever it was, it was most definitely dangerous and shouldn't be repeated. We'll have to find something to keep him occupied. You seem to have quite a connection with him though, Lily. Any suggestions?'*

*Lily frowned and shook her head.*

*'Anyone else? Anything? Face painting isn't going to cut it for long.'*

*There was little more than a murmur.*

*'It's such a shame. We've had a fantastic time all summer and now it's going to end like a damp squib.' Sandra was not her usual upbeat self.*

*One of the girls spoke up. 'What about like Dirty Dancing?'*

*Sandra stopped what she was doing. 'We'll not have any of that, thank you very much.'*

*'No.' The girl clarified. 'They finish the season with a talent show. Why don't we get the kids to choose an act and put on a show on Friday?'*

*'Do you know? That's not a bad idea. I could see most of them getting involved. What about Brandon though? Do you think it would hold his attention, Lily? What could he do?'*

*Lily was proud to have her opinion sought on such a matter. 'I think it would, as long as it was kept fun and wasn't too complicated.'*

*'Right then. We'll stick to the old favourites this morning, but then come up with a plan with the children this afternoon. Perhaps I could make Brandon your particular responsibility? Would that be alright?'*

*Before Lily could answer, the first of the children arrived and it was all hands on deck.*

***

The ombudsman bunny-hopped the footage from scene to scene. 'We're almost at the end of this stage now.'

'And I haven't learned much yet, apart from that Marie blinking Wilkie was still on the scene creating havoc, and that one random person thought I'd make a good teacher one day. And, I was right about Adonis, wasn't I? I told you nothing good would come of it. Me and Harriet were doing fine until his gang got between us.' Lily sighed. 'What is this all about? Is there a point?'

'You haven't a great deal of patience, have you? Bear with me, Lily. Sometimes you have to save the best for last. Keep watching.'

*ALTERNATIVE LILY ARMITAGE - AGED FIFTEEN*

*The children were instantly enthralled with the idea of a talent show and those who didn't have a particular skill they wanted to show off, or were too shy, were roped in backstage, to manufacture props and scenery, and even costumes, from whatever could be conjured up from the stockroom. It was amazing what had been left behind by various hen parties, stag-dos and celebrations of the past, from feather boas to inflatable palm trees. A treasure trove.*

*Lily had her work cut out with Brandon. He was a pleasant enough little boy, but he was in a world of his own a lot of the time and, once he got an idea into his head, there was no shifting it. To begin with, he'd been happy rifling through the junk they'd rescued from the cupboard but, once he saw others rehearsing, he was determined to perform in one way or another. But what was he to do? The grown-ups were at a loss.*

*'Would you like to sing a song, Brandon?' Sandra was trying to steer him clear of dancing after his earlier performance.*

*The boy bounced on the spot. 'Nope.'*

*'Ok. Do you know any magic tricks? You could guess somebody's card or something. People always like card tricks,' she continued.*

*He stopped bouncing and squeezed her arm, excited. 'I could cut someone in half.'*

*'Oh no, I don't think we can do that.'*

*He started jumping again, shouting rhythmically. 'Cut in half, cut in half, cut in half.'*

*'Shoot, I've started something now.' Sandra turned to Lily. 'Help.'*

*Lily thought hard. 'I think you need to be a superhero, Brandon, because that's your favourite thing, isn't it?'*

*The jumping continued, perilously close to three girls doing warm up exercises before their ballet routine, but the shouting changed. 'Superhero, superhero, superhero.'*

*'Right, come and sit down and we'll list superheroes and work out which one you should be.'*

*He instantly returned to her side and held out his hand, ready to be led away.*

*'Lily, you're amazing. I think you're the superhero.' Sandra laughed.*

*Brandon glared at her. 'No, I am.'*

*Suitably chastised, Sandra quickly backtracked. 'You're right, Brandon. I guess Lily must be your sidekick, like Batman's Robin, eh?'*

*'No, I'm going to save her from the baddies. Aren't I, Lily? I'm going to fly across and save you from the baddies.'*

*Lily shot a glance at Sandra. This was an idea which would be hard to do away with. 'Not all superheroes fly, you know?'*

*'This one does,' he stated.*

*Sandra bit her lips together, to stop herself laughing. 'Right, I'll leave this with you then, shall I? Once you've decided which superhero we're dealing with, perhaps you could write a little scene for him. You've got such a way with words. And one or two of the others might not object to being extras.'*

*'Oh.' Lily found the idea a little daunting. 'Ok. I'll see what I can come up with.'*

*Lily needn't have worried, Brandon had plenty of ideas of his own and by the end of the day he'd come up with a plan. He was happy to search for props to build his dream backdrop and it didn't seem to matter if the reality fell short of his description, his imagination did the rest.*

*It was Harriet who was the source of a real breakthrough, the day before the show. Her needlework skills had been thoroughly tested during the preparations, and while looking for fabric to fashion into clouds for a particular dance act, she pulled out the remains of a Superman costume.*

*'Lily, is this any good to you?'*

*Brandon looked up from the scene they were painting and squealed, grabbing Lily's attention. 'Is that for me? Is that for me? Is that for me?' He jumped to his feet and jiggled, as if sprinting on the spot.*

*The girls held the costume up between them. It was huge, adult size, probably the remains of someone's fancy dress effort, and had a few rips and a couple of dubious stains, but it showed promise.*

*'Wow, this would be great, if you can fix it. What do you think?'*

*Brandon looked from Lily to Harriet, desperate for her response to be positive.*

*'I'm sure I can do something with it, bits anyway. Can I measure it against you, Brandon?'*

*Without answering, he stood bolt upright, arms out like a scarecrow, ready to be measured.*

*Harriet laughed and separated out the items, trying each in turn. 'We could fit you in this twice over, Brandon.' She chewed her lip as she considered the issues. 'The cape's fine, apart from needing a wash. I can probably just cut the ends off the sleeves because it's Lycra sort of stuff, and I wouldn't have to take it in much, but we'll have to take about a foot off the bottom. I could use the leftovers to patch up the tear in the back.'*

*'It's lots of work. Have you got time?' Lily was in awe of Harriet's abilities with needle and thread and knew what was required was far beyond anything she could manage herself.*

*'Well...'*

*'Please, please, please.' Brandon squeezed his hands together in prayer, his face taut with the threat of his ideal costume being lost.*

*'I suppose so, but I'm supposed to be making clouds... unless you could paint clouds onto the sheets instead?'*

*He turned his attention to Lily. 'Can we? Please?'*

*Lily kept her face straight. 'We'll have to do it right to the end. We won't be able to stop halfway through. Can you do that?'*

*Without even considering the possibility of an alternative response, his head flew into a flurry of energetic nodding.*

*Lily was doubtful he would be able to keep his side of the deal, but she didn't have the heart to refuse him. 'Ok, then. Let's do it.*

# CHAPTER TWENTY

*ALTERNATIVE LILY ARMITAGE - AGE FIFTEEN*

*The following morning, Harriet produced a patched-up, but wearable version of the costume and Brandon could barely contain himself. He was allowed to try it on, on the understanding it would then be put away, to be kept safe for the afternoon's show, but once he was wearing it, his adherence to the rules fizzled out. He shot around the room, one arm held out in front, zig-zagging around huddles of other children still trying to finish their own preparations, yelling at the top of his voice. Lily chased him, but his small body was able to take corners far more nimbly than hers and he was constantly one step ahead. Giving up, she collapsed into a chair and watched his progress, in the hope his energy would eventually run out.*

*Sandra stood in the centre of the room; arms spread in disbelief at the havoc he was creating. He circled her twice, before skidding to a halt only a few centimetres away from Lily, hands on hips, chest puffed out like a cockerel.*

*'I'm Superman and I'm going to save the world.'*

*In spite of everything, Lily had to stop herself laughing. 'Brandon, you wear me out.'*

*'My mum says that.' He pulled the cape over his shoulder and smoothed it down one arm as if it were a pet rabbit. 'I want to show my brother.'*

*Lily sat forward and made eye contact. 'Your brother can see it at the show, but now you need to take it off.'*

*His bottom lip thrust forward.*

*'You promised. You know you did, and it's only for a little while. After lunch you'll be able to put it on and keep it on until you go home.'*

*'Can I keep it?'*

*'I don't know. We'll have to talk to Sandra about that, but she definitely won't say yes if you keep knocking people over and running into things.'*

*His chin dropped.*

*'I'll ask her. You go and get changed.' She pointed him in the direction of the changing area, and he went without another sound.*

*Lily was true to her word and went to speak to Sandra.*

*'Of course he can have it,' she said. 'It'll be no use to anyone else now it's been cut down and, to be honest, it's on its last legs. Maybe we should use it as a "bribe".' She mouthed the word. 'He can have it if he stays calm. I've a feeling we might need a bargaining chip or two this afternoon. The excitement is certainly building.'*

*Lily looked around the room at all the children engrossed in their work. 'I'll miss this. It's been far more fun than I imagined.'*

*Sandra half turned away in response to a tug on her shirt. 'Remember that later when all hell breaks loose.' She laughed.*

*Harriet joined them, arms loaded down with bags. 'Where's Brandon off to?'*

*'What?'*

*She twitched a shoulder towards the door. 'I just saw him heading down the side path…'*

*Lily squealed. 'Brandon. I thought I could trust you.' She pointed the way Harriet had entered. 'That way?'*

*Sandra's mouth had opened to speak, but Lily was ahead of her.*

*'It's alright. I'll find him.'*

*All week she had kept a close eye on the boy, checking he was where he should be, keeping him occupied and out of trouble. Now it seemed, at the last fence, he had gotten away from her and, although they were in a pretty safe, enclosed environment, there was plenty of potential for things to go wrong.*

*The wind and rain didn't help. Within seconds her hair was flattened to her face, and she swiped it away to see, in time to spot a flash of Brandon's red cape disappearing around the corner of a chalet. At least she knew which way to go. She held one hand above her head to keep off the worst of the weather and ran, skidding as she took a shortcut across the sodden grass, in an attempt to close some ground. Brandon seemed to know exactly where he was going and was not slowing down.*

*Finally, she joined the main walkway along the bottom of the camp and the straight path stretched out in front, revealing a bedraggled Brandon a couple hundred metres ahead. He had slowed to a trot and then stopped, directly outside of the cabin.*

*Lily's breath was ragged in her throat. Despite the weeks of exercise, playing rounders and tennis, sprinting for this distance was outside of her comfort zone, as was the territory. She slowed down too, anxious about who may be hovering around the building, regardless of the downpour.*

*Brandon stood facing the entrance of the cabin, his hands twisting around each other. Lily could see his lips moving. He must be talking to someone under the veranda, but she couldn't yet see. Reluctantly, she continued on. No matter what, she had to get this little boy back to the hall, both for his sake and Sandra's. There would be ructions if word got out that one of the children was running around the park unattended.*

*As she came up level to the structure, she saw a small group huddled on the decking and right in the middle of them was Marie. Lily's heart dropped.*

*'What are you looking at, kid?' Marie hadn't seen Lily. She was focused on Brandon.*

*'My brother,' Brandon muttered, his hands writhing even faster.*

*'What's that?' Marie leaned over the handrail into the rain.*

*'My brother,' Brandon repeated, no louder than before, his chin sinking into his chest.*

*Marie muttered something to the group behind her, then turned back to the boy. 'I don't know what you're on about. Get lost, freak.'*

*This was too much for Lily. It was one thing for the girl to make Lily's life a misery, but she wasn't to speak to a child like that. She strode forward and grabbed Brandon's hand, aware in the corner of her eye that another person had walked out of the cabin. 'He is not. He's a lovely little boy. If anybody's a freak, it's you, talking to a kid that way.' Pulling him away, she ignored any response Marie could possibly offer. 'Come on, Superman. You can show your brother later, but if you stay out here any longer it'll be too wet to wear on stage.'*

*Marie shouted something, but the wind was blowing in the other direction and Lily was glad not to be able to decipher it. Brandon didn't need to hear any more abuse, whether it be directed at him or her.*

*They hadn't gone far though when the pad of speedy footsteps came up behind them, and Lily steeled herself for confrontation, but as the person drew level and put a hand on her arm to stall her, it was a young man. He was about her age, maybe slightly older.*

*The boy ushered them into the shelter of an overhang from a chalet roof and crouched in front of Brandon, who immediately threw wet arms around his neck in a hug.*

*'Alright, buddy? I didn't recognise you in that get up. You look amazing.'*

*Brandon stood back, tall and straight. 'I'm Superman.'*

*'I can see that.'*

*'Are you going to come and watch me later? I'm going to be great.'*

*The older boy chuckled. 'I bet you will. I wouldn't miss it.'*

*He stood up and Lily could now detect similarities between the two faces, the same colouring and matching dimples in their cheeks, but the older version had a ring through his eyebrow and a floppy haircut that gave him a different kind of cute to the younger one. She blinked as rain dripped down her face, and hoped the damp hid the sudden blush to her cheeks.*

*Briefly, he made eye contact and patted her shoulder awkwardly. 'Thanks.' He gestured with his chin toward the cabin.*

*The blush increased. He had the most incredible blue eyes, when his fringe wasn't hiding them. 'It's ok. She shouldn't be like that. I guess you're Brandon's brother.'*

*It was his turn to pink. 'Blimey, have I got a reputation already? I've only been here a week.'*

*She shook her head. 'No. Brandon ran away because he wanted to show you the costume.*

*His face took on a serious expression. 'Brandon. We've talked about this. You only get to do these fun things if you follow the rules. You mustn't run away.'*

*'I wanted to show…'*

*'It doesn't matter what you wanted; you mustn't run away. Got it?'*

*Brandon gazed at the floor but nodded.*

*'You and the lady are wet through now. Go on. Go back and do as you're told.'*

*'You won't tell Mum, will you?'*

*'As long as you don't do it again, right? Go on. Off with you.'*

*They parted ways, Lily and Brandon heading to the hall and his brother back toward the cabin.*

*He leant in to speak quietly in her ear as he passed. 'Hey, thanks again.'*

*Lily glanced over her shoulder to smile in response and found him far closer than she expected. A wave of something warm flooded through her. A grin plastered itself across her face as she continued to walk, she had a feeling Marie might get a talking to of a very different kind.*

# CHAPTER TWENTY-ONE

*ALTERNATIVE LILY ARMITAGE - AGED FIFTEEN*

*From the level of excitement backstage (the little huddle behind a screen, off to the right of the make do platform), you would have been forgiven for thinking a Royal Variety performance was about to begin. It took all the group leaders' efforts to keep their wards in line which, thankfully for Lily, meant she didn't have time to be nervous about her own part in proceedings.*

*Contrary to the usual order of things, Brandon was serene. He had been ready before anyone else, sat on a bench and stayed there, oblivious to the squealing girls in their tutus, whirling around him as their nervous energy overflowed. It was as if he was born for this sort of thing.*

*Lily checked on him frequently, having expected a very different experience for the afternoon, but rather than having to turn to others for support, she was able to assist them with their wayward prodigies instead. With only minutes to go, she slipped onto the bench next to him.*

*'Did you want to run through your lines one last time?'*

*His gaze remained fixed on the stage, only the shaking of his head showing he had heard.*

*'Do you need a last-minute glass of water, or trip to the loo? The guests are almost all here so we'll be starting very soon.'*

*'Is my brother here?' His head shot round to try and see through the hinged area of the screen.*

*'I don't know. Do you want me to check?' She was quite interested in whether he had arrived too.*

*He sat back down, nodding briskly.*

*Lily picked her way past bundles of clothes and small bodies littering the floor and peered around the screen. Brandon's brother was lounging against a pillar at the back, hands in pockets, intermittently flicking his fringe out of his eyes. He was the epitome of cool and Lily felt a blush rise up her neck into her cheeks. She returned to the space next to Brandon.*

*'Yes, he's here. I can't see your mum though.'*

*The boy shrugged. 'She usually sleeps after lunch.'*

*'Oh, ok.'*

*Sandra appeared from somewhere to give a quick pep talk to all concerned, then mounted the platform to get thing started.*

*Brandon's snippet was towards the end of the schedule, and although he remained calm throughout dance routines, songs and magic tricks, as the time for them to do their part approached Lily's knees shook.*

*He must have noticed her discomfort because he leaned over to her and said, 'Don't worry, Lily. You'll be fine. I'll be there with you.'*

*She couldn't help but smile at his reassurance. He really was a special little boy.*

*At last, the moment arrived, and they took up their positions. Sandra was to narrate, and Lily's role was to walk across the stage as if she were merely out for an afternoon stroll. Another, bigger boy had been roped in to play the part of a robber, who wanted to steal Lily's handbag, at which point she was to shout for help and Superman was to race to the rescue.*

*Sandra began to read the background story; Lily stepped out from the side, heading for centre stage and, at that point, glanced up and saw the audience looking straight at her. Her mind suddenly flipped back to the last time she had stood on a stage in front of a crowd and the humiliation she had felt then. She froze, her mouth completely dry and she missed her cue*

*Unsure what was happening, Sandra repeated the cue and, when Lily still didn't move, waved the would-be robber on to do his bit. Rather too exuberant in his role, the boy ran in, grabbed Lily's bag, shoving her hard and, as her mind was elsewhere engaged, she was totally unprepared and lost her balance. What was supposed to be an acted minor stumble became a real major topple and she crashed across stage, careering over the edge and landing at the feet of onlookers in the front row. Taken aback, the robber stopped short, clutching the bag to his chest, staring at Lily's prone body.*

*Brandon hurtled onto centre stage like a wrecking ball, where he struck a pose and announced that Superman would not allow such injustice and bad behaviour as long as he was around. He then grabbed the other boy and dragged him off in a headlock.*

*Although the platform wasn't far off the ground, Lily's breath had been forced out of her chest with the impact and it took a few seconds to get her bearings. She looked up and realised she was directly at the feet of Brandon's brother. He gazed down, firstly in shock, then, once he realised she was not injured, in amusement. Standing up, he held out his hand to help her to her feet.*

*'You ok?'*

*The light in his eyes told her he was holding back a grin, which made them even more attractive. Rather than embarrassment, she felt something else entirely and it was difficult to draw her gaze away. Hopefully everyone would put her blushes down to the accident and not the quickening of her heart as she became aware her hand remained gripped by his.*

*Brandon had run back onto the stage. 'Lily. Lily.' His voice was an extremely loud whisper and the audience laughed. 'Come here, Lily.'*

*His words drew Lily back to reality and she freed her hand and turned to Brandon, who was waving frantically for her to come closer. She moved towards him, and as he was on the platform, but she was not, they were now at the same height.*

*Brandon threw one arm around Lily's shoulders and raised her handbag into the air with the other. 'Don't worry, lady. I have got your bag back from the robber and slammed him in jail so he can't do it again. Here you are.'*

*He gave her the bag and she was pleased to find her nerves had reduced, figuring the worst had happened already and things couldn't get any more embarrassing. 'Thank you, Superman. You're my hero.'*

*He leaned forward. 'You may kiss me, if you like.'*

*That wasn't in the script.*

*He jammed a finger into his cheek, showing where she should be kissing, and stuck out his chin.*

*There seemed little option. She leaned in and gave him a peck on the cheek.*

*Brandon's brother chuckled in his seat. 'That's my boy.'*

*Sandra finished the narration and the cast slipped back behind the screen, while the last couple of acts did their bit. In some ways, Lily was glad it was over, but it also meant the end of the season, and she was going to miss the job and the friends she had made doing it. The show finished, the audience broke into enthusiastic applause and Sandra shouted over the noise for all the acts to come and take a bow.*

*As she stood shoulder to shoulder with Harriet, with Brandon and the others, she knew this was a moment she would remember forever.*

# CHAPTER TWENTY-TWO

The ombudsman peered at Lily to gauge her reaction. 'Well? What do you think?'

'Yes, it was actually quite… nice.' She struggled to find an appropriate word. 'Boy, it was scary though. I'm glad it wasn't real. My heart's still pounding now.'

'Nice? Nice?' he blustered. 'Don't get carried away, will you? That was beyond nice. It was fun. It was touching. It was a valuable experience.'

'Ok. Ok. Message received.'

'Considering the alternative was sitting in your bedroom for six weeks reading… What was it? Ugh. The Pickwick Papers.' He shuddered. 'That's hours of your life you'll never get back.'

'I actually quite enjoyed it.' She was offended on Dickens' behalf.

He slapped his forehead with his palm. 'It gets worse. Let's weigh it up.' Holding his hands out, one on either side, he mimicked a set of scales. 'Pickwick Papers or first kiss? Pickwick Papers or first kiss? I know which I'd choose.'

She tutted. 'Hang on. I'd hardly call that a first kiss. Brandon was a child, and it was part of a show. I don't think that counts.'

The ombudsman's eyes widened, and he inhaled sharply. 'Oh, shoot. I switched it off too soon. Quick, headset back on. There's more.'

'Really? More?'

'Oh, yes. You don't want to miss this. It's the best bit.'

*ALTERNATIVE LILY ARMITAGE - AGED FIFTEEN*

*There were hugs all round as the group parted company, and promises to keep in touch. Lily stayed behind to help Sandra clear away, while some headed home and some had prior arrangements for a rendezvous at the surfer cabin. It was going to be tough for Harriet and the like, who had struck up relationships with some of the boys but would now face the challenges of finding time to see each other when back in the old routine.*

*Finally, Lily retrieved her rucksack and headed off, with the promise of a job the next summer if she wanted it. She hadn't got far when she heard a voice calling her name, from behind. Turning, she saw Brandon's brother pelting towards her, and her heart fluttered.*

*He skidded to a stop in front of her. 'Hi.' His breathing was fast and heavy from the exercise, but for some reason it turned Lily's insides molten.*

*'Sorry. I didn't think I was going to get back in time.'*

*'Is Brandon alright?'*

*He laughed. 'Yeah, he's alright. I've left him eating toast with Mum. He's absolutely starving.' His face straightened. 'Look, I wanted to say thanks again, for, you know, sticking up for him this morning and, from what he's said, you've pretty much been looking after him all this week. I know he's not everybody's cup of tea...'*

*'No, he's lovely.'*

*'Yeah, right. I love him to bits, but he can wind people up, so, thank you for being patient with him, and not letting that cow down at the shack get away with it.'*

*Lily was embarrassed by the praise. 'She's like that with everyone. I just didn't think she should pick on someone smaller than her.'*

*'That's a rule most people stick to.'*

*'Marie's not just anyone, she has her own rules.' Lily sneered.*

*He studied her face, looking into her eyes as if searching deep inside her. 'You're not just anyone either. I think you're quite special.'*

*She couldn't hold his gaze, letting her focus dip to her shoes, but then, desperate to read his thoughts, looked back up. He was still staring, and as their eyes met, he leaned in and planted a soft, slow kiss on her lips.*

*Pulling back, he turned to walk away, but looked over his shoulder, smiling. 'I couldn't let my little brother be the only one to get a kiss today, could I?'*

*Lily was glued to the spot, legs too weak to move, staring after him as he disappeared among the chalets. She pulled air slowly into her lungs and put her fingertips to the place on her mouth where his lips had been. Today was officially the best day ever.*

***

'Now what was that you were saying? Nice, was it? Yes, I think it was something along those lines.' The ombudsman's voice was as lofty as his superior eyebrows. 'Would you like to amend your verdict at all?'

Lily's throat was dry, and she couldn't form clear words. She coughed. 'Water. Water, please.'

He jumped up, poured a glass of water and passed it to her. 'Are you alright? We're not going to have any passing out shenanigans, are we? I can't stand it when you humans pass out on me.'

She swallowed several gulps then cradled the glass in her hands. 'No. I'll be ok in a minute.'

The ombudsman watched as she took another couple of sips and sat back down, reassured.

She looked at him, a doubtful frown heavy on her brow. 'That was all made up, wasn't it? It didn't actually happen, right?'

He nodded. 'Complete fabrication.'

'But it seemed so real.' She put a hand to her chest. 'It was almost as if I was actually there.'

He pursed his lips. 'Well, I suppose in a way you were. After all, it was another version of you we were watching. Had you taken a different path in life, you would have lived that experience. I suppose it's only natural for you to feel a strong connection.'

She blew a silent whistle. 'Well, in that case, I think I've seen enough.'

'Sorry?'

'I don't think I want to see any more. I don't know if I could handle it. That was a roller coaster ride, making friends, dealing with Marie blinking Wilkie, appearing on stage and then…' She waved a hand at thin air. 'then… that. Besides, I'm sure it was all very lovely for those few seconds, but I bet I was mooning after the guy for weeks after.'

'You say mooning, I say reminiscing.'

'No, I can't take any more. If I've got to go back, I might as well get on with it.'

The ombudsman bit his cheek and peered at her. 'But I want to show you more. You clearly haven't seen enough to change your attitude, because you're still afraid now. Afraid to view another scene, let alone live it.'

'No, send me back.'

He picked up the tablet and scrolled through several pages, muttering to himself. 'You can't please some people. One minute it's "no, no, don't send me back", and the next it's "send me back this instant". Fickle humans…'

Something caught his attention and he stopped abruptly, peaking at her out of the corner of his eye. 'I know something you might like to see.'

'I doubt it.'

'Oh, ok. I thought you might be interested in seeing a certain Mr Darren Chantilly, but if you don't want to, that's fine.'

Her interest was piqued. The man she could have married. What sort of man would he have been? Was he handsome? Was he funny? What had attracted her to him? And what had he seen in her? She had to know. 'Wait. What, Darren?'

The ombudsman feigned confusion. 'What? Is there a problem?'

She bit her lips together, sensing she'd been manipulated, but unable to switch off her curiosity. 'I want to see.'

'What? You want to see now?'

'Yes. I do. Just get on with it.'

He was enjoying her discomfort. 'Are you sure?'

She groaned. 'Yes. Do it.'

He shrugged. 'Ok. Here we go.'

# CHAPTER TWENTY-THREE

*ALTERNATIVE LILY ARMITAGE - AGED EIGHTEEN*

*Harriet was drumming her fingers on the table, struggling to retain her patience. 'But Lily, the whole point of us going to the same uni was so we could go out and have fun together. It's Freshers' week! We've got to sign up to some of the events or it's a complete waste of time being here so early.'*

*When she'd sent off her application, attending university had been such a distant prospect it had seemed like a good idea, but in the weeks leading up to leaving home, and now Lily was here, it was all a bit much. 'But I've got masses of reading to do.'*

*Harriet rolled her eyes. 'Nobody expects you to do it during Freshers' week. The whole idea is to go out and meet people and settle in, get to know what's what. There'll be plenty of time for work the whole of the next three years.' She stood up to give emphasis to her plea. 'Please, Lily. Please, let's just go to a couple of events. That won't take too much time.' An idea occurred to her. 'I know, you choose one event and I'll choose one and then I won't nag you anymore. Please, please, please.'*

*Lily could resist no longer. She'd been listening to Harriet's pleading for three days and knew it wasn't an unreasonable request. They'd talked about and planned their uni experience for months in advance and it was Lily whose enthusiasm had dwindled, not Harriet. 'Alright.'*

*Harriet grabbed her. 'Really?'*

*'Yes, alright. One thing each, but don't go mad. I'm not going sky diving or paragliding or karaoke or anything scary like that.'*

*'No. That's fine by me. Quick, get your coat.' Harriet bustled Lily out of the door before she could change her mind.*

*Their accommodation was on different levels of the same building, twenty minutes' walk from campus if the brochures were to be believed, but they covered the distance in fifteen, Harriet ushering Lily along every step of the way.*

*Lily came up with more sanctions every few metres. 'No dancing. I'm not doing dancing of any description. I've got two left feet and I couldn't bear people watching me make a fool of myself.'*

*'Everybody would be making fools of themselves.'*

*Lily halted. 'Harriet...'*

*'Ok, no dancing.' Harriet grabbed Lily's arm to keep her moving.*

*'Absolutely no public speaking. That means no debating society, or drama clubs or political groups or...'*

*Harriet threw an arm around Lily's shoulders as they pushed through swing doors into the foyer. 'Chill out, Lils. I'll see if there's a breathing club. Or are you not doing that either.'*

*'Ha, ha.'*

*The lobby was swarming with excited young bodies, soaking up the atmosphere, revelling in the freedom of being in a fresh environment, with new people and pretty much nobody to answer to about their comings and goings.*

*Harriett was agog, basking in the stew-pot of swirling testosterone in its many forms.*

*'So, where do we start?' Lily was verging on the overwhelmed.*

*A tall, broad-shouldered guy, with slicked back blonde hair, had made brief eye contact with Harriett and there was nothing holding her back.*

*'There.' She pointed and dragged Lily by the elbow. 'What have we here?' Her face dropped as she read the sign propped on the table. 'Ooo, get legless with the Snake Pit.' She glanced at the props alongside it. 'Yuk, are they actual snakes.'*

*'Yes, they are.' The guy leaned over the desk at them. 'Fascinating, aren't they?'*

*Harriett shuddered. 'No, actually, they're not.' She pulled Lily away. 'Let's go stand to stand until we see something we fancy.'*

*Lily was well aware of Harriett's motivations. 'That'll be pretty much anything in trousers then.'*

*'Oi.' Harriett nudged her and moved on.*

*Lily trailed behind.*

*'Chess club, no. Harmonising choir, no. Rowing club, no. Although…' A dark-haired youth in shorts, with extremely toned thighs stood up from behind the desk.*

*Lily pushed Harriett past. 'No. Keep going.'*

*'But…'*

*'Keep going.' Lily took the lead, pulling Harriett along, until they'd completed a full circuit. 'Right, there's nothing here.'*

*'What? I counted almost thirty stalls. I could have signed up for at least half of them.'*

*'Yes,' Lily was unimpressed. 'The tall one, the blonde one, the one with tattoos.'*

*'Honestly, anyone would think I was boy mad, the way you go on.'*

*'No. Really?'*

*They mounted stairs to a mezzanine level so they could look down over the ground floor, reviewing each stall from a safe distance.*

*'Come on, Lily. There must be something.'*

*Lily huffed. She didn't want to let her friend down, but this was extremely difficult for her. Then again, with Harriett beside her, it was actually an opportunity to meet new people who were perhaps on a similar wavelength, which was something Lily would find impossible alone. She dug deep. 'Ok. There were only really three which showed any promise.'*

*Harriett perked up. 'Really? What were they?' She craned over the barrier to check out the representatives behind the relevant desks.*

*'Shakespeare Club.'*

*'No way. Uh-uh. That's a never in a month of Sundays. Me and Shakespeare are never going to be buddies.'*

*Lily pouted. She hadn't considered the idea that bad. 'Ok, then. Campus newspaper? Or Scrabble Club?'*

*Harriett scowled. 'Which were they?'*

*Lily pointed into the crowds. 'The desk at the back, with the girl with the glasses. Or the one by the pillar, with the two boys…'*

*'Ok, pillar it is. Let's go.' She marched down the stairs, turning halfway down. 'Which was it by the pillar? Newspaper or Scrabble?'*

*'Scrabble.'*

*Harriett shrugged. 'So be it. I'll probably get thrown out after a week for my spelling, but I'll give it a go.' She marched straight to the desk. 'Ok, boys. Sign us up.'*

*Sheets of paper were thrust under their noses, pens provided, and the deal was done. Lily was satisfied she had done her bit.*

*'We'll just sign up for my one, and then be off. In fact, we can pop to town on the way back to find something to wear.'*

*'Sorry?' Lily was confused.*

*'I've signed up for Scrabble Club for you, now you have to sign up for the Social Club for me. The first night out is Friday at the Student Union bar and I haven't got a thing to wear, and I can't imagine you have anything suitable. Come on. Let's go.'*

*Harriett made a beeline for the busiest stall in the building and joined a queue, waving for Lily to keep up.*

*Lily stared in horror. She should have seen this coming, should have known the type of thing Harriett would have in store for her, but instead she'd walked straight into it and now there was no way out.*

***

Lily was hyperventilating. The mere idea of being forced into clubbing by her so-called friend had tipped her over the edge.

The ombudsman, hearing her laboured breathing, halted the footage and removed the equipment, first from his own head, then Lily's. Her eyes were staring, one hand-held to her heaving chest, her mouth opening and closing like a fish out of water. He jumped to his feet grabbed the remains of a glass of water and launched the contents into her face.

She squealed, inhaling sharply, returning her breathing to a natural rhythm. He watched as her face relaxed, liquid dripping from her hair, down her forehead and onto her shoulders.

'This is getting to be a regular occurrence.'

'Works though, doesn't it?' He smiled. 'I'll get Blessing to bring another towel in a minute. Are you alright now?'

She whistled a breath in and out, concentrating on keeping it steady. 'I can't possibly go clubbing with a bunch of strangers, with all that drunkenness and goodness knows what else.'

'You're not going to. Remember, it's all pretend. None of it's real.'

'I keep telling myself that, but it's not helping.'

'I understand.' He tapped his chin in thought. 'Listen, the next part is only the first outing at Scrabble Club, where you meet this Chantilly fellow. I'm sure nothing untoward can happen at something as innocuous as that. Let's watch that and then pause. If you don't want to go on, we'll stop, and if you do, we'll go on, one small chunk at a time. What do you think?'

She swiped damp hair out of her eyes. 'I would like to see what Darren's like.'

‘Then, let’s give it a go. Yes?’
The temptation outweighed her anxiety. ‘Yes, alright then.’

# CHAPTER TWENTY-FOUR

*ALTERNATIVE LILY ARMITAGE - AGED EIGHTEEN*

*While Lily studied the letters lined up on a wooden stand, Harriett was stretching her neck to look around the hall.*

*On arrival, they'd been separated into small groups at tables dotted around the room for a mini-Scrabble tournament. The games were played on a timer and, at the end, scores totted up and submitted, before the players moved onto another table. They were on their third rotation. Harriett had lost interest halfway through the first.*

*A mature student with a spindly goatee, who seemed to be in charge, stood up and rang a handbell, indicating the event was over. A flurry of minions scurried around, collecting up results. 'That's a wrap people. Great start. We've got some impressive scores coming in. We're going to use those to sort you into regular match groups to make sure you're playing opponents of a similar level. It's boring if you win hands down every time without at least a decent fight.' He snorted a laugh, but no one joined in.*

*Pointing at a run of tables against the wall, he coughed his embarrassment away. 'Help yourself to refreshments while we finish off, then check your levels at the judges' desk on your way out.' He stepped away and joined a huddle with the other organisers.*

*Lily was quick to leave her table to join Harriett who, having been positioned close to the refreshments, was already leaning against the table eating crisps. 'That was fun, wasn't it? How did you get on?'*

*Harriett rolled her eyes. 'There are some right prigs here, and yes, that is a word and I do know what it means, because one of them used it on my second game. I thought he'd spelt it wrong and should have had a "ck" at the end.' She put another handful of crisps into her mouth and crunched a couple of times before continuing. 'And what's the big deal about using swear words? Matey with the blue jumper reckons it's not "de rigueur".' She put on higher-pitched posh voice.*

*'Oh dear.' Lily was disappointed Harriett hadn't enjoyed herself.*

*'I told him, if I can't add "bol" to the word "locks", he definitely shouldn't be chucking poncey French phrases around.'*

*'What did he say?'*

*'Nothing. The bell went.'*

*The pair moved away as the crowd around the food grew. Harriett rubbed her forehead and ran fingers back through her hair to the base of her neck. 'Come on, Lils. Let's get out of here. If we're quick, we could get to the pub before it closes. I could do with a stiff drink.' She lowered her voice. 'And a bit of eye candy... speaking of which.' Her face perked up, as an average looking young man approached them.*

*At the last minute, he dodged around Harriett and stopped in front of Lily. Bending down slightly, he checked the name badge on her chest. 'Ah, Lily. I've got the right one. Good. I'm Darren, part of the campus first team.'*

*She blushed for no reason whatsoever. 'Hi.'*

*Harriett bobbed around behind him, making faces, eyes wide as she gestured at him with her head. Lily tried to ignore her.*

*'Your scores are pretty impressive. Have you played on the circuit before?' He continued.*

*'No. I just play for fun.'*

*Harriett mouthed the word fun and grimaced behind his back, pretending to vomit.*

*'Really? Ok. How would you feel about joining the team? It's not a massive commitment, a match a month or so, though it heats up in the winter with a couple of big regional tournaments. We lost a couple of our stalwarts because they graduated last term, so we need new blood.'*

*'Oh. Umm. I don't know.' Lily was more used to standing on the side-lines than being selected for anything. It was a strange feeling, but not an unpleasant one.*

*He took her reluctance as concern for interference with her work schedule. 'Don't worry. We all have deadlines, so there's no pressure. Study always comes first, but you'd be a great asset to our wordsmith bank, even if only as a reserve.'*

*His enthusiasm was catching. 'Yes, alright. Why not? What do I have to do?'*

*He patted her shoulder, clearly pleased she had agreed. 'Excellent. Great news. I'll pop round some info tomorrow; we've got your accommodation details on your sign-up forms. But basically, come along here on a Thursday evening and we'll keep you up to date with fixture meetings and stuff then.' He patted her again. 'The team will be pleased.'*

*As soon as he had walked away, Harriett grabbed her friend's hands. 'OMG, he is so into you.'*

*Lily blushed. The thought hadn't crossed her mind. 'No, he's not. Shut up.' She wished Harriett would keep her voice down.*

*'He so is. Good for you, girl.'*

*Grabbing Harriett's arm, she steered her towards the door. 'Come on. I thought you needed a drink.'*

***

'Ta da! There you have it.' The ombudsman announced, pleased with himself, throwing his headset aside. 'That's how you met Darren Chantilly.'

Lily's head tipped to one side. 'Really? That's *the* Darren?'

He confirmed. 'The one and only. Actually, there are probably several the world over, but that's the one who would have whisked you off your feet.'

She was still confused and removed her own equipment to check the ombudsman's expression. There had been such a lack of emotion in the scene they'd witnessed, nothing to give the slightest inkling of what was to come. 'There wasn't any whisking going on, as far as I could see.'

'No, well, that's all movies and romance books, isn't it? Real life tends to be less… ostentatious.'

'Ostentatious? That was more "blink and you miss it". In fact, I did blink and miss it, if there was any connection there whatsoever. There must be some mistake.'

The ombudsman scrolled through information on his tablet, then closed it and shrugged. 'No. That's the man of your dreams. At least, it could have been, for a while anyway.'

'Go figure.' Lily was bemused. 'I can't for the life of me imagine how we went from that, to being married.'

He chewed on his cheek, trying to prevent a smile. 'Well, I could show you more, if you think it would help. Only if you want to though, obviously.'

Her eyes narrowed. She was suspicious she had been coerced into continuing, but, at the same time, she was curious. 'Maybe just a scene or two, to help me understand.'

He nodded, straight-faced. 'Your wish is my command.'

# CHAPTER TWENTY-FIVE

*ALTERNATIVE LILY ARMITAGE - AGED EIGHTEEN*

*The social club night out was everything Lily and Harriett had anticipated it to be, loud, sweaty, and packed to the rafters with half-drunk students. Harriett was over the moon; Lily hated every minute.*

*Harriett headed straight for the bar. 'Come on, Lils. We've got some catching up to do.'*

*Lily, uncomfortable in a minute dress and heels chosen by her friend, hobbled to keep up, trying to pull the skirt down and the neckline up, while still staying upright. The only good thing was, she was so focussed on maintaining a level of decency, she hadn't had the opportunity to feel anxious about the hordes of people.*

*'What're you having? The first round's on me, seeing as I talked you into it.'*

*'Orange juice.' Lily hollered to be heard over the noise.*

*'Yeah, right.' Harriett turned back to the bar and shouted. 'Double Vodka and orange.' She turned back to Lily. 'Trust me, a couple of these and you'll feel much more comfortable.'*

*'A couple more and I won't feel anything.' Lily muttered under her breath.*

*Harriett backed out of the crowd at the bar, drinks held aloft to avoid being knocked. She leaned in close to Lily's ear. 'Spotted anybody you know?'*

*Before she could answer, Harriett nudged her elbow. 'There's Sarah from my floor. Come on. Let's go.'*

*Harriett forged ahead and, as soon as she was spotted by Sarah, was pulled into a hug. 'This is my mate, Lily. Lily, Sarah.'*

*Lily nodded, there was no way her voice would be heard above the drum and base anyway. It didn't stop Sarah, who proceeded to make her way around the table introducing all the bodies squeezed onto the haphazard array of sofas and benches. Harriett searched for more chairs to force into a gap, but a lad on the far side patted the arm of his sofa and waved her round to sit next to him. There clearly wasn't room for another person and, as Lily suspected, Harriett was forced to sit half on the arm and half on him, but Harriett didn't seem to mind. Lily hovered next to Sarah, who seemed the least inebriated of the group, and forced her face into a smile, praying she wouldn't have to talk to anyone.*

*Hours later, she was still there. Pitchers of coloured liquids had appeared, disappeared and been replaced many times over on the table in the centre, but Lily kept her glass to herself, holding up a hand and taking a pretend sip, whenever anyone tried to top her up. The others were slowly sinking into the upholstery, onto the floor, or against each other, to the extent Lily wasn't quite sure where to look. Harriett seemed to now be surgically attached at the face to the lad on the sofa and Sarah was asleep, her cheek pressed up against a pillar. Lily wished she could leave, but at the same time, felt responsible for making sure Harriett got back in one piece which, without her, was by no means likely.*

*Someone behind her got up and Lily leaned forward to give him room to pass, but at the last moment he seemed to think better of it, tapping her on the shoulder. Lily tensed. The last thing she needed was to have to dodge the grubby paws of a drunken letch, she was having enough trouble staying upright in her shoes. He leaned close and she thought about punching him, but it turned out to be purely to facilitate her hearing him.*

*'Do you want my chair before someone else nicks it?'*

*She turned to thank him and found her face far closer to him than she'd anticipated and pulled away abruptly. 'Thanks.'*

*He chuckled at her reaction but reached down to manoeuvre the chair.*

*She looked at him more carefully. He had a nice face, short dark hair and a beard, with a dimple just above it, high on his cheek. He seemed familiar, but she couldn't place him. More than likely, he'd been at one of her induction meetings. Thanking him again, she sat down. Her feet would be forever grateful to the thoughtful stranger, while her eyes followed him all the way to the exit, where he paused briefly to exchange brief words with another face she knew, Darren.*

*A particular song was the catalyst for half the group to rouse themselves and stagger to the dancefloor, Harriett's new beau among them. Harriett however stayed put. Without another body to keep her upright, her torso toppled sideways into the middle of the cushions, and it was only Lily's swift actions which prevented another reveller from sitting on her head.*

*Sarah had come to and grabbed Lily's arm. 'That girl is plastered,' she slurred.*

*Lily couldn't help thinking that was rather the pot calling the kettle black, but she nodded. 'I should probably get her back. How about you? Are you done for the night?'*

*'Nah. I'll get my second wind in a minute.' She stifled a belch, stumbled and grabbed the pillar for support. 'Can you manage her on your own?'*

*Lily thought Sarah would be more of a hindrance than a help with the state she was in. 'Yeah. If I can just get her up.'*

*Helpers appeared from nowhere, levering Harriett onto her feet and Lily slipped her shoulder under Harriett's arm, gripping tight around her middle to keep her vertical.*

*Harriett looked across at her and smiled. 'Hi, Lils.'*

*Lily couldn't help but smile back. 'Hi, Harry. Time to go home.'*

*The fresh air had a reviving affect as they stepped out and, for a few minutes, Harriett was able to bear her own weight, although her sense of direction was history. The walk to the bar had seemed short, but in the small hours, and in their current condition, the distance had increased massively. With that in mind, Lily took a short cut through a car park, afraid that at any moment Harriett's legs would give way again and, as they mounted the pavement at the far side, her fears were realised. Harriett leaned against her and, despite Lily's best efforts, slid down into a heap at her feet.*

*'Oh, Harriett. Now what am I supposed to do?' Lily crouched down, keeping one arm around her friend, and craned all around for assistance, but found none. There was no way she could manhandle her all the way home, so the only choice remaining was to continue alone to the main road and either find help or flag down a taxi, although it was dubious whether a cab driver would permit someone in Harriett's state in his car anyway.*

*Swearing under her breath, she hurried through an alley to the road. There was no one in sight and no cars driving past, but as it was almost two in the morning that was hardly surprising. She marched into the centre of the road so she could see around a bend and beyond, but there was nobody. Her only option was to go and put her efforts into getting Harriett back on her feet, even if it took all night.*

*As she exited the alley back into the car park, she heard whistling and, without sparing any thought to the possibility of serial killers or the like, ducked around a van to request the help of whoever was making the sound. It was the mysterious chair provider from earlier in the club.*

*Lily sighed in relief. 'Thank goodness it's you.'*

*He looked around and stopped whistling. 'It was the last time I looked.'*

*'Can you help me? My friend's had one too many and I can't get her moving on my own. We're only going five minutes down the road, or a taxi would do if you know where I can find one.'*

*He chuckled, making his dimple even more pronounced, even in the dull light provided by the streetlamps. 'Go on then. Where is she?'*

*'Over by the railings.' They both hurried to the edge of the car park.*

*Instead of leaning against the iron rails, where Lily had left her, Harriett was now on her hands and knees, head firmly stuck between them, presumably having regained consciousness at some point in Lily's absence, but now she was back in the land of nod.*

*Lily's hand flew to her forehead. 'Harriett! What have you done now?'*

*The handsome stranger found the situation so amusing he was bent double with laughter. 'There's one too many, and there's a shedload too many and I think we both know what she's had.'*

*'I can't believe it. We've only been here a week and we're going to be in trouble already. Her mum's going to kill her, or me, in fact, probably both of us.' Lily looked around for inspiration. 'What am I going to do?'*

*'Don't panic. We'll sort this out.' Grabbing Harriett's shoulder, he gave her a shake. 'Hey, you.' He turned to Lily. 'Harriett, is it?'*

*At her nod, he continued, louder. 'Hey, Harriett. Wake up. Come on, wake up.'*

*Harriett grunted and snored, but otherwise remained oblivious.*

*'Got a bottle of water I can throw over her?'*

*Lily wriggled in her tiny dress. It was pretty obvious she had nowhere to conceal anything, let alone a bottle of water. 'No.'*

*'Hmm.' He stood up straight and thought for a moment. 'Ok, the only thing we can do is try and lift her out. If that doesn't work, it's going to have to be the fire brigade.'*

*'What? No. We've got to do it ourselves somehow. I couldn't bear having to call out the emergency services for such a ridiculous thing as this.'*

*He waved her concern away. 'Hey, it's Fresher's week. They expect it.'*

*'Not from me they don't.' Lily crouched down to feel around Harriett's head to see what space there was between skin and railing. The bars nestled firmly behind her ears. 'How the heck did she get in there like that?'*

*He crouched beside her and examined the scene. 'Hmm, it looks like they taper as they go down. The gap at the top is wider. If we could lift her up, nearer the top, she should just pop out.'*

*'You think?'*

*'You go that side. I'll go this. Get your arms under her…' Between them they brought her legs in and shuffled her body slowly up the railings. 'That's it. Stop her bum leaning over or she'll bash her neck. Bit more. Have you got her?' Without letting go, he staggered to his feet to lift her higher.*

*'I think so. Hang on, let me get underneath…'*

*'That's it. Mind her ear and, she's out.'*

*As her head came free, they lowered her back to the pavement so they could take a break.*

*'She owes me big time after this.'*

*He was pragmatic. 'Ahh, she'll probably do the same for you one of these days.'*

*'Hardly. I can't see me getting in this state at Scrabble Club.'*

*He laughed. 'I don't know, that Scrabble lot are a wild crowd.'*

*'Really?' Lily was about to rethink her position regarding joining up.*

*'Nah.' He laughed again. 'Anyway, let's get her on her feet.' With one huge effort he lifted her from the pavement, holding her close against his side for stability.*

*At that moment, she came to, opened her eyes and shoved him away. 'Hey, buster. Take your hands off me.' She turned to Lily, swaying. 'Did you see that? What a liberty! Come on. Let's go.' With that, she grabbed her bag and marched off.*

*Lily couldn't believe Harriett's behaviour. She turned to her rescuer in shame. 'I'm so sorry. She has no idea how helpful you've been.'*

*He shrugged and laughed. 'Never mind. Besides, she'll be paying for it in the morning with the hangover from hell.' Turning in the opposite direction from that which Harriett had headed, he gestured with his head. 'I'm that way. I'd get her back quick if I were you, before she passes out again.'*

*Lily watched as he strolled away. His whistling restarted seconds later, as he stepped between parked cars and disappeared down a path. She didn't know who he was, but he had certainly been a Godsend to her tonight. No doubt they'd bump into each other again, after all, she'd run into him twice in one night already.*

*From some distance she heard Harriett's voice shouting. 'Lily? Lily, where are you?'*

*Lily stepped out to silence her friend before someone called the police, but as she did so, she kicked something into the path ahead of her. It was a wallet. It must have been his, probably fallen from his pocket as they were moving Harriett. She glanced at the path he had taken, considering running after him, but then Harriett yelled again. Picking up the rectangle of brown leather, Lily put it in her handbag, slipped off her shoes and sprinted in the direction of Harriett's dulcet tones.*

# CHAPTER TWENTY-SIX

*ALTERNATIVE LILY ARMITAGE - AGED EIGHTEEN*

*Lily had spent what remained of the night propped up against the bed in Harriett's room, a bucket at the ready, fearful her friend may come to harm left to her own devices. It came into operation at about eight in the morning, when Harriett came to with a sharp cry. She sat up, grabbed a handful of fringe and groaned before throwing up. Luckily, Lily was a light sleeper and had been quick to get into position.*

*'I swear somebody spiked my drink.' Harriett moaned.*

*'I don't think so. You were among friends all night.'*

*Harriett tried to shake her head in an emphatic manner, but instantly had to use both hands to hold it still as the movement caused too much pain. 'No. I shouldn't feel this bad after what I had to drink. I only remember having four... maybe five drinks all night.'*

*Lily was the voice of reason. 'Yes, but I think those five drinks might have interfered with your memory. You definitely had more than that. I told you to have a soft drink in between each alcoholic one...'*

*'Yes, alright, mother.' She threw herself back on the bed, placing a pillow over her eyes. 'I've got a headache. I don't need a lecture now.'*

*'The pain will have far more impact than any lecture I could give you.'*

*'Did I say mother? I should have said grandmother. Aaaahh, my head.'*

*Lily sighed. It would appear her friend was not appreciative of her ministrations, at least, not yet. 'Listen. If you think you'll be alright on your own for a minute, I'll empty that.' She nodded at the bucket. 'And get you some painkillers, water and dry toast. That should sort you out.'*

*Without uncovering her eyes, Harriett waved at the door, clearly keen to be left alone.*

*Lily set about her business, hoping the way Harriett was feeling might prevent future recurrence. She certainly never wanted to spend another night in the same way. When she returned to Harriett's room, Harriett was sitting up, examining the wallet Lily had retrieved from the car park, which had been left on the bedside cabinet overnight.*

*Harriett's face was serious. 'What is this?' She closed it and waved it at Lily. 'Did I ...? Was I ...?' She breathed deeply, as if steeling herself. 'Did I come back here with a stranger last night? Did some sleaze-bag take advantage?'*

*Rolling her eyes, Lily banged a glass of water and plate of toast down on the surface, no longer caring if it caused discomfort to her friend's fragile head. 'No. This…' She grabbed the wallet and waved it back. 'This belonged to your knight in shining armour, actually, not that you're grateful.'*

*She brought Harriett up to date with her antics the night before. 'So, in the process of scraping you out of the gutter, this "Mr Peacock" lost his wallet. He's probably worried sick, but I've got no way of tracking him down.'*

*Harriett had the courtesy to look slightly ashamed. 'Is there no address or phone number in it?'*

*'No, only a bank card and some cash.'*

*'Is it a lot?'*

*'No, but enough to be missed, especially if he's a student, which I assume he is. Here, have these.' Lily handed Harriett two paracetamol, then helped herself to a slice of toast, taking a bite as she thought. 'Right, well. I'd better get back to my room and get changed and then nip up to campus to see if admin can track him down, though they probably won't give me any details.'*

*'Just hand it in and let them sort it. It's not your problem, is it?'*

*'Maybe not, but I do feel responsible, and I'd like to thank him again. Goodness knows how I'd have managed on my own.'*

*Harriett grinned. 'Looker, was he?'*

*Lily felt a blush rise up her cheeks. 'Honestly, Harry, you've got a one-track mind.'*

*She laughed at Lily's response. 'Ooh, he was. Ok. Give me half an hour to have a shower and we'll go hunt for him together.' Harriett went to get up and was forced to grab the wall to maintain balance. 'Make that an hour.'*

*Her stilettos were even more uncomfortable the morning after than they had been the night before and, after leaving Harriett's section, Lily slipped them off and carried them up the stairs to her own floor. As she rounded the landing to the entrance to her room, two lads passed her, on their way down, nudging each other and smirking.*

*'Oi, oi!' One of them hollered at her before carrying on.*

*She glanced over her shoulder at them, confused. Darren was standing outside her door, leaning against the wall, writing on a piece of paper. He looked up as she arrived.*

*'What was that about?' She asked.*

*'Aah.' He pointed at her. 'The outfit, at this time in the morning. Looks very much like the walk of shame, if you don't mind my saying so.'*

*Lily blushed to the roots of her hair. 'Great. I spend the night stopping my friend inhaling her own vomit and it's me who gets a reputation. Thanks, Harriett.'*

*He grimaced at the image and changed the subject, handing her the document he was holding. 'As promised, club information sheet. I think it's all straight forward, but if you have any questions, I'd be happy to answer them.'*

*'Oh, right.' Accepting the form, she looked it up and down. She was eager to shower and change, but he was clearly waiting for her to read it.*

*Another student topped the stairs and the pair moved in to allow him past. He glanced at Lily, then Darren and winked. 'Alright, mate?'*

*Lily blushed again. The sooner she was back in jeans and a jumper the better or, at least, out of public viewing, but she wasn't about to allow this almost stranger access to her bedroom. She pointed to another door at the end of the corridor. 'Could you give me five minutes and I'll meet you in the kitchen?'*

*He shrugged and trundled off. Lily rushed into her room and shut the door firmly. How embarrassing. What sort of impression was she giving of herself? Ripping off the dress, she pulled on jeans and checked shirt with one hand, while taking her make up off with a wipe with the other. She read the document Darren had given her, at the same time as running a brush through her hair, and in a few minutes was as near normal as she could be after only two hours sleep.*

*Darren was perched on the sofa, looking at the view from the window to one side.*

*'Sorry about that.'*

*He didn't seem bothered at having to wait. 'Don't worry. Do you want me to go through the details with you?'*

*The information provided was actually so basic, Lily couldn't imagine there ever being any explanation required. 'No. I don't think so. Like you said before, turn up at the weekly meeting and hang around until the end for a short briefing and that's it, isn't it?'*

*'You've got it.' He stood up. 'I've written my details on the back, in case you want to get hold of me, should anything come up. Don't hold back. We want new members to feel as welcome as possible.'*

*'Oh, ok. I think I've got it though.' Lily wondered if every new member got this level of attention.*

*'Good, good. I'll be off then.' He headed for the door but paused in the doorway. 'If you want to know any more, we could always meet for a coffee or something.'*

*Harriett's comment at the club meeting about him being "into her" suddenly burst into Lily's thoughts, setting her cheeks aflame. 'I think I'm good, thanks.'*

*'Right, ok.' He paused again. 'You're sure?'*

*It seemed she was going to have trouble shifting him, when all she really wanted was a shower and a good breakfast, before heading up to campus to try and track down her knight in shining armour. Oh yes, the knight. She'd seen him talking to Darren at the club the night before. 'Actually…'*

*'Yes?' His reaction was a little too enthusiastic for her liking.*

*She pulled the wallet from her bag and opened it up. 'Do you know a Mr A Peacock? I think he's a student here.'*

*His face dropped. 'Peacock? No, I don't think so. Why?'*

*She shook her head. 'Oh, he helped me get my friend back last night and dropped his wallet. I wanted to get it back to him, that's all.'*

*'No, I don't know any Peacocks. What a shame. I'd hand it in to lost property. They'll sort it out.'*

*'I guess. It's just…I thought I saw you talking to him earlier in the evening at the club, by the door. You were coming in and he was going out.'*

*Darren made a face like he was thinking hard, but for some reason Lily wasn't convinced. 'Not that I can remember.' He pinched his chin. 'Tell you what. I'll have a good think, see if I can remember, and maybe we could meet for a drink this afternoon to see if I've come up with anything.'*

*Her eyes narrowed as she studied his face. Was this simply an excuse to ask her out? If so, she really wasn't interested, but then, what if he could provide the answer about the tall, dark stranger? 'I suppose I could, but perhaps I should just hand it in. He's probably worried about his bank card and stuff.'*

*'Do you know? It's ringing a bell now. Talking to someone by the door, you said?'*

*'That's right.' She sensed a breakthrough.*

*'No, maybe not. But given time to think, I might remember.' He was watching her out of the corner of his eye. 'Shall we say three o'clock at the campus café? If I haven't got a name for you by then, you can go straight to lost property as you'll already be in the building.'*

*There didn't seem to be an argument against such a plan, except she didn't really want to meet him and she certainly didn't want to give him the wrong idea. He was not her type in the slightest. 'Ok, then. Three o'clock.'*

*'Excellent. See you there.' He was gone in a second, as if he didn't want to give her the opportunity to change her mind.*

*Lily didn't see him go. She was too focussed on the idea she had "a type", when such a thing had never crossed her mind before. Right now, if she were to be asked, she suspected her "type" might be tall, dark and handsome, with the cutest dimple she had ever seen.*

# CHAPTER TWENTY-SEVEN

The image froze.

'How are we doing?' The ombudsman's voice cut through Lily's thoughts.

'Ok. I think. But this isn't clarifying anything. You're sure I end up with this Chantilly guy? I mean, from what I can see, there's no attraction whatsoever.'

There was a pause and Lily assumed the ombudsman was checking the records. 'That's what it says, but, you know, feelings can change over time. Perhaps he grew on you.'

'Like a parasite,' she murmured under her breath.

'Sorry? What was that?'

'Oh, nothing.' She huffed. 'But I don't like his attitude. It's a bit creepy, don't you think? A bit persistent?'

'Can't blame a guy for trying - or can you? I don't know, there comes a point where he should take no for an answer, but then, you didn't actually say no, did you?'

'I guess not.' It was strange watching her life and yet having no influence on it. Something inside her wanted to tell her young self to run a mile from this would-be husband. She had to know how it turned out. 'Could we see more? I'd like to know what happened about the wallet, you know, make sure it got back to its rightful owner.'

The ombudsman let out a burst of laughter. 'And I suppose it's got nothing to do with wanting to see Mr Peacock again. Hah.'

'Think what you like.' She hoped the ombudsman was still wearing his headset and couldn't see the colour of her cheeks. 'I'd like to know I did my duty, that's all.'

The ombudsman continued to chuckle as he instructed the footage to play.

*ALTERNATIVE LILY ARMITAGE - AGED EIGHTEEN*

*Lily eventually arrived at the campus café five minutes late, thanks to Harriett, who had been flip-flopping about accompanying her, but at the last moment backed out, pleading a relapse of the hangover. Lily would have liked the support, but she was determined to get to the bottom of the mystery of Mr Peacock. It was more than simply the fact he was attractive, when she first saw him there had been something, a familiarity she couldn't quite put her finger on.*

*Darren was in the centre of the café, his eye on the door and, as soon as she walked in, he bobbed up, waving frantically, drawing the attention of everyone in the room, much to Lily's dismay. She nodded to show she'd seen him and sat the other side of the table.*

*He shuffled to the edge. 'Tea?'*

*'No, thanks. Just water please.'*

*'Good for you. Keeping hydrated. None of the old additives.'*

*Lily had the impression he wanted to pat her on the head for being a good girl. She didn't know what it was about Darren, but he put her slightly on edge.*

*He returned with their drinks and sat down. 'Are you feeling better now you've had lunch and so forth? You're certainly looking more refreshed, if you don't mind my saying so.'*

*'Yes, thanks, I'm fine.' She wasn't looking for compliments. 'Anyway, did you remember who you were talking to last night? A Peacock?'*

*'Aah. Not yet, I'm afraid.' He moved swiftly on. 'I don't know if you'd be interested, but we have our first fixture a week on Friday. It's against a local seniors' team and is held here on campus. Would you be interested in coming along as first reserve? They're a formidable crowd, but we generally win out. I don't think they'd be too big a challenge to someone like yourself.'*

*Lily was confused by the sudden topic change. 'Um, I suppose I could. But are you sure you can't remember who this guy was?'*

*'No. I've racked my brain, but nothing.' He shrugged.*

*'Well, in that case, I should be getting to lost property. I've held on to his stuff too long already.' She made to stand.*

*He delayed her with a hand on her arm. 'The problem is, I spoke to so many people last night, it could have been any one of them. Perhaps if you could give me more details?'*

*She sat back down; eyes narrowed. His attitude was annoying her. 'For a start, it was a male, so you can rule out the females you came into contact with.'*

*He smirked. 'Of course. Unfortunately, I know a lot of people. You do if you're involved with something social like Scrabble Club, but it tends to be first names only. Rarely do we exchange surnames, so Peacock, well, it could be anyone.'*

*She was certain he was being intentionally obstructive. 'Let's look at the information we do have then. His first name begins with the letter A, so what could that be? Andrew? Adrian? Alexander?'*

*'Aloysius?'*

*She frowned. 'Do you know anyone called Aloysius?'*

*'No.'*

*'Then I think we can overlook that particular one. Think about it, Darren. Do you remember speaking to someone with a name beginning with A?'*

*He pursed his lips and stared into the distance. 'Not that I can think of.'*

*Her patience was wearing thin. 'He's tall and slim, with dark hair, a beard and…' She was afraid giving too much detail of his appearance might also suggest alternative reasons for her interest in him, but she needed to get to the bottom of it. 'A dimple in his cheek.' Her finger pressed against her own cheek in emphasis of the fact.*

*'No bells are ringing.'*

*She'd had enough. 'Right. I'm going to lost property, now.' She grabbed her bag to leave.*

*Darren looked at his watch and tutted. 'Oh dear. I think you might have missed it for today. I've a feeling they close early at weekends.'*

*'What?'*

*He grimaced. 'Sorry, my bad. I've kept you talking too long. Anyway, you might as well stay and finish your drink. They won't open again until morning.'*

*'What? Oh, Darren…' She was convinced he had delayed her on purpose, and it took some restraint to stop herself giving him what for. 'That's really not on. Why didn't you warn me they'd be closing? You know I'm concerned about this.'*

*He had the decency to look sheepish, but she was not in a forgiving mood.*

*'I'm going to check the office in case it's still open.' She turned to walk away.*

*'Actually, now you've mentioned the dimple, I might know who you mean.'*

*She huffed. Was this another delaying tactic? She looked him straight in the eye. 'Really?'*

*'Yes. As it happens, I seem to remember bumping into someone like that. A friend of a friend of a friend. I only know him as Poppy?'*

*'Poppy?'*

*'Yes.' He scratched his head. 'I think it's because of his surname. Yes, Poppy Cock instead of his actual name Peacock. Lily, I think we have your man.'*

*A wave of relief washed over her. 'So, you do know him? How can I find him? Can you put me in touch with him?'*

*'Aah, well, now then.' Darren was avoiding her eye, staring at the table.*

*'What is it? Can you, or not?'*

*'Well, I could, but...' He shrugged.*

*'Darren, what is it. For goodness' sake...'*

*'The thing is, he's got quite the reputation.' He screwed his face up as if it was something he didn't want to say aloud. 'I'm not sure he's the sort of chap you want to get involved with. Different girl every night, sort of thing. You know, probably not someone a girl like you, who values her reputation, would want to be associated with. Why don't you give me the wallet? I could pass it on for you. No need for you to ever go near him again.'*

*Lily found herself cornered. She wanted to tell Darren to cut the crap and put her in touch with this Poppy character, but at the same time she was dependent upon him for the introduction and couldn't risk putting his nose out of joint. She bit her tongue. 'I'm sure I can look after myself, Darren, and I really should make sure the wallet goes directly into his hands, besides which, no matter what sort of person he is, I owe him thanks for his help. Please can you put me in touch with him?'*

*He shook his head, and for a moment Lily thought he was going to refuse. 'Alright. If you're sure, but don't say I didn't warn you. Wait there.'*

*Lily watched him retrieve a mobile phone from a briefcase on the bench beside him and stride out into the lobby to make a call. She could see him talking through the glass in the door and hoped progress was finally being made. When he came back, he sat down and put the phone carefully back into its home without speaking.*

*'Did you manage to get hold of him?'*

*'No…' He shook his head and her heart dropped. 'But I have it on good authority he'll be at a party this evening, at my friend, Jake's, digs.'*

*'That's great. Can you give me the address and I'll drop it in to him?'*

*'Sorry, no can do.' His chin lifted in challenge. 'It's invitation only, I'm afraid, and if you want to go, the only option is for you to come as my guest.' The last few words were stretched out, as if he knew he was in a position of power and was revelling in it.*

*She stared at him. Should she challenge him? No. He would shut down and she would be left no further forward. If she wanted to see Poppy again, it would have to be on Darren's terms. 'What time and where?'*

*The breathless laugh which escaped him showed he couldn't believe he'd got away with it, but he had. 'Tonight. Eight o'clock. I'll pick you up.'*

*Without responding, she grabbed her bag and walked away.*

*'Ooh, and that dress you were wearing last night would be suitable attire.'*

*She turned to glare at him, then continued on her way.*

***

'There is no way I'm marrying that man.' Lily was livid.

The ombudsman chewed his cheek. 'Yes and no. You missed the boat obviously, because you never actually went to university so no, you won't marry him, but on this particular life pathway, you most certainly would have. It's in the records, in black and white.'

'But he's horrible. I don't want to be married to him. I want to be married to someone lovely and kind and handsome…' Her chin stuck out in disappointment. 'And with a dimple. I like dimples.'

'You know they're actually a weakness in a muscle, don't you? Strictly speaking, they're not a positive characteristic.'

'I don't care about that.' She sighed. 'I can't believe I even agreed to go to the party with him and, even if I did go, surely I would have made a run for it at the first opportunity?' Was there no hope for her other self?

'Hmm.'

She guessed the ombudsman was reading notes by his tone.

'The thought did cross your mind, but… I might as well show you. Do you want to see what happens next?'

Lily was dubious whether she did or not, but curiosity won out. 'I don't think I have any choice, or I'll spend the rest of my life wondering.'

'You won't, because once you go back to your body you won't remember any details, only the essence of the experience, but your reasoning works for me. Let's see if we can get to grips with the inner workings of alternative you. Who knows, it might make sense in the end.'

'I sincerely hope so.' She muttered. 'Because it makes none whatsoever at the moment.'

# CHAPTER TWENTY-EIGHT

*ALTERNATIVE LILY ARMITAGE - AGED EIGHTEEN*

*Curtains twitched as Lily trailed behind Darren to his friend's party. The digs were in a predominantly residential area and, considering they'd been able to hear music thumping from the property as soon as they entered the cul-de-sac, Lily could imagine these particular students were not popular neighbours.*

*Darren was grumpy and had been from the moment he collected her, probably because she had ignored his instructions about the dress. What to wear had been an issue. First and foremost, she wanted to be sure not to give Darren the wrong impression, but on the other hand she didn't want to dress down to the extent of making herself repulsive to her knight in shining armour either, presuming he did actually put in an appearance. In the end, she had opted for trusty jeans, a sparkly, strappy top supplied by Harriett, and a suede effect jacket to hide inside whenever she felt the need.*

*As they approached the front door, Darren put a hand under her elbow and leaned in close. 'Stick close to me,' he said. 'I'll make sure old Poppy doesn't get his claws into you. Although knowing him, he'll have his hands full already.'*

*The door opened before she had a chance to reply, and they were ushered in. Drinks were distributed and Darren pulled Lily through the crowds to a gap at the back of the lounge. The proximity of so many people, the loudness of the music and heightened atmosphere would usually have sent Lily running, but she had alternative motivation for staying and her anxiety levels simmered at a level where she remained in control.*

*Darren knew most of the people present and he contributed to the conversations going on easily and naturally. Lily began to relax in his company, apart from having to repeatedly unhook herself from his arm, which kept sneaking around her shoulders. She didn't partake in the interactions herself, but was content to listen, one eye always on the door, looking for dimple guy to appear.*

*An hour and a half in, there was still no sign of him, and Lily was beginning to think she'd been lured there under false pretences. Darren's hand crept round her waist for the third time in fifteen minutes and, rather than slap him, which was her first instinct, she edged away, craving space.*

*'Where's the loo?' She had to lean into him to be heard.*

*He pointed into the corridor and up the stairs.*

*Even though she had to push her way through, somehow, she felt freer simply being away from Darren's wandering hands, and she took her time in the bathroom, before returning downstairs. As she reached the ground floor again, she was delayed by a scrum of drunk people between her and the door and, while she waited for it to clear, she spotted the person she'd been waiting for, in the kitchen, perched on the edge of the worktop. At last. Now, all she had to do was navigate a path to him, hand back the wallet and then make her excuses to Darren and leave.*

*All at once, a pathway opened up in front of her. She hurried through it, only pausing in the doorway as someone pushed through, drinks held high at arm's length to prevent being knocked but, as she made to continue, another female got there first, throwing her arms around him and drowning him in kisses. The channel had closed behind Lily, and she found herself trapped in a corner staring right at the snogging couple. She desperately tried to backtrack, but there was no escape, and she felt herself growing more and more flustered.*

*In the end, she decided the best thing was to interrupt them and get the wallet exchange over and done with and leave them to their evening. She coughed to get their attention, although if she was in the girl's situation, she was pretty sure it would take more than a cough to drag her away. 'Excuse me.'*

*There was no response.*

*'Excuse me.' She tried again. This time the guy opened one eye, looking at her from around the side of the girl, who was still engrossed with kissing his face off.*

*He pushed the girl away. 'Fancy meeting you here.'*

*Lily felt herself blush, firstly from the warmth of his gaze and secondly from the infuriated face of his disgruntled companion. 'Hi. Umm, sorry to interrupt.'*

*'That's alright.' He patted the girl on the bottom, nudging her away. 'Tiffany was just going anyway.'*

*Tiffany glared at him but didn't speak.*

*He shrugged. 'What? Goodnight kiss, you said.'*

*She shook her head and flounced away.*

*Lily grabbed her chance, pulling his wallet from her jacket pocket. 'I think this is yours.'*

*'Hah!' Recognition crossed his face in an instant and he jumped down from his perch to Lily's level, and much closer than he had been before. 'Where'd you get that?'*

*'The pavement in the car park. I think you must have dropped it when we were sorting Harriett out.'*

*He took it from her and slapped it against his other palm. 'Ideal. I thought I'd left it at the bar. I've been waiting for a call back. Thank you.'*

*'No. Thank you for your help. I don't know what I'd have done if you hadn't been there.' She watched as he opened the wallet and did a quick check of the contents. 'It's all there.'*

*He pushed it into his back pocket and met her gaze. 'I never thought it wouldn't be.'*

*A surge of bodies pushed Lily forward and she put her hands against his chest to stop herself falling. She blushed and grew breathless, but his smile broadened.*

*'It's a bit busy in here. Let's go somewhere we can hear ourselves speak.'*

*Lily pushed herself away but was immediately knocked forward again. 'It's worse than the January sales.'*

*He took her hand and snaked past, pulling her towards the door. 'Let's get some air.'*

*She had little choice, the crowd ebbing and flowing around her as she was pulled forward. It was like he had a magic wand, parting the waves, which closed again as soon as they'd passed, and she was surprised there wasn't a pop as she emerged onto the front yard.*

*He retained hold of her hand. 'There, that's better.'*

*She couldn't deny it. The thudding of the music subsided with the closing of the door. She could still feel it through the soles of her shoes, and her heart seemed to be beating in time, but the tension in her body reduced. 'Yes.' That was all she could manage.*

*'I'm Adam, by the way.'*

*'Ah, not Aloysius then?'*

*He smiled through a confused frown. 'No. Do I look like one?'*

*'No.' To come up with an explanation would mean bringing Darren into the conversation and she didn't want to think about him right now. 'I was trying to track you down from the name on your bank card, but it seems like everyone calls you Poppy?'*

*He grunted. 'Not to my face, they don't. At least, the last one who did got a black eye.'*

*She grimaced. 'Sorry. I didn't know.'*

*'Why would you? You don't know me at all, do you? At least, not yet.' He pulled her towards him, to allow new arrivals access to the front door, but once she was there, didn't release her. 'Do you want to go somewhere else? A walk along the canal or something?'*

*Lily was tempted, but she couldn't help remembering a certain girl being attached to his face only minutes earlier. 'What about... Tiffany, was it?'*

*'I don't remember.'*

*His gaze didn't waver from her own and she felt herself weaken.*

*'She's probably moved on to another sucker by now.' He tilted his head to one side, studying Lily's face, only pausing at her lips. 'Whereas you, I wouldn't be letting out of my sight.'*

*Her mouth was so dry, she couldn't ignore the natural instinct to moisten her lips with her tongue and she realised he was watching every minute move, like she was prey.*

*'Lily, there you are.' Darren's voice cut the atmosphere like a bucket of icy water.*

*Lily's eyes flew to him as he walked down the steps to join them, and she automatically stood back.*

*'Poppy.' Darren coughed. 'I mean, Adam. There was a tall, blonde looking for you in the kitchen.'*

*Adam's eyes narrowed, but he didn't speak.*

*Darren turned to Lily, cutting Adam out of the conversation. 'I've had enough of this racket so I'm heading back. Are you coming?'*

*First Tiffany, now a tall blonde and goodness knows who else. Darren had warned Lily that Adam was a player and, tempted or not, Lily had no intention of becoming the next notch on his belt. That was only asking for heartbreak, although there might be fun to be had along the way.*

*'I guess I should make sure Harriett's ok.' Walking home with Darren would be the safe thing to do. If her heartrate was anything to go by, spending time with Adam would not.*

*He didn't try to talk her round; he merely shrugged and mounted the steps to go back inside. 'Another time then, Lily. See you around.'*

*'Yes, see you.' At least she hoped so. Then again, perhaps it would be better if she didn't. In fact, to be on the safe side, if she did see him again, she'd make sure to give him a wide berth, for the sake of her mental health.*

***

The screen went dark, and Lily waited for it to restart.

'Blast it.' The ombudsman grumbled under his breath.

She pulled off her headset to see he had done the same.

'Blasted batteries. You'd think modern technology would come up with a better alternative, wouldn't you? They always go flat at inopportune moments and it's such a nuisance recharging the things.'

'Do you know what I've realised?' Her brows were low in anger. 'Darren knew he was called Adam all along. The whole "I only know him as Poppy" thing was made up. When he came down the steps, he called him Adam straight away.'

'So he did.' The ombudsman was only half listening, his attention still on the equipment. 'Does it matter?'

'Yes, it does. That means Darren lied.' She slapped a palm to her forehead and left it there as she did her calculation. 'And, if he lied about that, he very well might have lied about other things as well, like Adam being a player. Adam may, in fact, be a decent guy. I was led astray.'

He threw the headset onto the floor and crossed his arms, patience exhausted. 'To be quite frank, I think you were either going to be led astray by Darren in one way, or by Adam in another. Choose your poison. If you're going to live your life according to what other people tell you rather than finding out for yourself, there's always a danger you'll be misinformed.' He scratched his chin. 'Then again, if you don't listen to warnings, you could make mistakes that way.'

'Great, so you're damned if you do, and damned if you don't.'

'That's going a bit far. Mistakes come in different shapes and sizes. The main aim is to keep to small, manageable ones rather than enormous, monumental ones. If you can do that, you've got it made.' He pushed himself off of the sofa and selected more boxes from the stack in the corner.

'Do you see what I'm up against? Do you see why I find life so petrifying? Mistakes don't come with labels. How am I supposed which one is less nasty than the other?'

He stood still, cradling the cartons in his arms. 'Yes. I do see where you're coming from. It's quite a conundrum, isn't it?'

'At last! Thank you!' Lily threw her arms wide. 'Does that mean I can forget this nonsense and move on to the next place?'

'No, afraid not.' He slumped onto the sofa. 'As much as I can empathise with your situation, unfortunately it's something every human has to deal with every day.'

She allowed her arms to drop. 'And that's all you've got to say on the subject?'

'Yes, basically, Lily, suck it up. You have to do the best you can with what you've got, and you haven't done that. In fact, you've avoided doing anything at all if you possibly could.'

'I was afraid.'

'But look how it turned out for you. Things couldn't possibly have gone any worse if you'd forged ahead and made stupid, massive, colossal mistakes. Surely you can see that? In your current state you have nothing, apart from the roof over your head, a job you're bored out of your brains in and a cat who shows less loyalty than a goldfish. What's the point?'

'Well…' She couldn't think of anything to say. The silence stretched. 'I don't know.'

'No, and I don't know either.' His voice was pleading. 'It's such a waste of life, Lily. I see people going through here who would give anything to have the chances you've had, to have the extra time that you have available to you, and yet you want to throw it away.'

'I understand what you're saying, I really do, and if I could donate that extra time to someone more deserving, I'd be more than willing to do so.' Her eyes narrowed at the prospect. 'I don't suppose that's an option, is it?'

'Aaargh!' The ombudsman finally lost his cool.

Lily bit her lip. 'I'll take that as a no.'

When he didn't respond, she continued. 'I wish I could enjoy my life. I wish I could have lived it to its full and not wasted a second, but it's too late now. I can't undo what I've done, or what I've not done, or… Now, I'm confused.'

The ombudsman spoke slowly and succinctly, making sure she took in every word. 'Lily, the past is the past. Nothing can change that. Even if we play this little game of "what could have been" until the cows come home, the facts remain the same. You will still have been the person you've been until now and carried out the same acts you carried out until now and missed the opportunities which you missed. What I'm trying to do is to put you in a position where you can be a whole new you; where you can lead a more fulfilling life, where you don't miss any more opportunities. That's got to be worth a try, hasn't it?'

'I suppose, but deep down, I can't help thinking I'm a hopeless case. I'm beyond redemption.'

He closed his eyes and breathed three deep breaths slowly in and out and when he opened them again, he took her hand in his own. 'Lily, there is no such thing as a hopeless case. There is always hope. You just have to search for it.'

Her face was a picture of misery, but she had no further argument to throw at him.

'We can search for it together. You and me, in the short time we have left together. Let's push ahead a little further and see if we can't find that glimmer of hope. Do you trust me, Lily?'

'Yes?' The word was a positive, but her tone was doubtful.

'All I need is for you to be willing to try.'

She gripped both knees and concentrated hard. 'I suppose I'd be mad not to, wouldn't I?'

He nodded. 'Completely bonkers.'

'Go on, then. Quickly, before I change my mind.'

'Right. I'm going to jump forward a bit, see if we can't get to the bottom of this Chantilly conundrum. At some point, you must have fallen for him. Let's see when that was and what lessons can be taken from it. Perhaps images of true love might give you the enthusiasm you need to take life by the horns.'

'Ok, but…'

'What now?'

'I don't want any rude bits, ok? Love, yes. Rude bits, no.'

He rolled his eyes. 'Lily, this is not a peep show. Come on. Here's a fresh headset for you, fully charged and ready to go.'

Lily wished she could say the same about herself.

# CHAPTER TWENTY-NINE

*ALTERNATIVE LILY ARMITAGE - AGED TWENTY-THREE*

*Harriet was wearing a flouncy, floor length, peach bridesmaid's dress which did nothing to conceal the bump protruding from her middle. Of course, when the pattern had been chosen and fabric selected it hadn't been with a heavily pregnant woman in mind. Her current condition had been a surprise to everyone, Harriett included.*

*From her hiding place, Lily could see Harriett and various other helpers scurrying backward and forward, but they couldn't see her, and that was exactly as she wanted it. A mere ninety minutes before her wedding ceremony was due to take place, a switch had flicked inside her head, and it suddenly became very clear this whole debacle was a massive mistake. She panicked, there was no other word for it. Panic had taken over her whole body, the result being she'd concealed herself in a large wardrobe, in the room she'd been allocated, at the fancy Tudor Manor House where she was to be married. She was hot and sticky, but she was convinced no one was going to find her, provided she didn't give herself away somehow.*

*A conversation was taking place only metres away, between Harriett and Lily's stepfather. It would appear Lily's mother had completely freaked out when she heard Lily was missing and been given a sedative and put to bed. Nothing new there.*

*'Rack your brains, Harriett love. Has she not given you any clues what's going on in her head? You must have some insight into her state of mind, if anyone does.'*

*Listening to herself being discussed by two people she loved most in the world, when they didn't know she was there, was not adding to Lily's comfort. She certainly wouldn't have been happy having some of the comments she'd made about her friend, in the past, being heard by Harriett's ears. Sometimes, what came out of your mouth sounded different from how the thoughts in your head seemed to, the sentiment kinder than the words.*

*'I'm sorry, Ray, I haven't got a clue, but then, what goes on inside her head where Darren's concerned has always been a mystery to me. I never have been able to understand it.'*

*'You're not a fan, are you? I can't say he would have been my choice for her either, but it's not ours to make, is it? The heart wants what the heart wants, and I daresay my friends and family have wondered at my decisions on the love front, over the years.'*

*There were a few moments of silence, where Lily imagined Ray thinking back over the roller-coaster ride of his life with Marion. There had been plenty of nail-biting moments, for sure.*

*'Well, I don't see anything for it, but to go and break it to the man. As much as he's no favourite of mine, it won't be easy telling him his bride-to-be has done a runner. For all his faults, he's besotted with the girl.'*

*Harriett clearly didn't have as much deference for Darren's feelings. 'I'll tell him, if you want, with relish. I don't owe him any favours since he told my ex about this little bundle, without my say so.' Lily could imagine Harriett rubbing her enormous belly in slow, circular motions. A habit recently formed, but ingrained, nonetheless. 'It wasn't his secret to tell. It was mine, and I should have had the opportunity to do it when it felt right, not when Darren Chantilly wanted me to.'*

*Lily had no doubt Harriett would have enjoyed imparting every syllable too, but that wasn't what Lily wanted. Although she had doubts about Darren's character, and she certainly had doubts about her feelings for him, she didn't want to hurt him more than necessary. At the same time, there was no way she could face him herself.*

*'No.' Ray's tone was firm. 'There'll be none of that. Now's not the time for revenge. Besides, it's a father's job and I'm the nearest thing Lily's ever had to a father, bless her.'*

*There was some rustling and a squeal of springs as if someone had sat heavily on the bed.*

*'Do me a favour, lovey. Check the other rooms one last time and get someone to do a circuit of the grounds. Not you, mind, not in your condition. Then, if there's still no sign, I'll do the deed.'*

*'Alright, Ray. Leave it to me.'*

*'Keep it low key. I don't want word getting to Darren until we know she's definitely gone.'*

*'Alright.' Harriett's voice was muffled by the closing of the door she'd walked through.*

*Lily settled back into the corner of her wardrobe, resting her head against cushions stored there. A few more minutes and it would be over. As soon as things died down, she would nip out, get into ordinary clothes and make a run for it. She didn't know where she was going to go. Somewhere miles away. Somewhere she didn't know anyone and wouldn't have to explain herself. Somewhere away from all the tension and stress, which was rendering her exhausted. Anywhere but here really.*

*She didn't know how much time had elapsed, but instinct told Lily it was substantial - the intensity of the light trickling through the gap in the wardrobe door had subsided and she felt like she'd been asleep for hours. She could have slept for many more too, if she hadn't woken up, choking on one of her own snores.*

*In the quiet which followed, she listened carefully for signs of life in the room beyond, but could hear nothing, apart from her own breathing. She didn't know what to do. Obviously, she couldn't stay hidden forever, but how would she know when it was safe to emerge? Would there ever be a right time? Her bladder told her it would be sooner, rather than later, and her first priority would be to find a bathroom, then get out of her wedding dress and into something less attention grabbing. Then, perhaps she could slip away.*

*She pushed the door open an inch, and then another, ready to duck back at the first sign of anyone entering the room or passing in the corridor beyond, but there was nothing. Although still alert, she breathed a sigh of relief, and pushed it wide to facilitate the dress fitting through the gap. At that moment, she looked up and saw Ray, staring right at her, from his perch at the end of the bed.*

*'What are you doing here?' She was shocked by his presence, having been pretty sure her family would have been long gone by now, and completely overlooked the fact her situation was far more incongruous than Ray's.*

*His face was blank. 'Believe it or not, for your wedding.'*

*He was talking as if it was something which could still take place, as if the event hadn't been written off already, which confused her further. 'What time is it?'*

*'About eleven thirty.'*

*Still half an hour before the start of the ceremony. She must have slept for little more than five minutes, ten at the most, and the lack of light was purely down to a cloud blotting out the sun. Now what was she to do?*

*'What were you doing in there, Lily?' He pushed himself up from the bed slowly, as if his legs were too weary to hold him. 'We've all been going frantic looking for you. Your mum... Well, you know your mum.'*

*How did she tell him? How did you tell people the wedding you've been planning, and talking about, and looking forward to, for more than a year, wasn't going to take place; that you suddenly realised it could be the biggest mistake you would ever make?*

*She opened and closed her mouth, like a fish out of water, then flopped onto the edge of the bed. 'I needed to get away. It was all… all too much. I just needed…' She searched around for the right words but failed.*

*Ray slipped his arm around her shoulder and sat next to her. 'It is a very big day for you.' He chuckled. 'Big day for us all. It's only natural to feel a bit overwhelmed, but here, we've got five minutes to ourselves before we need to get going. It won't do young Darren any harm to be kept waiting a short while, make him all the keener in fact, not that he needs reminding what a lucky chap he is. He already knows, that's for sure.'*

*Lily knew this was the moment she should speak up, make her feelings known, call a halt to proceedings, but she couldn't find a way.*

*Ray tightened his grip and his tone deepened. Lily could detect withheld emotion in his voice. 'I know I'm not your real dad, but I have to be honest, Lily. I couldn't be prouder if I was, and there's no doubt about it, I love you as if you were my own. I hope you know that, and I hope you know I've done my best with your mum.'*

*'Ray…'*

*He was on a roll and wouldn't allow her to interrupt. 'It hasn't always been easy, you know, with everything, for me, or for you, come to that, but I've tried to be a steadying hand in yours and your mum's life. I'm sorry if I've let you down today. I know your mum so wanted to be a part of your big day and, no doubt, you wanted her here too. I don't need to tell you how excited she's been. Perhaps that's the problem, but just like you're feeling the strain, so's she. You know she can't cope with any sign of trouble and, the minute you weren't right on schedule, she couldn't deal with it. I've had to put her to bed. Try not to be too disappointed.'*

*His arm had slipped from Lily's shoulders and instead his hands gripped his knees tight, waiting for her to vent her disappointment. She didn't have the heart. He'd always done the best for her, come what may, and he had nothing to apologise for.*

*'Ray, honestly, it's fine. I know…'*

*'Truth's told, she's been finding life even more trying than usual recently. I don't know if another little stay in hospital might not be called for. I hope not but, you know…' He removed one hand from his knee and patted hers instead. 'I knew you'd be like this. You've always been a good girl, always stayed on side with your mum, even when she's not treating you like she should. You understand she can't help it. But she will be very proud, when she watches the video, when she sees the photos. I know she will. It'll buck her up no end.'*

*The sun suddenly freed itself from the dark cloud and flooded the room with light and warmth and Ray jumped to his feet. 'I think I hear Harriett coming back. We should get ourselves ready, can't be seen all maudlin on a special occasion like this. What would people say?' He winked at her. 'Come on, lovey, show me your best smile.'*

*What could she do but give him the smile he was requesting?*

*Harriett burst into the room, with a bevy of helpers, and their excitement and relief at finding Lily present, took over.*

*Ray waved his arms to quieten the questions. 'It's alright, girls. She'd only stepped away for a few minutes' peace. No drama. Come on, everyone get your things and we'll go downstairs and get this party started.'*

*The mass of bodies left as quickly as they'd arrived, and Ray pulled Lily up from her seat, tucking her hand in the crook of his arm, and whisking her towards the door. He paused for only a moment on the landing, to pull her closer, as he chuckled and spoke low, for her ears only. 'I should have known where you'd be. When you were little, whenever and whatever gave you cause for concern, it was always straight to the wardrobe with you. I suppose it was your safe place.'*

*He patted her hand and led her on. 'That'll be Darren's job now. From this day forward it's Darren'll be your safe place. I'll never have to worry about you again.'*

*Lily's heart was in her shoes. It was too late. She couldn't pull out now, even if she was sure Darren wasn't right for her, even if she was pretty sure Adam was. It would cause too much pain to all concerned and she couldn't be responsible for that.*

# CHAPTER THIRTY

The ombudsman halted the footage abruptly and Lily heard the edginess in his voice. 'I didn't see that coming.' He rushed on. 'I thought I was showing you something lovely and poignant and heart-warming, not…not…not. That'll teach me to do my research before rushing on.'

Lily was thoughtful. Yes, it was unpleasant to see an alternative self heading to a wedding she didn't want to be part of but, at the same time, there had been beautiful moments too. 'No, don't worry. I needed to see it. In my world, Ray and I never had that conversation and it's one I think we should have had. I've always had a thing, a bit of a chip, I suppose, about not having a "real" dad, and Mum being the way she is. In some ways, I've felt like an orphan all my life, but to know Ray felt that way about me is quite something. I loved him too, like a dad, but at the same time, I didn't feel I wholly had the right to. It would seem I did. I wish he was still around for me to tell him so.'

'Ah, he passed away?' The ombudsman's words were soft.

'No, he moved to Bognor Regis when my mum threw him out. He had her sectioned one too many times and the last time, when she got out, she sent him packing. It was her house, you see, inherited when my gran died. Mum might have been deemed sane enough to come home, but she wasn't in a place where she could be a sound judge of what was actually good for her.' Lily sighed. It was ancient history to her, but it still wasn't easy. 'Poor Ray. I should have stayed in touch with him, but Mum wouldn't have liked it.'

'It's never too late. Perhaps that's something you can sort out when you get back.'

'Not so fast.' She could tell what the ombudsman was thinking, that he had her right where he wanted her, keen to go back to her body to rekindle her relationship with her stepdad, but she had other fish to fry before that happened. 'I'm not finished with that period of my life yet. There are things about the wedding scene which didn't make sense, questions which need answers.'

The ombudsman was taken aback. 'Such as?'

Lily scratched her head. 'Why was I still harping on about Adam? Surely the wedding is a good while after the uni encounter. I would have thought I would have moved on by then, particularly if I agreed to marry Darren. If the Adam thing was an ongoing infatuation, which lasted years, I can't see why I would agree to the wedding in the first place. Something else must have happened.'

'Good point. I hadn't considered that.'

'Can you find out? I'd like to know.'

'I suppose I could.' He seemed unsure. 'But I don't see how it will help. The whole point of watching the wedding was to encourage you to embrace life and love and all it has to offer. Watching your love-life fall apart isn't going to strengthen my point, is it? I don't want you backsliding after all my hard work.'

'I hate to disappoint you, but I'm not convinced there's been any forward movement to allow for backsliding yet. Just because I'm becoming resigned about going back, doesn't mean I'm any happier about it.' She realised her comments might not encourage him to allow her to view what she wanted to see. 'Perhaps it's more a case of letting me see myself going through these scenarios and how I deal with them. Now, that might give me confidence for the future.'

'Lily, a few minutes ago you were having panic attacks at the idea of watching yourself at a spelling bee, now you want to see your love-life unravel? Are you sure?'

She frowned at the idea of this new, determined her. 'I think I must. I may be a scaredy cat, but I'm also a curious one. I need to know.'

'I won't remind you what curiosity did to the cat,' he muttere'd as he took the necessary actions to continue. 'At least I learnt something in the last few minutes.'

'You did? What was that?'

'The mystery of why you appeared in the staffroom broom cupboard. You've got history.' He chuckled. 'Ok. Let me find some relevant events. Alright. Here we are. On your head be it.'

*ALTERNATIVE LILY ARMITAGE - AGED TWENTY-THREE*

*Lily had driven through a lengthy avenue of trees and pulled up outside a magnificent Tudor Manor House, in a parking space punctuated by potted shrubs and spiky, strutting peacocks. The grounds were lush with green growth and late summer flora, and the early autumn sunshine highlighted the frontage beautifully, while areas of shadow zigzagged across parts of the lawns.*

*It was a pretty place, no doubt about it, but she still wasn't sure it was really her. Darren had picked it, having been told about it by someone in his office, but right from the start she'd made it clear, she wanted a simple, straightforward ceremony. Any function which took place here would have to be an extremely grand affair, or risk being lost among the box hedges and topiary. Darren said it was all about appearances - you didn't have to have twenty bridesmaids and champagne fountains, but you should make an effort, show the world how special the occasion was. Personally, she thought the fact they were promising themselves to each other for eternity was special enough, and if the world didn't agree it could mind its own business. But it was Darren's day too and, as his family were paying for the whole shebang, who was she to deny him?*

*She was early and the woman who had taken the booking had warned her not to be. They had a full day of viewings by prospective brides-to-be and wanted to ensure each lucky lady was treated to a full tour experience without feeling rushed, and neither did they want to keep her waiting. Rather than intrude on the previous tour, Lily decided to walk around the outside of the house, to get a feel for it. Perhaps its grandeur would grow on her when viewed from a different angle.*

*She followed a public path past her car, dodging one particular peacock who seemed to have his eye on her, through what was signposted "The Folley", to the side and rear. The gigantic building didn't reduce in stature, and her heart didn't grow any fonder, so she slipped off the path and across the lawn to view it from a distance. There were people wandering around there, probably guests of the tearooms which, according to brochures, sat in the old stables, providing an income for the business year-round rather than it being solely dependent on functions.*

*Standing away, she viewed the rear facade. It was a pleasant enough place, and she could see why people would want to come here for a lazy afternoon stroll, but she simply didn't feel a connection with it.*

*A male voice cut through her thoughts. 'Marvellous old pile of bricks, isn't it?'*

*'Mmm, yes, it is.' Although it wasn't to her taste, she saw no reason to disagree with the passer-by.*

*He moved away, as if he were going to walk on, then stopped. 'Lily, is it?'*

*The sound of her own name grabbed her attention, and she looked at him only to realise the face was very familiar. 'Adam.'*

*At her acknowledgement of him, he turned and held out his hand to shake hers.*

*'Fancy seeing you here.' He didn't let go of her hand.*

*'Yes, long time no see.' She was at a loss what to say and the fact he remembered her at all had blown her away. He had left university at the end of her first year and she had spent most of that year keeping her distance, although their paths had by necessity crossed from time to time. Since those days, he had cropped up in her thoughts on and off. She had even imagined bumping into him somewhere unexpectedly, maybe he would walk into the library where she worked, or perhaps they would find themselves at adjacent pumps at the petrol station, the variations were endless, but she had not foreseen his presence today. 'You're not from this neck of the woods, are you?'*

*'No.' He seemed to realise he had been holding her hand a little longer than politeness required and dropped it. 'Or, I suppose, I am now. I've relocated for work.'*

*'Really? Where are you working?' This was safe territory; she could make small talk about careers. What could be more normal?*

*He spread his hands. 'Here.'*

*'What, right here?' At the place she was considering getting married?*

*'Yes. I mean, it's not a permanent thing, but I'm here as a consultant.' Standing back, he put his hands on his hips and looked around. He was clearly confident in his situation. 'They're wanting to expand, you know, maximise income, attract more business, diversify maybe, and I'm here to come up with a proposal.'*

*'Wow.' Where to go with the conversation. 'I hope they're not going to make too many changes. It would be a shame to overdevelop it.'*

*He put a palm to his chest. 'That's why I'm here. I've worked on a couple of projects at old country estates before this and, you're right, it's easy to get carried away. Next thing you know, you've got modern holiday flats squeezed between the Elizabethan mansion and Renaissance gatehouse, complete with faux Victorian lighting and satellite dishes. It's a travesty.'*

*'Is that what you do then? Architecture? Planning?' She never had found out what he was studying at university.*

*'No, not really. I love history, but my thing is business development. When I can combine the two, like here, it's all my dreams come true.' His eyes zoned in on her for an extended moment. 'Most of them, anyway.'*

*He hasn't lost the charm, she thought. If she didn't know him, or about his reputation, she would have been lost, in that one, single, loaded look.*

*'So, what are you doing here? Afternoon stroll? Or meeting someone at the café?'*

*She realised it had been her turn to speak, but she'd missed her cue, too busy concentrating on how immune she was to his wiles. 'Oh, me? No, I'm here to do the tour.' A blush came to her cheeks. For some reason she found explaining her presence embarrassing. 'They do weddings. Of course, you already know that.'*

*'You're getting married?'*

*Had she imagined it? Or did some of the colour drain from his face. His smile certainly shrank. 'Don't sound so surprised.' She covered her embarrassment with a joke.*

*He briefly took her hand again. 'No. Good grief, no, I'm not surprised at all. If anyone was going to get snapped up it was going to be you. It's just strange I should run into you like this and then…' His explanation stalled. 'Who's the lucky guy?'*

*The depth of colour in her cheeks deepened, and again she couldn't put her finger on why. 'You remember Darren? Chantilly?'*

*His face gave nothing away. 'Ahh. Yes, Darren. Hmm. Well, lucky Darren.'*

*'Thanks.' She wasn't sure what she was thanking him for. Suddenly the conversation felt stilted.*

*The mention of Darren's name seemed to have brought the meeting to a full stop. Neither of them had anything further to say.*

*Lily swung her arms as her mind searched for something to add. 'Umm, actually, I suppose I should get on.' She glanced at her watch but had no idea what time it showed. 'My tour is due to start any minute now.'*

*'Oh, yes. Don't let me hold you up.'*

*There was an awkward moment as neither of them knew how to part company. Lily held out her hand, at the same time that Adam leaned in to kiss her cheek. They both laughed and he shrugged, shaking her hand and planting a peck below her ear.*

*'Good luck with that. Nice to see you again.' He put his hands in his pockets, as if he wanted to make sure they behaved themselves.*

*'Thanks. You too.' Lily walked away without a backward glance. She closed her eyes tight for a second, cross with herself. All these years she'd imagined seeing Adam again, and it had to be here, today, in these circumstances, and she had dealt with it like that. Her stomach gurgled with a cocktail of emotions, so thoroughly mixed she couldn't tell one ingredient from another, but the predominant flavour was disappointment. She'd missed an opportunity. She didn't know what that opportunity was, but she knew it had passed her by.*

*'Hey, Lily.'*

*Adam's voice sent her spinning to face him, now a hundred metres apart. 'Yes?'*

*He jogged to catch up with her and she waited, breathing on hold.*

*'I know it's cheeky, but....' His grin was lopsided and heavenly, and his dimple deepened. 'I wonder, once you've done the tour, if you'd meet me for coffee in the tearooms. As a bride-to-be, it would be great to get your input about what's on offer here, your overall impression of it. It would help me out no end.'*

*Lily knew she was on dodgy territory. She did want to see him again, but not to talk about this place or her wedding, just to spend more time with him, and, in her current situation, it wasn't the right thing to do. It wouldn't be fair to Darren or to herself.*

*'My treat. I could even throw in a slice of their famous Key Lime Pie?'*

*What the heck? It was only coffee and cake and maybe half an hour of her time. What was unfair to anybody about that? In fact, it could mean she'd finally get this cool, charismatic and thoroughly gorgeous man out of her head for good. That had to be a positive thing, right?*

*She shrugged and shook her head. 'Why not? I'll probably be an hour though.'*

*'No problem. I'm pretty much living in the tearooms anyway – coffee on tap and the cake's too good, and I like to work with people around me rather than a sterile office. Come over when you're ready.'*

*'Ok.'*

*'I'll be looking out for you.'*

*'Ok.' As she walked away for the second time, the cocktail of emotions was still there, but the recipe was completely different.*

# CHAPTER THIRTY-ONE

*ALTERNATIVE LILY ARMITAGE - AGED TWENTY-THREE*

*The tour guide had only served to confirm Lily's worst fears. Contrary to the woman's constant sugary reminders that it was "all about the Bride and Groom and their special, special day", it was clearly all about the grandeur of the building, the fancy cuisine and an awful lot of pomp and ceremony. To be honest, Lily couldn't care less about the thread count of the serviettes or the provenance of the asparagus, but she'd smiled and nodded her way around, as seemed appropriate. She was glad to get out, and not only because she knew Adam was waiting for her.*

*It was difficult to tell if her stomach was aflutter with excitement or anxiety. If it was nerves, Darren had gone to some lengths recently to encourage her to ignore such signals and "man up", as he put it, so today she intended to do exactly that. As she stepped into the air-conditioned tearooms, she spotted Adam at a table in the back corner, and decided the butterflies were definitely positive ones, as a wave of pleasure washed through her at the sight of him.*

*He looked up from his laptop and stood the moment he saw her. How different he was from the teenager she'd watched snogging in the kitchen all those years ago. But he was still the same person. She shouldn't forget that.*

*'Hi. Sit yourself down.' He shuffled around the table and held out a chair for her. 'Coffee or tea? I'm not even going to ask if you want Key Lime Pie, you'd be mad not to.'*

*He appeared nervous, which somehow reassured her, and she chuckled at his comments. 'Tea, please and, trust me, I never say no to cake.'*

*His eyes swept her body from head to toe and back again. 'It doesn't show.'*

*Her composure fled and she made use of the time he was at the counter giving their order to bring herself back in line.*

*When he returned, he was all business. 'So, how did the tour go? Are you in love with the place? Tell me what you think, the good, the bad and the ugly.'*

*She did exactly that, and he took copious notes, so that almost an hour had passed before they'd finished.*

*Adam pushed his pad and pen aside and rested back in his seat. 'This really is invaluable, you know?' He waved at what he'd written. 'An outsider can come up with lots of ideas, but until you actually want to make use of the facilities personally, you're only getting half the picture. Thank you.'*

*She shrugged. 'That's ok.'*

*He drained the dregs of his Americano. 'I take it you're not going to have your wedding here, considering your first impression?'*

*'Oh no. It will be here. Darren desperately wants it to be, and his parents are keen too, so, you know…'*

*'I thought it was generally the bride who ruled the roost on these things.' His cup clinked as he replaced it on the saucer.*

*'Only if the bride is prepared to put her foot down and I prefer an easy life to an argument, and I'm not that bothered. It's the marriage that's important, not the wedding.'*

*'And the Bridezilla award for this year goes to anyone other than you.' He chuckled. 'I suspect there would be far fewer divorces if more people thought like that. In my experience, it's usually all about the bling. But you should have the day you want, you know? It doesn't have to create a battlefield.' He pursed his lips and tapped his notepad with his pen. 'In fact, I've already got some ideas brewing, some of which could be implemented quite quickly, and they may benefit you.'*

*'Really?' She was intrigued.*

*'I don't want to say too much right now. I need to percolate for a while, work out the finer details and probably have a chat with the management team too.' He paused. 'Would it be too much to ask you to meet me again once I'm further forward, so I could run it past you?'*

*'I don't know…' She'd enjoyed their time together. He'd been easy to chat with and had been a very good listener – not once had she suspected him of thinking about the next scrabble fixture or tomorrow's board meeting when she'd been venting about the superior attitude of the tour guide.*

*'It would be a great help, and we could do it here, or somewhere closer to where you live, if that would be easier.'*

*It was a trek to the manor house, but it was probably best Adam didn't come any closer to her home. It was a small town and secret assignations quickly became the talk of it, not that they would be having a secret assignation as such, although something told her Darren wouldn't approve, even if it was just business.*

*'No, here would be fine.' Darren would probably be pleased she was taking an interest in the place, having made it clear previously that she wasn't keen.*

*'Fantastic.' In his excitement, Adam grasped her hand where it sat on the table, then his face fell as he realised what he'd done, and he quickly turned the grasp into a pat. 'Thank you. This is the first big project I've managed on my own and I want to do it right.*

*Having the insight of a consumer like you is bound to give me an edge.'*

*She could still feel the warmth of his hand on hers and it disturbed her somewhat, so she turned her attention to her bag, pretending to check for something inside and getting ready to leave. 'That's fine. My pleasure.'*

*'Do you want to take my number? Or shall we arrange a date now?'*

*A date? He only meant a note for the calendar, but somehow putting Adam and "a date" in the same sentence sent a thrill through her, an inappropriate thrill, she reminded herself. On the other hand, if Darren saw Adam's name on her phone, it would not go down well. 'Same time next week? I don't work on a Wednesday. Or is that too soon?'*

*His face lit up. 'No, next week will be perfect. I'll be right here, waiting.'*

*'Fine. See you then.'*

*Her heart was beating fast as she crossed the car park at the front of the house towards her car, but progress was stalled by the arrogant peacock which had been watching her earlier. She stepped left to go around it, but it matched her move, so she stepped right, but once again, it copied her. At a loss, she backed up. It dipped its head, staring up through long lashes, and suddenly opened its feathery tail into an ornate display. She had the horrible feeling she had caught the eye of more than one Peacock today, but the attentions of this particular one she could do without. The one she had left in the Tearooms? Now, he had made a much better impression.*

*Holding her bag against her chest, she ducked backwards and around a small white van, running like the clappers to the rear of her car, almost dropping the keys as she fiddled with the lock. The bird had followed at a much more sedate rate, proudly displaying his wares. Her heartrate didn't return to normal until she had locked the door and started the engine, the music on the radio drowning out her troubled thoughts.*

***

'I don't want to see any more.' Lily interrupted the ombudsman as he leapfrogged from one scene to the next.

'You don't? I thought you were desperate to understand what was going on in your alternative head.'

'I think it's perfectly clear what was going on in my head and other parts of my body, and I don't like it. I don't like it one little bit.'

'It might be perfectly clear to you, but not to me. I can see you're attracted to Adam, but obviously you overcome that attraction because the wedding to Darren still goes ahead. What's the problem?'

'I'll tell you what the problem is, Adam and I are going to have an affair, aren't we? I'm going to do the dirty on Darren.' Her breathing was too fast, and she put a hand to her chest in an attempt to control it. 'I've never actually been in that sort of situation in real life, but I always thought, if I was, I'd be a better person and do the right thing. I'm very disappointed in myself.'

'Am I going to need another glass of water? Because, if so, there's going to be very little left to top up the percolator.'

Lily found his attitude annoying. 'No, you're not going to need another glass of water. I'm soggy enough as it is, thank you very much.'

'You're welcome.' He completely overlooked her sarcasm. 'As a matter of fact, you should have more faith in yourself, not less.'

'How so?'

'The issue is not the fact you were tempted. Everybody faces temptation in one form or another at some point in their lives. It's inevitable. The issue is how you react to it, and so far, I don't see any lines being crossed and, according to my records, you stay firmly on the right side of propriety throughout.'

Lily's jaw dropped open. 'I do? Because that's not the direction it looks like I'm headed in that scene.'

'As I said, you need to trust yourself. Lily, you have more strength than you know.'

'Do I?' She shook her head. 'I wish I could believe it.'

'You don't have to just believe it. Focus, and you'll see it with your own eyes.'

# CHAPTER THIRTY-TWO

ALTERNATIVE LILY ARMITAGE - AGED TWENTY-THREE

*'So, you're heading out for another look at the Manor today?' Darren had one eye on the newspaper and one on Lily, across the breakfast table.*

*She felt her cheeks flush, conscious the draw was Adam rather than the venue, and collected up the dishes, carrying them to the kitchen sink to conceal the glow. 'Yes. It's one thing to do the tour, but I want to see it without all the formality.'*

*His tone was smug. 'You're warming to it, I can tell. I knew you would. Who wouldn't love a place that's that expensive? A bit of bragging fodder. You're very lucky, you know? Not every girl has parents-in-law prepared to throw that sort of bash. If it was left to your tribe, it would be a quick jaunt down the Registry Office and a pie and pint at the pub.'*

*'It would still have been special. You don't have to spend a fortune.' It jarred that he took every given opportunity to point out her family's financial status.*

*'Of course you don't, but it doesn't hurt to throw a bit of wonga at these things, especially if you're inviting the bosses. You can't expect people like that to turn out for a shindig at The Dog and Duck, and it's always good to rub noses in a social setting with*

*the powers that be, puts you a notch ahead of the opposition when promotion's in the air.'*

*Lily bit her tongue and dropped the tea-towel on the worktop. 'Darren, a wedding is about the bride and groom and no one else. It's not supposed to be a political campaign.'*

*He must have realised he'd spoken out of turn, as he folded the newspaper and viewed her with a frown. 'Of course not, darling. The main priority will always be you and me.' Grabbing her hand, he pulled her towards him. 'But there's no harm in networking, that's all I'm saying. After all, it's work that puts bread on the table.'*

*He was like an old man, not an excited twenty something groom-to-be, and it grated on Lily. She pushed away and returned to the sink. 'If you say so.'*

*He stood up and slipped his arms around her waist from behind, his lips close to her ear. 'Now then, sweetie, don't be like that.'*

*She ignored him, holding a bowl under the running tap.*

*'I tell you what. Shall I take the morning off and come with you? It's a beautiful day and I'm sure the office could do without me for an hour or two. We could sign on the dotted line while we're there and set the date for definite.'*

*Lily felt a prickle of panic flood through her. If Darren came along, she would have to ditch Adam, or worse, they'd run into him together and then she'd have some explaining to do, even if it was all innocent.*

*She turned in his arms and smiled. 'I wouldn't want you to get in trouble with those bosses of yours.'*

*'Don't you worry about that. I'm high enough up in the echelons now that I can take the odd morning off if I feel the need. There's got to be some perks to all the slogging I've been doing.'*

*'But surely they can't do without you at such short notice? I thought you were vital to operations.' A bit of ego plumping wouldn't go amiss.*

*Darren considered the matter. 'I am pretty important.'*

*Her shoulders relaxed as she sensed a win.*

*'But if I leave them to it for a couple of hours it'll serve as a good reminder of how much they depend on me. Absence makes the heart grow fonder and all that.'*

*Foiled. She could think of no other response. 'If you want to then.'*

*'If I want to? You don't sound too pleased. Anyone would think you didn't want me to come.'*

*For goodness' sake, not only was he going to gate-crash her morning out, she was supposed to be enthusiastic about it too, but then, he was her fiancé, and it was their wedding venue. He had a right to expect some excitement and togetherness. It was her who was out of order, wanting one last outing with an old crush. She felt ashamed and slipped an arm around his shoulders.*

*'Of course I want you to. I just didn't want to put you out. It'll be lovely to have company.' Apart from the fact she would have one eye on the lookout for Adam at all times, this time to avoid him, rather than spot him.*

*'Good. That's that then.' He looked at his watch. 'How long do you think it'll take? Could we be back in time for me to grab lunch with James?'*

*Now he was going to rush her. So much for togetherness. An idea struck her. 'I'm sure we could at a push, but I was thinking, if we're going together, we could make use of some of the facilities, maybe go for a couples' massage.'*

*'Couples' massage?' He was instantly suspicious.*

*'Mmm, one of the girls at work said about it. You both go in and strip off. They provide you with these lovely fluffy matching dressing gowns. Then you get rubbed all over with fabulous aromatherapy oils. It sounds heavenly.' She knew to Darren it would sound like hell.*

*'Aromatherapy oils?' He grimaced. 'I can't go back to work smelling like I've spent the morning in a brothel.'*

*She allowed her gaze to wander off as if she was blissfully lost in the idea. 'You probably wouldn't want to go back at all, you'd be so relaxed. We could both have a treatment while we're there too. They do everything to buff up a body you could possibly think of, exfoliating, waxing. What do you say? Shall I phone ahead and book?'*

*His face had taken on a wan hue. 'Do you know? On second thoughts, I probably ought to show my face at work first thing. We've got a big meeting with clients tomorrow and I need to make sure everyone's on top of their game.'*

*'Oh, really? What a shame.' Lily had never considered an acting career before, but she felt pretty confident he would take her response as disappointed. 'I can picture it now: me having my eyebrows done; you having your chest waxed.'*

*He visibly winced, leaned around her and reached for his keys. 'Yes, well, maybe next time. I'd better shoot.' Hastily kissing her forehead, he ducked out of the kitchen. 'Enjoy... whatever you decide to have treated.'*

*Collapsing, chuckling, into the chair he had recently vacated, her body shook with mirth. She should feel guilty about what she'd just done to her husband-to-be, but she didn't, not in the slightest.*

*Adam was in the same position as at their last meeting, his laptop open on a table at the back of the Tearooms, a pile of files spread across the surface next to it. When he saw her in the doorway, he snatched them up to tidy away and closed the lid of the computer, so all his attention was on her.*

*He made her feel important and she knew her face was glowing with pleasure as she crossed to where he was. As she reached the table, he leaned across and kissed her cheek.*

*'Thanks for coming. I wasn't sure you would.'*

*'I said I would.'*

*'I know, but, you know, plans change, people change their minds. I wouldn't have blamed you if something had cropped up or you'd had a better offer.'*

*She studied his face as he spoke. He seemed a little flustered, not the calm, collected individual she'd expected. 'No, no better offer.'*

*'Good. I've been looking forward to seeing you again.' His mouth spread into a wide smile. 'Let me get you some tea.'*

*Her heart felt as if someone was squeezing it tight. That's what his smile did to her and she knew she was in trouble. If she had any sense, she would get up and run for it, leave before he came back. She didn't move a muscle.*

*'How's the research going?' The least she could do was keep the conversation on topic and, if the pile of papers on his desk were anything to go by, he'd been busy.*

*'Yes, good.' He rested the end of a tray on the edge of the table and shifted cups and plates off with one hand, before sliding into his seat. 'Take your pick.'*

*There was a mouth-watering display of cakes to choose from. 'Good grief, I don't know where to start.'*

*'In that case, the cream horn's mine, and you can take as long as you like working through the rest.' He snatched up the pastry and bit into it, an ooze of cream immediately shooting out the side and down his shirt.*

*Lily exploded with laughter, as Adam's eyes widened in horror and he grappled around for a serviette, his hands covered in sticky cream. She came to his rescue with a tissue, wiping down his shirt and removing his tie from a blob on the table, chuckling at the same time. He sat still, allowing her ministrations, like a child at the hands of his mother but, when she glanced up, she found he was staring right at her, studying every inch of her face. The intensity of his gaze brought turmoil to her insides, her heart jumping in her chest and she sat back heavily in the seat.*

*He coughed and looked away. 'Sorry about that. I think I'm going to have to go and clean up. Can you give me a minute?' With that, he got up and disappeared through swing doors near the till, to the toilets.*

*The feelings pulsing through her weren't right for a woman engaged to someone else. What was she doing here? Drinking tea and eating cake with an almost stranger?*

*Lily grabbed her bag to leave but was blocked by a waitress with a damp cloth.*

*'Honestly, them cakes should come with a warning.'*

*Lily felt obliged to laugh in response as the young woman lifted a plate to wipe underneath.*

*'I'll get you more napkins.'*

*As the woman turned away, Adam re-entered and Lily realised she'd missed her chance to make a swift exit, without having to offer an explanation. She put her bag back down on the chair and fixed a smile on her face, while Adam and the waitress exchanged banter about his messiness. One hour and she would be on her way home and would probably never see this man again. One hour to hold herself together, maintain a safe distance, and not do anything stupid.*

*'Right, back to business.' Adam reached for some paperwork and gave it all his attention.*

*If she didn't know better, she would have said he was avoiding eye contact with her too.*

*He explained his ideas at some length, and she took it all in. His descriptions were interesting and enthusiastic, the changes he was proposing well thought out and sensible and it didn't take long for her to forget the previous awkwardness. She gave some counter suggestions which he scribbled in the margins of his notebook, drawing rings around some, as if they were of particular import. But, in spite of everything, she could see nothing which would make her more inclined to hold her own wedding here and she told him so.*

*Adam smiled and held one finger in the air. 'Aah! Yes. I was coming to that.' He restacked his papers on top of a closed laptop. 'I want to show you something.' Turning to the waitress, he waved at his equipment, hand signalling that he was going to leave it there and for her to watch over it.*

*The woman nodded back and waved him out, as if it were a regular occurrence.*

*'It's only a short walk, but it's worth it.'*

*Intrigued, Lily followed him into the grounds.*

*They followed the path for a few steps and then he ducked beneath an ivy-clad, low arch, cut out of the wall of the gardens into a sprawling lawned area. 'This way.'*

*It was clear this part of the grounds wasn't frequented by many visitors and Lily wasn't surprised. If Adam hadn't led the way, she wouldn't have given the arch a second glance and no doubt many people walked straight past without knowing it was there. The space had a climate all of its own too, high walls enclosing it holding back the breeze and the noise of the outside, giving it a peace, a sereneness which she hadn't experienced elsewhere on site.*

*She took a long slow breath. 'Wow! This is quite lovely.'*

*'Isn't it?' He backed away from her and turned in a circle, arms spread wide, a new light to his eyes. 'It's my favourite spot in the entire estate of goodness knows how many acres, and hardly anyone knows about it. It's like my own secret garden.'*

*The lawn was far from flat, with bumps and slopes and random shrubs with no divisible design, completely at odds with the formality of what she'd previously seen here. It was pretty, rather than handsome; verdant rather than grand. It was romantic. It was Lily. It was perfect for a wedding, if only British weather could be relied upon. She told him so.*

*'Aah. Yes. Follow me.' He raced across the grass to a point where the wall curved away, concealing another swathe of lawn.*

*'The area extends right around this corner and then opens out to this.'*

*Her eye was immediately caught by a run-down octagonal construction, resembling an old-fashioned bandstand, complete with ramshackle roof. 'Oh, my!' She hurried past him, towards the building, and up the few steps to the centre.*

*'Be careful.' He rushed after her. 'Not all the boards are sound.' He caught up and stood next to her. 'It needs work, but it could be…'*

*'It is magnificent.' She moved to the outer edge, picking her way through a complete circuit of the stand, taking in the three-hundred-and-sixty-degree view. 'The bride and groom would stand here, with the view of the river behind them, and the guests seated in rows here.' She waved her arms to demonstrate her comments. 'How many could you fit in?'*

*He shrugged. 'Between twenty and thirty I'd say, so it would only be suitable for smaller functions, but it would be great for the estate. They could still have the big, grand affairs in the main hall, while holding more intimate ceremonies here.'*

*'Intimate. Yes, that's the word.' She gripped a length of balustrade and leaned over, taking in the extent of the ground. 'Oh, Adam, this is perfect.'*

*'I knew you'd like it.' He tested his weight against the same section of woodwork, checking it was safe before relaxing against it. 'Not everybody wants full on splendour. I could tell from what you were saying before, you're looking for something with more depth than polish, more meaning than drama. I understand that. It's what I would want, if I'm ever lucky enough to meet the right girl.' His eye caught hers, then swiftly moved on. 'At the right time.'*

*Her heart was full of the beauty of the place, and she couldn't think of anything to say.*

*'You are lucky, you know? To feel so much for one person, to be so sure about your feelings, to see your future laid out before*

*you and know that it's right.' He briefly laid a hand on her shoulder, before walking away and back down the steps.*

*After a pause, he reverted to facts and figures about what the plans for the garden were, the amount of work, the length of time it would take before it was ready for use.*

*Lily was glad to be distracted from her own thoughts, glad to be led back to the mundane, because his comments had struck a chord. Did she feel enough for that one person? Or, had she fallen into line with what that other person wanted? Was she sure of the future in front of her? Or resigned? Did she know it was right? An uncomfortable response reverberated around her brain in answer to all those questions. She needed to get away. She needed to get her head together.*

*'I should get back.'*

*Her interruption pulled him up short and he frowned at her sudden change of tack. 'Of course. Let me show you the right path.'*

*She was very much afraid he had already done that.*

# CHAPTER THIRTY-THREE

*ALTERNATIVE LILY ARMITAGE - AGED TWENTY-THREE*

*The trek back to the car park was more march than leisurely walk, Lily hurrying on, desperate to get away, Adam matching her stride for stride.*

*As they re-entered the main grounds, he interrupted her thoughts. 'I hope I haven't taken up too much of your time, but it has been invaluable, you know, getting your input. Between you and me, this job is quite an important step for me, setting out on my own. Under normal circumstances I would have probably stuck with the company I was working with for a bit longer, but I really needed the extra income.'*

*She was too deep in thought to reply, and his comments went over her head.*

*'It's a struggle for mum. She's been ill on and off for years so can't hold a job down and, well, you remember Brandon. He's got his own issues.'*

*Lily stopped short as his words sunk in. 'Brandon?'*

*'Yes. I thought you might remember him after spending so much time with him that summer at the camp, but I guess you worked with loads of kids, even if he does usually stand out from the crowd.'*

*'Brandon? As in Superman Brandon?' The penny dropped. That's why Adam had seemed so familiar when she met him at uni. He had grown up, filled out and what with the beard too, it must have confused her. She'd met him before. That summer. That kiss. Her stomach churned. 'Of course I remember him, I just didn't realise you... Good grief! How is he?'*

*Their walk resumed, slower, less frantic.*

*'Yes, he's fine, but, you know, he had special needs. They finally diagnosed him as being on the autistic spectrum a couple of years ago, which was a relief, because until then we didn't know what his issue was. It means mum gets more support, but there are always limits and with her health too, she finds it hard.'*

*'I can imagine.' Lily was thoughtful. 'I can't believe I didn't realise who you were when we met at uni.'*

*'I was sure you did. I thought maybe that was why you kept your distance. I know you were really nice to Brandon and me before, but sometimes people give the whole family a wide berth. They don't want to get involved.'*

*His comments bit. She would have hoped nobody would bundle her in that sort of selfish bracket and felt she needed to prove she wasn't "people". 'No way. Brandon was a sweetie. Besides, I never kept distance. As far as I recall, you always had more than enough company.'*

*'What do you mean?'*

*'I seem to remember a skinny redhead all over you in the kitchen at that party, and wasn't there a blonde waiting for you, which Darren told you about?'*

*Adam's eyebrows raised. 'Tiffany, I'll grant you. The redhead, that is,' he qualified. 'We went out a few times in the first year, but she had a tendency to go home with someone else at the end of the evening, so that was short lived. She quite often seemed to seek me out at a party, until a better option came along, but I don't believe in that sort of relationship. You're either together, or you're not. But a blonde?'*

*Lily was pretty sure of her memory. Darren's comment had stuck, mainly because she had been so attracted to Adam and it had disappointed her to think of him being such a player.*

*'Oh, yes. I remember now. The blonde was my flatmate, Paul. I wondered at the time what Darren was going on about. Just a joke, I guess.'*

*A joke? Darren wouldn't waste his energy doing anything simply as a joke. Without being disloyal, she had to admit he wasn't averse to painting a picture in a particular manner to get his own way and if he had suspected her of being interested in Adam, it might have been something he would say to give her a certain impression. If so, it had worked. 'You could be right.'*

*'And you were tied up with Darren even then, I know. I asked him about you, and he told me you were an item.'*

*Had he now? They hadn't been an item until long after that. In fact, it had taken a good two years for Darren to wear her down, and even then, it had involved a particularly rough patch with her mother and an awful lot of alcohol at a post scrabble tournament celebration. She had an uncomfortable feeling she had been manipulated and that only added to the confusion whirling in her mind.*

*'There's my car.' She paused a few yards away and rifled in her handbag for her keys.*

*Adam stood by, hands clenched fists by his sides. 'Will you come and see me again, do you think? For an update, I mean?'*

*'Maybe. I've got quite a lot on over the next few weeks.'*

*'Ok, then. Well, thanks again.' There was a smile on his face, but it didn't reach his eyes. 'You know where I am if you're ever up this way.'*

*He thought she was giving him the brush off, she could tell by his stance, and in a way she was. It wasn't safe for her to see him again anytime soon, especially with the way she was feeling about Darren right now, but that wasn't his fault. She put her hand on his arm without thinking. 'Of course. It was lovely to see you again too.'*

*Adam leaned in to kiss her cheek as Lily began to turn away and his lips inadvertently brushed hers. It was like an electric shock, pulsing through her whole body, and she pulled away abruptly.*

*'Sorry about that.'*

*She waved his apology away, laughing, making light of it, when her insides were in uproar. 'It's ok. See you again.'*

*The dreaded peacock was once again standing guard by the door to her car, but this time she was having none of it. She rushed towards it, stamping a foot and shooing it away, the incentive to find refuge inside stronger than her fear of its pointy beak. She couldn't get away quick enough, but she was taking the turmoil with her.*

***

The action paused on alternative Lily's car reversing out of the parking space, Adam watching from the side-lines, hands in pockets, shoulders slumped.

The ombudsman broke the silence. 'That was it. You drove away and didn't go back, even though you wanted to. You see, you're stronger than you think.'

Lily blew through her lips. 'Is that what strength looks like?'

He chuckled. 'It comes in all sorts of guises and isn't always pretty. But let's face it, you could have completely ignored your sense of right and wrong and that could have been even uglier.'

'Would it though?' Lily's head tilted to one side as she took in the scene.

'What do you mean?'

'I'm afraid…'

'Nothing new there.' He talked over her.

Lily pushed her point, louder. 'I'm afraid I'm slightly confused about things. I'm not convinced I did do the right thing.'

The ombudsman's chin contracted as he frowned. 'What, you think you should have had an affair with Adam? I hardly think so. The wrong thing to do is rarely the right thing to do. The clue's in the words.'

'No, that's not what I mean.' She shook her head. 'What I mean is, although it was right not to have an affair, I don't think it was right I went back and married Darren. You said yourself, he wasn't my soulmate, and I've a funny feeling Adam might have been. So, what we've actually just watched is me walking away from possibly my soulmate and potentially ruining my life.'

His chin gradually re-emerged as she completed her speech and the ombudsman gripped it with one hand. 'Hmmm.'

'Well, am I right or am I wrong.'

'That's a very good question.' He walked around the scene, studying it from several different angles.

Lily followed his lead but couldn't see why he was doing it. 'Does that help? Walking around like that?'

'No, it would appear not.' He stopped and placed his hands on his hips, pursing and unpursing his lips as he considered the conundrum. 'Ok, here's my verdict. Yes, you were right not to have an affair with Adam. We have to take that as read, you know, "do not commit adultery" and all that, although of course at this stage you weren't married, but that's beside the point.' He waved a hand to indicate he was moving on. 'Then you were wrong to go ahead with the wedding, although it's clear you made that decision for laudable reasons.'

He walked back around the static scene, waving at it. 'The ideal scenario would have seen you leave here, go and be honest with Darren, dumping him in the process, and then moving on with your life.'

‘But then I wouldn’t have had Darren or Adam, or anywhere to live, I would have upset mum and Ray, as well as Darren’s family. That would have been a right mess.’

‘I suppose it would, but in the long run, it would still have been for the best. Wouldn’t it?’

‘Well, if you don’t know, I certainly don’t.’ Lily shrugged. ‘Now do you see why I find life so blooming scary? Half the time you can’t do right for doing wrong.’

‘You do have a point. A very little one, but a point nonetheless.’ He scratched his head.

‘But you’re still going to send me back, right?’ She said the words but was under no illusion they would achieve anything positive.

‘It’s out of my hands, I’m afraid.’

‘I thought it would be.’ She sighed. ‘But so much for you proving the value of being brave. In the alternative version of my life, I ended up just as alone as I am in my real life. It does sort of back me up, even if it doesn’t change anything.’

‘Wait a minute, who said anything about you ending up alone? You’re rather jumping the gun there, if you don’t mind my saying so. As a matter of fact...’

A small voice interrupted the debate. ‘Excuse me. Sorry for barging in…’

Lily swung around to where the words seemed to emanate and was surprised to see the peacock, still frozen in one spot with its tail on full display. ‘I beg your pardon?’ This was a turn up, even in the strangest of situations she had found herself of late.

‘Ah, Blessing. There you are.’ The ombudsman disappeared from the scene and Lily assumed he’d taken off his headset.

Blushing, Lily followed suit. Of course, the blinking peacock couldn’t be butting in. That would be beyond ridiculous.

Blessing was hovering in the doorway, arms full. ‘Sorry to disturb you, but you wanted a towel?’ She dropped a heap in the middle of the sofa. 'I thought I'd bring a few to save my legs. The way this morning's going, I'm guessing you might be needing 'em.'

'Thank you, Blessing. Very thoughtful.'

Lily helped herself and dabbed at her soggy hair, cheeks still glowing at the idea of a peacock having its say on the state of her life. She half wondered whose side it would have been on.

Blessing turned at the door, one hand on the push-plate. 'Oh, and Grace asked me to mention the time. There's been a bit of activity down below, if you'll excuse the phrase. Neighbours have noticed Lily's out for the count, and someone's called the emergency services. Assuming she's going back, we don't have to send her right now, but the clock's ticking. So, if you could bear that in mind.' She waved her hand at the virtual reality equipment.

'Don't worry,' the ombudsman reassured. 'We've made significant progress. I don't think we'll need to review a great deal more. If you can keep an eye on things and let me know if anything changes, I'll keep you posted when we're through, ok?'

She shrugged. 'You're the boss.'

He leaned towards Lily after Blessing had departed. 'Of course, I'm not the boss really. I answer to the Powers That Be, like everyone else.' Sitting up straight, he picked up the headset and wiggled it in her direction. 'Anyway, where were we?'

Lily tipped her head to one side. 'I was sad and alone and despairing of the future, and you were trying to convince me it was rosy.'

'Aah, yes!' He pointed a finger at her. 'I was going to show you that sometimes it's a question of being patient. The fruits of our labours can take time to come good. Rome wasn't built in a day, you know?'

'In my experience, it wasn't built in thirty-six years either. When exactly am I going to see some of this fruit?'

He pursed his lips. 'If you put your headset back on, I might show you.'

# CHAPTER THIRTY-FOUR

*ALTERNATIVE LILY ARMITAGE - AGED THIRTY*

*The sealed envelope sat on the table in the library staffroom between Lily and Kiki, who were perched on the edges of their seats, looking at it.*

*'Are you going to open it then?' Kiki was nibbling the tips of her fingernails, poking through the ends of rainbow-coloured fingerless gloves.*

*'No. I can't. I've had it since Saturday morning, and I can't bear to read it. What if it's a no?'*

*'It'd better not be! The Government's constantly throwing money at some rubbish scheme or another. It's about time they recognised a good thing when they saw it.'*

*I know it's a good scheme, I'm not worried about that,' Lily said. 'It's whether they think we're good enough to run it.' She shook her head. 'I still can't believe you dropped me in it with the presentation, I told you I'd make a pig's ear of it.'*

*'I'm sure you did no such thing. Anyway, I can't help it if Gertie's got a mind of her own.' Kiki and her camper van were on first name terms, but it was a bumpy relationship. 'If she decides she doesn't want to go, she doesn't go.'*

*'You need a reliable car.'*

*'Hush! Gertie might hear you.'*

*'Assuming she's parked in the car park off the High Street as usual, she'd have to have supersonic hearing.' Lily accepted Kiki's need to humanise her transport but couldn't fully climb on board.*

*Kiki was oblivious. 'Gertie is psychic. I'll probably have to walk home tonight now you've said that.' She tapped her tie-dye clad knees. 'Come on. Open it. You're driving me crazy. What's the verdict?'*

*'No, you do it.' Lily recoiled further into her chair.*

*'It's addressed to you.'*

*Lily picked it up and launched it at her friend. 'You do it. You have my permission. Go on.'*

*'Honestly!' Kiki tucked her long blonde dreadlocks over her shoulder and straightened up, wiggling the letter in her fingers before ripping it open. 'Here goes nothing.'*

*Silence reigned as Kiki pulled out a stapled collection of papers and examined the contents. Lily watched with eyes wide. Surely the length of the letter was a good sign, it only took a one-liner to say no.*

*Kiki flicked to the second page.*

*'Well?'*

*'Hmm.' Kiki allowed the letter and her hands to drop into her lap and sighed. 'Basically, there's good news and bad news.'*

*'What's the gist?' Lily almost bounced on her cushion.*

*'They are prepared to give us funding...'*

*'Yes?'*

*'But only half of what we asked for. It'll cover the rental costs, but nothing else.' Kiki frowned and continued to read.*

*'That's that then.' Lily shrugged. 'We'll have to shut it down.' She slumped in her seat.*

*'Not so fast.' Kiki muttered as she read but didn't look up.*

*Lily was not easily placated. 'We've put in so much hard work. The group are making so much progress with their reading, and it's all for nothing. What's the point of half funding something? I guess it's a way of saying no without saying no, so they don't look bad, because it's obvious if you only offer half of what a project needs it's doomed to fail. Never mind the fact we've put in hours of unpaid work. Never mind...'*

*'Shut up, Lily.'*

*'What?'*

*'Don't be such a defeatist.' Kiki was peering from beneath heavy brows.*

*'But...'*

*'They're offering us half the money we need. That's a good thing. They've also provided details of a host of other funding possibilities, pots of cash, through various organisations, which we might qualify for.'*

*Lily shook her head. 'More hoops to jump through...'*

*'It's a worthwhile project, so I don't mind a bit of blood, sweat and tears. Are you with me? Or are you putting all your effort into all this "woe is me" nonsense?'*

*This was unusually straight talking on Kiki's part and Lily bit back the string of complaints which had been brewing. 'Sorry. Yes, I'm with you. I'm just disappointed, that's all.'*

*'Well, don't be. Celebrate small victories and work towards the next one.' Kiki pulled a long-handled patchwork bag from the floor and retrieved a notepad and a pen with pink feathers attached to the end. 'Right. Action Plan.' She wiggled the feathers in Lily's direction. 'You can get hold of all the contacts the council have provided, to get the applications for funding. You're good with form filling.'*

*'Ok.' Lily was too cowed to argue.*

*'And I'll call a meeting of all the volunteers and service users to see if we can come up with fund-raising ideas. There's none so motivated as those who are benefitting from a scheme, and just because they find reading a challenge, it doesn't mean they haven't got good brains in their heads. We'll have all the money we need for the year in a couple of months. You wait and see.'*

*Lily rolled her eyes. 'That's all very well, but what about next year?'*

*'For goodness' sake! We'll worry about next year, next year. Let's get this one under our belts first. I'm going for some fresh air.' Kiki pulled the strap of the bag over her shoulder and climbed to her feet. 'Before I punch you on the nose.'*

*'Oh.' Lily watched Kiki stalk out of the room. Her friend generally prided herself on being "zen", but obviously on this occasion Lily had managed to push the wrong buttons. She picked up the letter and scanned the contents. Oh, well, best get on with it.*

***

The ombudsman interrupted the footage. 'I'm going to jump on a week or two.'

Lily sat back and waited, watching scenes appear and disappear in her eye-line. 'I'm assuming this is the literacy project Kiki and I talked about setting up years ago. I recognise her and the library staff-room, but in real life it never went ahead.'

'It never went ahead for you, because you gave up at the first sign of problems, but Kiki took it further. In this version, you made it past the initial bumps in the road, mainly thanks to Kiki's prompting, and the pair of you are trying to instate the group on a more official basis, to make it available to more users and over a longer period.'

'The library allowed a number of one-to-one sessions a week with people who found reading difficult. I used to love it. In some cases, it was really hard work for them, because of learning challenges, dyslexia and so forth. Others seemed to have simply fallen through the cracks of the education system and it meant going right back to square one, you know, the sort of learning which should have happened in primary school.'

Her smile grew as she remembered. 'It was usually rewarding, of course, but in one or two cases, it opened a whole new world for them. I can't imagine what my life would have been like if I hadn't been able to escape into a good book, and to be able to give that to someone else, that was incredibly special.'

'Then why didn't you pursue it? If you enjoyed it so much. I mean, from what you've said, you've found little joy in life, so why would you turn your back on what you did manage to find?' His concentration slipped from the controls as he tried to understand Lily's actions.

She thought deeply for a moment. 'I suppose I was afraid of failing.'

'Aah. That fear again. It's rather got in the way of a lot of things for you, hasn't it?'

'I thought I was protecting myself from pain.'

'Whereas, in actual fact, you were removing yourself from any chance of finding joy,' he clarified.

'I suppose so.' Although willing to accept his point, Lily wasn't prepared to allow him to win outright. 'I guess it's a two-edged sword. On one hand, I'm protected, and on the other, I'm restricted. I don't know what I could have done differently.'

The ombudsman harrumphed. 'Well, I do. You could have gone out and done something with your life instead of hiding it under a bushel.'

'Mmm.' She considered his comments, thinking about some of the times she could have been braver, taken a chance.

'Right, here's the next part of the tale of the literacy project. Are you ready?'

'I think so.' She paused. 'There's just one thing.'

'Yes?'

'What exactly is a bushel?'

The ombudsman rolled his eyes and instructed the film to play.

# CHAPTER THIRTY-FIVE

*ALTERNATIVE LILY ARMITAGE - AGED THIRTY*

*Kiki seemed to enjoy holding court. She sat at the head of the room, with everyone else in a semi-circle facing her. Lily had started with her chair pulled close to Kiki's own, but as numbers had increased, she gradually pulled away and now sat at right angles, neither at the front or part of the audience, but separate.*

*'Thanks so much for coming.' Kiki's hands were clasped together, as if in prayer, as she explained the issue of the hole in the finances.*

*The audience watched, entranced by her emotive appeal. Kiki had such a way with people, Lily thought. If it had been left to Lily to explain, they'd have all wandered off for coffee by now.*

*'So, the long and the short of it is, we need money, and that's not a request for you to put your hands in your pockets.' Kiki waved the idea away with an adamant hand. 'It's too much for us to cobble together on our own. We need to reach the wider public and muster their support and to do that, we need some really good ideas. Standing outside the supermarket with a bucket and a banner simply doesn't hit the spot anymore. Any ideas?'*

*There was a drawn-out pause and Lily began to despair of any response whatsoever. As she looked across at the crowd, their faces appeared pained at the idea of the loss of the service they had come to value, but no answers were forthcoming. Then a hand went up at the back of the room.*

*Kiki leaned from one side to another to spot who the hand belonged to. 'Ron. Yes?'*

*'What about a naked calendar? They seem to raise quite a bit.'*

*Lily gasped at the idea. She didn't know which was worse, the thought of having to strip off herself, or the image of Ron in all his naked glory. Kiki didn't miss a beat and jumped to her feet to scribble on a whiteboard erected for the purpose. 'That's definitely an idea. Not sure we could pull it off, but I'll write it up and come back to the practicalities later. Anyone else?'*

*Please let there be someone else, Lily repeated in her head. Otherwise, knowing Kiki they'd be setting up a photographic studio in the library staffroom in readiness for said calendar, and that was something she really didn't fancy being party to.*

*'Mavis? What have you got for me?'*

*A very timid, but lovely lady, Lily had only met once or twice, spoke up. 'Bingo's always a favourite. My nephew's done a bit of calling. I'm sure he'd step up to the mark.'*

*'Great, Mavis. We're on a roll.'*

*Kiki's excitement seemed to be growing, but Lily was yet to be inspired.*

*'How about a jam night?' A rough, husky male voice shouted, not far from Lily.*

*Kiki frowned, rubbing her chin. 'I'm not sure I understand. Making jam?'*

*'Nah, a jam night. Music. Acoustic guitar, bit of singing, that sort of thing. My local holds 'em now and again. Always draws a crowd.'*

*Lily's eyes flew from the man to Kiki's face to gauge her response and back again.*

*'How does that work, Elvis? How do you make money from a "jam night"?'*

*He stood up to address the crowd, seemingly quite comfortable with the attention. 'People like to get involved and there are a lot of amateur bands out there, just want a chance to show off their skills. They'll pay a premium to be given the stage for fifteen minutes. The pub'll let you use the premises free of charge because it draws the punters in. They might even give you a share of the beer profits.'*

*'You could do a raffle while you're there, as well.' Another anonymous voice chipped in. 'People love a raffle.'*

*Ideas were really starting to flow. Kiki didn't need to say much. She wrote the ideas on the board while the crowd floated possible plans between them.*

*Lily watched agape. She hadn't believed the service users would get behind them like this, but here they were, suggestion after suggestion firing around the room, until she didn't know who was saying what. In the midst of the chatter, Lily cast a glance at Kiki, who was scribbling furiously, but for a second their eyes met, and Kiki gave her a cheeky wink. Clearly, she had been right to have faith in human nature all along.*

*Eventually Kiki had to butt in or Lily truly believed they would have been there all night.*

*'Alright everyone. Thank you so much for your ideas. Let's bring this down for a moment and make some decisions about where to start.' She turned away from the crowd and tapped the marker-pen against the edge of the board as she thought. 'Here's what I think we should do. Elvis, can you make further enquiries with your local and come back with a response from them?'*

*'Aye.' He nodded, clearly proud of the part he would play. 'I'd love to.'*

*'I think we'll hold off on the calendar idea until the warmer weather. Nobody buys calendars at this time of year anyway, so we've got time to think on that one, and we can work on our all-over tans over the summer just in case. Now, who was it suggested a sponsored head-shave?'*

*There was no reply.*

*'Oh, I could have sworn someone said a head-shave. I must have thought of it myself. Anyone fancy shaving their hair off for char-i-dee?' Excitement had sent Kiki slightly into overdrive. 'No? Lily?'*

*Lily shook her head and waved a negating hand.*

*'No, I guess you'll be busy organising raffles and stuff anyway. Oh, well, have a think and if anyone fancies losing their hair for the summer, this is as good a cause as any. Perhaps we could meet again in a fortnight? Well done, everyone.'*

*Discussions continued over a post-meeting cup of tea and by the time the last stragglers had left, Lily was exhausted.*

*'This is a huge undertaking, you know, Kiki? Are you sure we're up to it?'*

*'Course we are. It's going to be grand. We'll share the work between us and before you know it, we'll be raking it in. Problem solved.'*

*'About that.' Lily squirmed. 'I don't mind doing my bit, but I don't want to do anything public, you know. It's not really my thing, public speaking and all that showy-offy stuff. You can give me as much paperwork and legwork as you like, but you won't make me do anything... I'm not comfortable with, will you?'*

*'Me? Make you do something out of your comfort zone.' Kiki tossed her head, as if the suggestion was unthinkable. 'Wouldn't dream of it. Come on, there's just time for a Guinness next door.'*

*Lily watched her friend grab her long, multi-coloured, crocheted cardigan from the back of her chair and march out the door and wondered if she could trust a word she said. One thing was for sure though. No one was touching her hair.*

***

'Do you see how this is building?' The ombudsman interrupted. 'Do you see why this was one of your more important life tasks? A scheme of this nature impacts so many people, and a fundraising event like this, brings the whole community together. It's so inspiring.'

Lily was gobsmacked by the scene. 'But it's so unlike me, it's so beyond anything I can ever imagine myself doing. In real life, I'd run a mile.'

'In fact, you did, didn't you?' He pointed at alternative Lily's image, now propped at the bar, nursing a pint of Guinness. 'But you see, this Lily keeps going despite misgivings. Although she's afraid, she still steps outside of her comfort zone from time to time, with the support of friends.' He turned to face real Lily. 'Whereas you haven't done that, and every time you retreat, your comfort zone contracts. It gets smaller and smaller over time, until you end up where you are now, alone and lonely, only going out to work and for essentials.'

'But is the other me happy? I mean, I looked totally stressed out during the meeting, and I don't even like Guinness.'

He pointed at the scene. 'But you look happy, with your friends. The stress was short-lived and the payback enormous. Can you imagine how different things would be if you had a social life?'

Lily could imagine, almost, but it was a stretch. She needed more evidence. 'So, what happens next? I suppose we manage to raise the money, and everyone lives happily ever after?'

The ombudsman laughed. 'Even fairy tales aren't that straightforward. Besides, it's not all about the end result, it's about the journey.'

'Right.' She tutted. 'Just my luck, I get travel sick.'

'You would.' He rolled his eyes. 'Strap yourself in. There's more to see, and it gets better. Trust me.'

# CHAPTER THIRTY-SIX

*ALTERNATIVE LILY ARMITAGE - AGED THIRTY*

*There was a widespread cringe as feedback squeal cut through the room.*

*'Sorry.' An unidentified musician apologised loudly, without the assistance of a microphone.*

*Other musicians continued to warm up, creating a cacophony of sound.*

*'I hope it's going to get better as the evening goes on.' Lily's teeth were on edge from the onslaught.*

*'Chill out and get a drink inside you.' Harriett was allowing it all to wash over her. 'This is my first outing in three months which doesn't include a nappy bag and an early night, so I intend to make the most of it, and you should to.' She waved a twenty-pound note in an attempt to attract the barman's attention. 'Lily, let yourself have fun.'*

*The band suddenly found common ground and the noise became a fast-paced tune. Kiki appeared with a long-haired man with a bushy beard, trailing behind. Her face was alight with excitement. 'They're good, aren't they?'*

*Lily couldn't honestly agree but smiled an acknowledgement.*

*Kiki pulled the man forward. 'This is Cosmo, my significant other.'*

*He shuffled forward and presented himself for inspection, nodding a greeting without speaking.*

*Lily introduced herself and Harriett, as she re-emerged from the scrum at the bar, having successfully purchased drinks.*

*'Go get a round in Cos, we'll grab the table in the corner before it all kicks off.' Kiki rubbed her man's arm. 'Come on, girls. It's a good spot to meet and greet people as they arrive. I've arranged with the licensee to make a speech halfway through to thank everyone.' She lowered her voice. 'And hopefully persuade them to put a couple of quid more in the bucket, but we ought to provide a welcome from the word go, to remind them what tonight's all about.'*

*The three of them ducked and dived around loitering drinkers to claim the table and settled in for the evening.*

*Kiki leaned in. 'What do you think of Cos?' As if he sensed he was being discussed, he turned at the bar and waved. 'Gorgeous, isn't he?'*

*'All men are bastards!' Harriett was currently particularly bitter, having found herself newly single and mother to three small children.*

*Lily nudged her with a firm elbow, then turned to Kiki. 'Don't listen to her. I'm sure he's very nice. Have you been together long?'*

*'I met him at a festival last September, he had an art stall there.'*

*'Really? What kind of art? Paintings?' Lily thought he looked like an artist.*

*'No, face painting. He did me a lovely glitter butterfly on my right cheek.' Tipping her head to one side, she studied the back view of her man. 'Very talented.' She winked at Harriett.*

*Lily coughed, uncomfortable with the tone. 'What does he do for a living?'*

*'Oh, something to do with camper-van conversions.' She waved a hand. 'I usually switch off when he talks about work. One mention of engines and I lose consciousness, although he's promised to give Gertie the once over for me, see if he can make her less temperamental.'*

*'I like a man who's good with his hands.' Harriett chuckled into her drink.*

*'Oh, believe me, he's got all sorts of talents.' Kiki joined in with the amusement.*

*Lily was about to excuse herself to hide in the ladies' loo, when Cosmo arrived at the table, laden with a tray of full glasses, putting a stop to the current leanings of the conversation.*

*'The bar's so busy I thought I'd get a couple of rounds in while I was there.'*

*'Oh, good man.' Harriett's eyes lit up as the drinks were lined up in front of her.*

*'Didn't I tell you he was special?' Kiki rubbed his arm again and squashed into the corner to make room for him on the wooden bench, winking at Harriett, while he was otherwise engaged clearing away empties. 'In fact, he's agreed to help out with another of our fund raisers, haven't you, Cos?'*

*His head bobbed and Lily detected a smile somewhere under all the hair.*

*'This amazing man has agreed to have all of this shaved off, face, head, the lot.' Kiki played with the tip of his beard and gazed into his eyes. 'I wonder what you look like under all that. I bet you're gorgeous.'*

*'That's very brave.' Lily had hoped the head shave idea had fallen by the way, but, as long as she didn't have to be involved, was happy for it to proceed.*

*'And not only that.' Kiki turned back to the table. 'He's only gone and talked a load of his friends into joining in. How many have signed up so far, Cos?'*

*He held up four fingers and nodded.*

*'Four. We're going to be raking it in. With any luck we'll not only cover this year's deficit, but maybe get ahead for next year.' Kiki was almost bouncing in her seat.*

*Harriett, nudged Lily, then leaned in confidentially. 'About these friends. Any of 'em single?'*

*Cosmo winked slowly. 'Every one of them.'*

*Harriett cheered loudly. Lily turned her attention to the stage and the new band lining up, praying for a change of subject.*

*As the evening went on, the music got louder, and the only way to hold a conversation was at shouting level. Cosmo kept the drinks flowing, resulting in Harriett and Kiki only remaining upright because they were propped against each other. He had retired to the bar, rubbing shoulders with a group of similarly hairy men.*

*Faces Lily knew had come and gone, popping up to say hello before disappearing to support the latest band showing off their skills. Lily was less drunk than the others, insisting on alternating soft drinks with the alcoholic ones, and was feeling decidedly mellow.*

*There was a lull as an eighties covers band packed away their electric keyboards and a heavy metal group lugged cases onto the low stage area. Lily was glad of the relative quiet, until the stout middle-aged landlord wandered towards her and leaned across the table.*

*'Are you one of the ones behind this charity thing?' His professional eye obviously recognised Lily as the most compos mentis of the group and he addressed her directly.*

*She nodded, actually feeling a little proud of the role she held in the night's proceedings, albeit very much behind the scenes.*

*'Right. Now would be a good time for that speech then, love. Remind people about the raffle tickets behind the bar. I'll go and introduce you.'*

*Her mouth dropped open, but dulled senses prevented her reacting more rapidly. She watched as the man made his way through the crowds, panic building in her chest. There was no way Kiki was up to addressing the masses, she could barely stay awake, but Lily shook her anyway, in the hope of a miracle recovery.*

*'Kiki, Kiki, you need to wake up.'*

*Kiki briefly opened her eyes and Lily felt a rush of hope.*

*'The landlord wants us to do the speech thingy.' The landlord was in fact addressing the audience as she spoke. 'Quick, you need to get up there.'*

*Turning her head at sloth speed, Kiki looked at the stage then turned back to Lily and opened her mouth to speak, but all that came out was a sigh, before she collapsed back onto Harriett's shoulder.*

*'Oh, no.' Lily breathed deeply, the only words her mind could form being expletives and totally unsuitable for the task she could currently see no way of avoiding. Unless she escaped to the toilet.*

*She jumped to her feet, ready to make a run for it, but as she did so the entire room turned to look at her, as the landlord had waved a hand in her general direction. There was no escape. Everyone was staring at her in anticipation, no doubt assuming she had stood up ready to address them.*

*'Come on up, missy.' The landlord shouted, when she didn't move.*

*I've got to do it, she thought, but I'm going to kill Kiki tomorrow, when she's conscious enough to feel pain. The crowd parted to allow her through, and she slowly approached, unable to form even the beginnings of a speech in her mind. A strong pair of hands at the front, assisted her onto the raised platform, and the landlord jostled her in front of the microphone. Everyone gazed up, giving them their full attention, while the musicians continued to set up a few feet behind. She was surrounded.*

*Her mouth opened, but nothing came out, so she closed it, and coughed, hoping that clearing her throat might kick-start something.*

*'You wanted to thank everyone for coming, didn't you?' The landlord prompted.*

*You can do this. You can do this, she repeated in her head, then opened her mouth again as she stared above the heads of those in front of her. 'Hi, yes, thank you.'*

*She ran out of breath and inhaled deeply. 'Yes, thank you for coming.' Her heart was thumping in her chest. 'The liter..ar..acy...' The alcohol she had consumed made her stumble over the word and she bit her lips as a warning for them to behave, before continuing. 'Project is really important to the people who use it and it's the only one in the area, and your support is absolutely essenen...essenential.' She was trying to add the depth of feeling she knew Kiki would have, but the words wouldn't come out right. 'So, thank you very much.'*

*She turned to leave the stage, but the landlord nudged her back. 'Raffle.'*

*'Oh, yes. Don't forget the raffle tickets at the bar. You can win...' She turned to the landlord with a harsh whisper. 'What can they win?'*

*He shrugged.*

*'You can win... things. Thank you.' For some reason, at that point, it seemed appropriate to curtsey and she did so, before stumbling off stage into the arms of an alert stranger. 'Oooh. Sorry.'*

*He helped her upright and their eyes met, with a flicker of recognition on her part and undisguised amusement on his. She couldn't place the face, so she unhooked herself and stumbled back to the table, where Kiki and Harriett were completely unaware of what was happening.*

*Cosmo approached from somewhere. 'I think it's time to make a move. Elvis says he'll stay to the end to sort the finances and ring Kiki tomorrow. Do you want a lift?'*

*The whole experience had exhausted her, and her body sagged with relief. 'Yes, please.'*

*She couldn't get away fast enough.*

***

Lily took slow, steady breaths, her hand pressed to her chest. 'You said it got better! That most definitely was not better. That was horrific. What are you thinking?'

The ombudsman's words were precisely spoken. 'I'm thinking how incredibly proud I am of you right now. Well done you.' There was a catch to his voice.

She spun round to look at him and was surprised to detect a certain glistening to his eye which she simply couldn't compute. 'You must be crazy. Alternative me was half cut, staggering all over the place, barely able to string two words together and you're proud of me? What…' She shook her head. 'No, I don't get it. That was the most embarrassing exhibition I have ever seen.'

'What, worse than a certain spelling bee?'

She groaned. 'Don't remind me.'

'Seriously. Ok, it might not have been the most inspiring oration, the most admirable presentation, the finest words, but you got up there and you did it. If that's not an achievement, I don't know what is, so yes, I'm proud of you.'

His words rattled around her head, and she gave them serious thought, before sighing. 'Shame it wasn't real then really, isn't it?'

'But it shows what you could achieve, if you put your mind to it, the different sort of life you could have.'

‘I wish I could say I’d like a life like that, but in all honesty, I would hate it. I would never enjoy public speaking, not in a million years…’

‘Oh, tush!’ He interrupted. ‘Stuff and nonsense. Nobody enjoys being put on the spot like that, but you’re missing the point. The stage bit was a very small part of a loftier story. You were giving your time for the benefit of others. You were putting your energy into something wholesome and of value. You were part of something. You had friends. You had hope. You had…life, and it was good.’

The idea struck her with some force. ‘It was, wasn’t it?’ She allowed the thought to percolate, becoming more comfortable with this sudden change of view. ‘Did we do it? Did we ensure a future for the program?’

The ombudsman smiled at her new interest. ‘Yes and no. The evening was a success. Dear old Elvis came good, but as a result more people came forward to make use of the program, so more funding was required to facilitate that. But you, and Kiki of course, took encouragement from it. You didn’t give up. Do you want to see the next event? You ought to, because there was something which you missed while watching this one, which becomes clearer at the next.’ He clenched and unclenched his hands in anticipation. ‘Go on, watch it. Go on. Let me show you.’

‘I’m intrigued…’

‘Good, I’m putting it on now. Pay attention.’

# CHAPTER THIRTY-SEVEN

*ALTERNATIVE LILY ARMITAGE - AGED THIRTY*

*Kiki was buzzing around like an agitated insect and Lily stood in one corner, maintaining a safe distance. Having been bitten once, there was no way she was being strong-armed into doing something she wasn't comfortable with.*

*The event was being held in the shopping mall, in an area cordoned off by the management team, out front of a fancy barbershop, to ensure as large an audience as possible.*

*'I'm not sure how to do this for greatest effect.' Kiki returned to Lily's side. 'There are six volunteers getting the chop, provided they all turn up. Only Cos and Felix are here as yet, but Cos says they'll be here soon, so I guess I've just got to trust him, because I've promised the journalist from the Gazette there'll be six and I don't want to let her down or she might not print the story.'*

*'Kiki, breathe.' It made a change for Lily to have to calm her friend, rather than the other way around.*

*'Yes, sorry. I don't know why I'm getting so worked up. Even if someone doesn't turn up, I'm sure we could quickly rustle up another volunteer. I don't suppose…'*

*'No!' There were limits, and having her hair shaved off, even if it was for charity, was beyond Lily's.*

*'Fair enough. It wouldn't be for me either.' She patted the thick dreadlocks, held in place by a shocking pink headscarf, tied at the side. 'It's taken too long to cultivate these babies. Besides, I think the fact it's all men losing not only their hair, but their beards as well, makes a far better story.'*

*Lily felt her friend was straying from the original point. 'So, what's the problem? What are you not sure about?'*

*'Oh, yes. Should we sit them all in a row and have them shaved one by one? Or would it be better to have each of them shaved by their allocated barber at the same time? You know, make a race of it.'*

*Lily stroked her chin. 'If you do them all at the same time it'll be over in a few minutes. If we spread it out, I'd have thought it'd attract more passers-by to contribute to the collection.'*

*'Good thinking.' Kiki tilted her head in a quick bob. 'Ah, there's someone with enormous facial hair. I bet he's one of ours.' She wandered away to greet the newcomer.*

*As Lily gazed across the growing crowd, she spotted Harriett, behind a buggy and juggling small children on either side. Her friend was looking rather pink-cheeked and Lily skipped to the barrier to offer assistance.*

*Harriett's face perked up. 'Good turnout. Where are your victims?' She glanced around, trying to spot the hairiest men.*

*'I think Cosmo and somebody called Felix are in the barbers, having a cup of tea before it all kicks off, and Kiki has run off to greet another who's just arrived. I guess the others will be along soon.'*

*'And which ones are single?'*

*Lily rolled her eyes. 'You're incorrigible. I thought all men were…' She pulled up short, remembering little ears were listening. 'You know whats?'*

*'Yeah, they are. What can I say? Can't live with 'em, can't live…' Harriett reached down to prevent the littlest attachment from pulling a sock off. 'Actually, just can't live with 'em, but they*

*have their uses. Anyway, which ones…' She craned her neck to look around the crowd.*

*'I have no idea which ones are single, married, gay or serial killers, I'm afraid. But I think we're all going to the beer garden after they've had the chop to celebrate, if you want to join us.' Lily lowered her voice. 'I could do with the moral support, to be honest. Kiki's crew can be a bit full on, for me.'*

*'I'd love to, but I'm otherwise engaged, as usual.' She pointed at the heads of her children. 'And they're not exactly man-magnets, even on a good day.'*

*Lily's head tilted to one side as she smiled. Despite the complaining, she knew her friend loved her children to bits, and would do anything for them. 'Never mind that. There's a playpark attached, and I'll give you a hand with them. It'd be good for you to get out and about.'*

*Harriett's eyes narrowed as she considered the offer.*

*'Go on,' Lily urged, then laughed. 'And if any of the guys are single and interested, they need to know what they're letting themselves in for from the word go. If they don't run a mile, you'll know they're a keeper.'*

*'Yeah, right. I'll think about it.' Her face suddenly turned serious, and she nudged Lily's elbow with considerable force, almost making her stumble.*

*'What the…'*

*'Isn't that…' Harriett jerked her head to one side, pointing with her eyes. 'You know who?'*

*Lily swung round to see who Harriett was referring to and spotted a bearded man ducking under the barrier and shaking Kiki's hand, then standing back with his hands on his hips. It was Adam.*

*She felt her face turn puce and repositioned herself so her back was to him. 'Yes, it is. Shoot, what's he doing here?'*

*'Aren't you pleased to see him? Last time…'*

*'Last time was a complete embarrassment. I must have made it so obvious how I felt, and there was me supposedly planning my wedding. What must he have thought of me?' Lily felt her blood pressure rising.*

*'Well, you're going to find out, 'cause he's coming over.' Harriett chuckled. 'Pull yourself together, Lils. This could be your chance to… Well, if it isn't Mr Peacock.'*

*As he reached their vicinity Adam frowned and studied Harriett's face for a moment, then his expression cleared. 'Aah! Last time I saw you, you were wearing a full set of railings. I assume the hangover must have cleared by now?'*

*'A twelve-year hangover? Mmm, that would be a killer. A gentleman shouldn't bring things like that up in polite conversation, you know?'*

*Adam sniggered. 'I never professed to be a gentleman.' He turned to Lily. 'Fancy seeing you here?'*

*'I could say the same about you.' Lily had pulled herself together enough to muster a reply but was still struggling to still her beating heart. 'I'm one of the organisers, and you?'*

*'Cosmo roped me in. He knows I'm a sucker for a good cause.' He shrugged. 'I saw you the other night at the jam night, but I don't think you recognised me.'*

*'What?' Her mind travelled back to that evening and one moment stood out, as she stumbled off the stage and a strong pair of hands steadied her. She knew she'd recognised the face, but the lighting had been poor, and she was several tequilas in. 'Oh! That was you.'*

*'It certainly was.' He must have noticed the increase in her blushes, as she recalled the speech palaver, as her whole face glowed, but he chose not to pursue it. 'It's a good thing you're doing here. Is Darren having his mop chopped too?'*

*Harriett interceded. 'If anything of Darren's was being chopped today, it would not be his mop.'*

*Adam's eyes slipped to Lily's hands, where the absence of a ring was apparent. 'Oh, shoot, sorry. Have I put my foot in it?'*

*A small frown appeared briefly on Lily's forehead as she looked at her feet but cleared as she pushed a smile through. 'It's ancient history. Don't worry.'*

*Kiki shouted from the other side of the area, where bar stools were being lined up, to get Adam's attention, and she waved at him to come and sit down, with the other participants.*

*Holding up a hand to acknowledge the request, he turned to leave, but paused, making eye contact with Lily. 'Are you hanging around here? Will I see you after?'*

*The intensity of his gaze set Lily's heart thumping again. She shrugged and smiled. 'I'm not going anywhere.'*

*'Make sure you don't. It would be good to catch up.'*

*Lily's eyes followed him as he retreated.*

*Harriett interrupted her thoughts with a gruff, comedy voice. '"Make sure you don't. It would be good to catch up." Roughly translated that means, "I fancy the pants off you. Don't run away". He so has the hots for you.'*

*'He hasn't.' Lily looked sideways at her friend. 'Has he?' She didn't dare to hope.*

*Kiki's concerns about the set up at the event proved unfounded, as it wasn't the barbers' first crack at a charity bash, and they had ideas of their own.*

*The volunteers were lined up on stools a few feet apart, with their own personal stylist behind them. The proprietor of the salon, an extremely butch specimen of a man, with very little hair himself, came forward to act as host. He walked around the edges of the cordoned off area with a portable microphone and whipped the audience into a state of excitement, encouraging them to throw their change into buckets strategically placed around the space.*

*Lily crouched next to Harriett, with Harriett's middle child resting on her knee as he pointed at the peculiar exhibition with one hand, while sucking the other thumb. Lily did her best to keep him calm as the noise levels increased, enjoying the building atmosphere.*

*'Victim number one. What is your name please?' The host approached the first chair.*

*'Cosmo.'*

*Lily noticed Cosmo was looking decidedly paler than she'd ever seen him before.*

*'Ok, everyone. I can reveal that Cosmo has raised a grand total of one hundred and seventy-three pounds for agreeing to part with this, I must say, magnificent example of facial hair. Is that enough?' His eyebrows rose as he waited for the crowd to respond.*

*There was a chorus of no's, closely followed by a collection bucket being pushed under the noses of those near to the cordon. As it returned to centre stage, the host shook it and there was a satisfying rattle of coins banging against each other.*

*'That's more like it. Now, Cosmo, to celebrate your de-bearding and full head shave...Ooooo!' He raised his hands, palm up, to encourage those watching to join him in a growing whoop. 'We're going to play a special song just for you, as your stylist gets to work. Are you ready?'*

*Cosmo forced a gallant fake smile. 'Yes?'*

*'Are you ready?' The man asked the audience, who replied with a resounding "yes". 'Then, let's go!' He disappeared to the side-lines, as a speaker started to thump out the bass of "Eye of the Tiger".*

*The stylist made a show of brandishing his clippers aloft, before lowering them and swiping them from forehead to nape of Cosmo's neck, leaving a bald stripe through the middle. Those watching clapped along, enjoying every moment. When Cosmo had nothing left to shave, the stylist stood back and Cosmo, caught up in the excitement, jumped out of his seat, raised his arms aloft and did a circuit of the perimeter before falling into Kiki's arms. The crowd went wild.*

*Harriett was laughing aloud. 'Oh, my goodness. This is fantastic.'*

*Lily chuckled, hugging the little boy in her lap, who was bemused by the whole thing.*

*'And next. Who is the next victim?'*

*Chair number two followed the same pattern as the first, the only difference being, this time the accompanying tune was "The Flight of the Bumblebee". By the time the stylist was done, great guffaws filled the air around the salon, attracting even more onlookers.*

*Chair number three belonged to Adam and Lily stood for a better view, Harriett's little boy clinging to her leg, but all her attention was on this man, who she'd known for such a large part of her life but didn't really know at all. She was intrigued by how he would react to being centre of attention, and in such circumstances.*

*The host was show-boating, strutting like a cockerel, driving the crowd into a frenzy of giving, the buckets filling to overflowing. 'Let's hear you all now, Adam, Adam, Adam.'*

*The crowd joined in the chorus of the name, only petering out as the music started, this time the sultry tones of "The Stripper". The whole building fell about laughing and Adam chuckled in his seat, even as the clippers were applied to his head. Lily watched his expression from afar, taking his reactions in, until he was hidden from view as his beard was removed. The stylist stood back with a flourish, making the big reveal and Adam stepped down from his stool to take a bow.*

The ombudsman paused the footage as Lily shot off the sofa with a squeal. ‘What’s the matter? What’s going on?’

She waved a pointed finger at the frozen image of Adam. ‘That’s… that’s… that’s…’

‘Now then, Lily. Take a breath.’

Doing as she was told, she inhaled through her nose and out through her mouth, twice in steady succession, until a level of calm returned.

‘Now, what were you trying to say?’ The ombudsman spoke slowly and succinctly, encouraging Lily to do the same.

She pointed again. ‘That’s Adam.’

The ombudsman pulled in his chin, confused. ‘Yes, obviously. That’s not really a surprise at this point in time.’

‘No.’ She shook her head in frustration. ‘I know that it’s Adam, from before, from the alternative world. What I mean is, that’s my Adam. The one who lives in my street. The one who asked me to go out with him on New Year’s Eve.’

‘Is it?’ He turned his head sideways and screwed up his eyes, as if that would provide a better view. ‘Are you sure?’

‘Yes.’ She walked around the static characters. ‘No doubt about it. It hadn’t occurred to me before, but now, without the beard, it’s obvious. Alternative Adam is my Adam, but I didn’t meet him until he moved into number eight a couple of years ago.’ Her hands spread in a questioning shrug. ‘What does this mean? Did you know?’

‘It hadn’t crossed my mind for a moment, but then, I don’t think we’ve discussed individuals involved in your current life, so why would it have? Hang on, let’s get these headsets off and get back to the sofa for a moment.’ With that, he did so, and disappeared from the scene.

With one last longing look at this new naked-faced Adam, Lily did the same.

The ombudsman was concentrating, tapping at his tablet, but Lily was highly suspicious he'd known about this turn of events all along.

'Be honest. You knew, didn't you?'

He raised an eyebrow without looking up. 'I wouldn't dream of being anything else. Honesty is my middle name.' His brow returned to its normal position. 'It's not actually, it's St Leopold, but the less said about that, the better. No, this is as much news to me as it is to you. Think about it, I've had no reason whatsoever to look up the people in your current life. It's been all about your past thus far.'

She had to admit the truth of his words. 'Ok, but this must mean something, for him to appear on so many different occasions in my alternative life and now in my real one. It can't be coincidence. Can it?'

The ombudsman's chin was resting in his hand, one finger stretched up, tapping the end of his nose. He spoke past it. 'No, no such thing as coincidence. Everything's part of the plan. Remember? The framework we talked about earlier?'

'Yes, yes. I know all about that, but that doesn't explain why he is where he is? I need to know.'

'Alright, alright, give me a chance. I'm looking it up. I don't hold all the answers in this brain of mine, you know. On the odd occasion I have to rely on technology.'

She closed her mouth and waited, her own mind flicking through the facts and trying to sort them into order, her foot tapping with ill-disguised impatience.

'Hmm. As I thought.'

'What? What? What did you think?'

He cast a warning look at her, the simmering of her stress levels still far higher than they ought to be. 'I thought this young man must be a fixture in your lifeline, and my investigations back up that suspicion. I've run a number of test scenarios, that is, a number of alternative life framework possibilities and he appears in every single one.'

She collapsed back in her seat. 'I knew it. He's my soulmate, isn't it?'

'Weeeeelll.' The vowels were drawn out as his face revealed the difficulty he was having putting an explanation into suitable terms. 'There's no such thing as a soulmate, per se.'

Lily shrugged, shaking her head in frustration. 'What does that mean? No soulmate per se? Am I supposed to be with him, or not?'

'Look, the straightforward answer you're looking for simply doesn't exist. There is no one person for each individual, it's more a calculation, a complex algorithm centred round physical attraction, ethics and character compatibility, and probability. There can be many people who score highly on the soulmate scale, not just one. You have to factor in suitability, availability, location and many other things too.'

Lily pursed her lips and stared him straight in the eye. 'Is Adam my soulmate?'

'Well, yes, probably, it's quite likely, there's a high percentage of likelihood. Far more likely than that Darren Chantilly character ever was. That's as far as I'm prepared to go on the subject.'

She slapped a palm to her forehead. 'I knew it. And I went and ditched him on New Year's Eve, because I was too scared of getting hurt. I've thrown away my chances of being with him in this life, in that life.' She waved the headset in the ombudsman's face. 'And probably every variation of a life I ever had the opportunity of living. What am I like?'

The ombudsman shook his head. 'No, you see, you're getting ahead of yourself again. No one said you threw away *all* your chances, in this life or that life. It's very rare for a person not to get at least a couple of bites at the cherry, if it's meant to be, I mean. I daresay, if we watch a little further there may be something more positive to see.'

‘Do you think so? Is there still hope?’ Lily was focused, waiting for an answer.

‘Oh, Lily. There is always hope.’ He smiled. ‘Let’s observe a scene or two more. You never know, perhaps alternative you can turn things around.’

‘I hope so.’ She huffed, pulling the headset back into position. ‘I really do.’

# CHAPTER THIRTY-EIGHT

*ALTERNATIVE LILY ARMITAGE - AGED THIRTY*

*The mood was buoyant at the beer garden, after the head shave event. The participants were simply relieved it was over, while the organisers were celebrating a fantastic financial result. First calculations suggested the literacy project had secured its future for at least several more months, an outcome far beyond Kiki and Lily's initial hopes.*

*Harriett was three drinks in and extremely comfortable in her current position, surrounded by Cosmo's single and attentive friends, while Lily chased Harriett's two older children around a large wooden fort and down numerous covered slides into a lake of coloured balls. She made a mental note to borrow the kids on a more regular basis, so she had a good excuse to repeat the experience. Her hair was plastered to her face in the late afternoon heat and, as the kids climbed over her, she laughed to the point of her legs giving way, her whole body disappearing beneath the plastic orbs.*

*Bobbing up for air, Lily sensed a figure beside her, and expected to find one of the children ready to pounce, but instead she saw Adam crouched on the edge of the ball pit, only a short distance from her head.*

*'Are you alright in there?'*

*She pulled herself upright, feeling too vulnerable to stay prone at his feet, and ran fingers through her hair to return some semblance of normality. 'Fine. I was thinking about joining a gym, but I reckon I've exercised every muscle in my body in here.'*

*An errant child grabbed her by the ankles and sent her sprawling forward, only Adam's fast responses saving her from hitting the deck, though as her face impacted his chest, she had to admit it was far from a soft landing.*

*'You're taking your life in your hands with this crew.'*

*Accepting his hand up out of the ball pit onto the side-lines, her cheeks glowed with embarrassment, or another emotion she didn't want to put a name to. 'Yeah, they're little barbarians, but I love them to bits, when they're not beating me up, that is. How's the head?' She patted the top of her own hair.*

*He rubbed his scalp. 'I was afraid I might feel the cold, but in actual fact it's a bit warm in this sun.'*

*'You'll have to get yourself a hat until it grows back.'*

*'Or stay indoors.' He jerked his head at the pub. 'Are you coming over for a drink?'*

*She was sorely tempted, but having talked her friend into joining the group, she now felt a responsibility for keeping the little ones occupied. 'I would, but…' She pointed at the small bodies ducking and diving around the pool. 'Somebody's got to keep an eye on this pair.'*

*'I guess Harriett's otherwise engaged.'*

*Harriett's laughter could be heard floating from the beer garden, but Lily didn't begrudge her some fun. 'She's had a tough time of it lately. It'll do her good to let off some steam.'*

*His eyes narrowed. 'You're a good friend to her, aren't you?'*

*'I guess. But she's been there for me in the past too.' She shrugged. 'What goes around, comes around.'*

*He nodded. 'How about I bring a drink to you? We can watch these tearaways together.'*

*That sounded perfect. 'A lemonade would be lovely.'*

*'Ok. Try not to let them beat you to a pulp while I'm gone.'*

*A ball appeared from nowhere, hitting her straight between the eyes. 'I can't promise.'*

*Adam reappeared with a tray of drinks and a couple of bowls of ice cream for the children, who he instructed to sit properly at a sturdy child-sized table and chairs. Without argument, they followed his instructions, sitting meekly, as they waited for their dishes.*

*Lily was more than a little impressed. 'You've got the magic touch. If that had been me, they'd have climbed my legs and got access to the ice cream before I was halfway across the lawn.'*

*'That's because they don't know me. They're afraid to play me up.'*

*Lily chuckled as she perched on a nearby wall to enjoy her drink. 'You mean, I'm a soft touch and they know it.'*

*'You said that, not me.' He leaned next to her, his legs long enough to reach the floor whereas hers dangled a few inches clear. 'You've got to remember, I have years of experience dealing with Brandon. He may be a grown up, but he still has a very childlike understanding of things. You have to say what you mean, no beating around the bush, and you have to say it like you mean it for him to pay any attention.'*

*'How is Brandon? I've got fond memories of him from that summer.' Her mind filled with images of those long hot days and the fun she and Harriett had had at the holiday park. They hadn't all been good times, of course, but for some reason those were the most prominent.*

*Adam's gaze was off somewhere in the distance. 'It was a good summer. Seems like ancient history now though. I suppose it is really. What was it, fifteen years ago? Sixteen?'*

*'Don't, you make me feel old.'*

*'Tell me about it.' He sighed deeply then took a long draught of his lager. 'Yes, Brandon's in supported accommodation now,*

*since mum... He's doing really well. It was hard for him, but he's turning it around. Spends loads of time in the gardens, planting stuff. He always loved the outdoors and it's become like a sanctuary for him now.'*

*Lily frowned. 'Sorry. Have you lost your mum recently? I didn't know.'*

*His eyebrows briefly raised. 'Why would you? But, yes, we lost mum about a year ago. It was a blow, not that I relied on her that much, but, you know, she was always there. Then suddenly she wasn't. It was just me and Brandon, and I had to work, I couldn't be there for him as much as he needed me.'*

*'Mmm, I can imagine that's tough. But it's good he's found somewhere to settle. It must be a weight off your mind.'*

*'Yes, it is.' He shook his head, as if to clear it. 'But enough about me. What's been happening with you? I admit, I'm shocked to hear about you and Darren. I thought you guys were in it for the long haul.'*

*'Three years were quite long enough, thank you very much.'*

*A squabble broke out at the table over one last spoonful of ice cream and Adam leapt in, removing the dishes and pulling colouring sheets and a small packet of pens from his back pocket. 'Here, you two. Let's see who can make the brightest picture. You need to let the ice cream go down before you start jumping around again.'*

*As if by magic they settled down to draw.*

*'Man, I am seriously impressed. Those are some skills you have.'*

*He laughed. 'I'm secretly a child whisperer. They can't resist my power.' Leaning against the wall again, he now faced Lily, rather than away. 'Do you mind me asking what happened? Or is it too painful?'*

*'No, as I said, it's all in the past. I guess he wasn't who I thought he was.' She shrugged. 'And I was never going to become*

*what he wanted me to be, so it was best all round we went our separate ways. No drama.'*

*'Oh, I thought from what Harriett said, he'd done the dirty on you or something.'*

*'Yeah, that as well, but I couldn't blame him. Neither of us were happy. I blame myself really, I should never have married him in the first place, but hindsight and all that.'*

*As she stared into space, sorting her thoughts into order, Adam faced the main beer garden, watching the comings and goings there. It was a topic which couldn't be rushed. 'You seem to have come out of it ok? You don't sound traumatised anyway. I've known one or two divorcees who've come out the other side as permanent man-haters.'*

*'I can't blame all mankind for mine and Darren's shortcomings.' Lily rolled her eyes. 'I let Harriett take care of that side of things for me.'*

*'She doesn't look like a man-hater from where I'm standing.'*

*Lily glanced over her shoulder to see Harriett cosying up with one of Cosmo's other friends and shook her head. 'You'd think she'd learn, wouldn't you?' She turned back to the view of the children. 'I've lost count of how many times she's been dumped on, but, hey, she watched her mum go through the pattern of one crappy relationship after another. She probably doesn't realise there's any other way. Or, she's looking for the father figure she never really had. I don't know. All I know is, when Darren let me down, quite spectacularly actually, she was there for me in an instant. In fact, if anything, I'm a stronger person because of her.'*

*'A friend in need, is a friend indeed.'*

*'Too right. I don't know what I'd have done without her. I didn't have anyone else.' She sipped her lemonade, trying to clear the sudden lump which had formed in her throat.*

*Adam was studying her, reading her expression. 'You don't have family?'*

*'I wish. My mother is alive and kicking and causing as much havoc as she always has. Honestly, I sometimes think I'd be far better off without...' Her hand flew to her mouth. 'Shit. Sorry, that was an awful thing to say, considering...'*

*Before Adam could respond there was a shout from the table, where the children had reverted to usual behaviour patterns and moved on from colouring their pictures to colouring each other's' faces.*

*Lily jumped from her perch to put a stop to the fracas, almost relieved to have a distraction from her hideously inappropriate faux pas. Both little ones were covered in vivid scribbles. 'Oh, you two. What's Mummy going to say when she sees the state of you? Come on, we'd better go and face the music. She'll probably never let me babysit again.'*

*Ushering them out of the play area, she only paused to glance back at Adam. 'Thanks for the drink. I'd better...' She grimaced and indicated the urchins now holding her hands, before carrying on to the beer garden, leaving him behind.*

*Outwardly, her attentions were all on the kids and the loud remonstrations from Harriett when she saw the damage. Inwardly, all she could think about was her big mouth and the unforgivably crass comments she'd allowed to pass out of it. What must he think of her? Wishing her own mother hither when he had only recently lost his own and was clearly still grieving.*

*One thing was certain. If Adam had had any interest in her before, he certainly wouldn't any longer. She'd gone and blown it, once and for all.*

'Oh, my goodness.' Lily's brow was deeply furrowed. 'That didn't look like hope to me. That looked more like the dashing of all hope. Why would you show me that?'

The ombudsman was bunny-hopping the footage forward at high speed. 'Don't panic. Don't panic. That's not the end. I know it didn't look great, but bear with me.'

'Didn't look great? It would take a mechanical digger to extricate my foot from my mouth after that shocking display. All of a sudden, I remember why I'm afraid to step outside my door in the mornings.'

'No. No. No. Here we are. Scratch that thought.' He took a deep breath, then spreading his hands palm down, he exhaled slowly. 'I would be very grateful if you would pretend the last few minutes didn't happen. Now. Let's move swiftly on.'

# CHAPTER THIRTY-NINE

*ALTERNTIVE LILY ARMITAGE - AGED THIRTY*

*Kiki's arms were folded across her chest as Lily side-stepped past a queue waiting to pay for entry into the social club.*

*'I know, I know, I'm late. Sorry.'*

*'Yes, you are. Everything alright?' Kiki's frown dissipated almost instantly. 'It's not like you. You'd be early for your own funeral.'*

*'Nice image.' Lily grimaced. 'No, everything's fine, I just didn't allow myself enough time to get across town.' She leaned back to take in the hordes making their way in. 'Good turnout. Mavis has done well. What is it, a tenner a head?'*

*'Yup, and thanks to Mavis's nephew we've got the club and facilities free, a cut of the profits from the bar, and all the prizes have been donated, so what you see here is pure income. What with this and the other events, we may have sufficient funding for the next couple of years. We could even expand, buy more resources and all sorts.'*

*'Excellent. Hopefully we won't have to do any more events for a while, they've stressed me right out.'*

*'You're always stressed out.' Kiki spotted a friend in the doorway and wandered away with a squeal of pleasure, arms wide in preparation for a hug.*

*'Do I need to do anything?' Lily called after her.*

*'Go and see Mavis's nephew, Graham, somewhere at the front of the hall. He's the one in the purple flowery shirt and turquoise bow tie. You can't miss him.'*

*Lily ducked past the ticket sellers, exchanging greetings as she went. 'Graham?' She mouthed.*

*Without interrupting the flow of ripping tickets from a book and dropping cash into a tin, the helper pointed to the front of the room.*

*'Ok. Thanks.' She hesitantly passed into the room, which by now was more than three quarters full, the atmosphere buzzing and the air filled with chatter and laughter. As Kiki had said, Graham was easily recognisable, as much for the perfectly coiffed and oiled hair as the outfit, and she headed in his direction. She hoped there was a nice simple job for her to do, behind the scenes, where she was always most comfortable. On this occasion though, her desire to hide was even stronger than usual, as she was afraid Adam might put in another appearance, as he'd turned up at the other events and, after the last time, she really didn't want to have to face him. He must think her a despicable person.*

*She introduced herself to Graham, who grabbed her by the shoulders and planted a theatrical kiss on the air surrounding each of her cheeks, as if he'd known her forever.*

*'Lily, darling, how lovely to meet you. You're a star, my dear, a veritable star. You've turned darling Aunty Mavis's life around, you really have. Her nose is always in a trashy novel these days. It's truly broadened her horizons.'*

*Lily didn't know how to deal with such loud and lavish attention. 'Oh, ok. You're welcome, I guess.' She rubbed her hands together in nervous anticipation. 'Do you have a job for me?'*

*'That's what I like to hear. More willing helpers.' He sucked in his cheeks and tapped his chin with a finger as he looked around to allocate her a task. 'Righto. You have a choice, you can either pop on stage to warm up the clientele with a few well-chosen jests?' He spotted her look of dismay and patted her clenched hands. 'Not your cup of tea? Don't worry, the limelight is not for everyone, although I must say you have the bone structure for it. Gorgeous.' He blew her an imaginary kiss. 'Ok then, how about packaging up some prizes, a bottle of bubbly with a box of choccies and a random other, all tied up with a ribbon, to look divine. Easy peasy. Though what we're supposed to do with a toilet brush and holder I don't know, even if it is top of the range and gift boxed.'*

*That was more like it. 'I can do that.'*

*'Good, good. Everything you'll need is tucked under the table, ribbon, cellophane, glitter – don't hold back on the glitter. Help yourself.' He spotted something awry on stage and strode away. 'No, no, darling. The microphone needs to be centre stage, the bingo ball tumbler to the left. No, my left, not your left…'*

*As Graham leapt onto the stage, Lily shuffled behind the gingham-clothed table and set about the task she'd been given. Out of the corner of her eye, she spotted Cosmo and a group of men with him, in the doorway. Moment of truth, was Adam among them? Yes, he was. Her stomach clenched and the blood drained from her face. He was bound to see her at the front, unless…*

*The voluminous stage curtain stopped just short of the table where Lily was working and she dived behind it, breathing deeply to regain her composure, but there was still work to be done, and she couldn't imagine Graham allowing slacking on his shift. What could be done?*

*Lily stretched to hook one ankle around the nearest table leg, ensuring the rest of her body remained behind the curtain, and tugged the table towards her. The weight from the many bottles of wine however, prevented it moving more than an inch. She tugged again. A couple more inches and she'd be able to continue packaging, completely obscured from view. Problem solved.*

*She had all but finished when a cry went up from Graham, from the other side of the stage. 'Heavens to Betsy. What on earth's happened here?' He strode to where Lily was hiding. 'Oh, this won't do. This won't do, at all.'*

*Stepping back, she clasped her hands together. What had she done wrong? Were her packages badly presented? Were the bows tied incorrectly? Had she used insufficient glitter?*

*'Darling, the prizes are the stars of the show. Come along.' He gripped one end of the table. 'Work with me. Out here, where everyone can see them, in all their glory.'*

*Lily hesitated. It wouldn't be only the prizes everyone could see, but her too, and Graham's voice had been at such a level it no doubt would have drawn everyone's attention.*

*'Come, come. Curtain up in five.' He tapped his watch.*

*She had no choice, but to take the other end of the table and do as he demanded. Focusing firmly on the task in hand, she moved it towards the middle, way past where it had originally stood then, at the earliest opportunity, scurried back behind the fabric.*

*Graham noticed. 'My, you are a timid creature, aren't you? Look here.' He grabbed her arm and tucked it under his own, pulling her out. 'Nobody's paying attention to you, my love. They're far too busy with their own business to mind what you're doing, pretty though you may be. Look.'*

*She looked up as instructed and, sure enough, everyone was busy greeting friends, chatting and laughing, drinking their drinks and preparing for the bingo to begin. Her shoulders dropped as she relaxed, realising her insignificance to the room.*

*Graham nudged her with his elbow and released her arm. 'You see? It's easy to disappear into the background. It's standing out in the crowd which takes effort.' He rolled his eyes. 'I should know. Right, time to kick things off. Wish me luck, darling.'*

*'Good luck.' A smile spread across her face as she watched him mount the steps onto the stage, ready to address his public. A hush fell across the room, and, stepping back, Lily dared glance out at the many faces, the majority of which were now turned to Graham. He was right. Although she was at the front and felt exposed, no one noticed her. She could study them all one by one and they were completely unaware.*

*Suddenly her eyes locked with a pair staring right back. It would appear someone had noticed her, after all. Someone couldn't seem to tear their gaze away, but then, neither could she, the warmth and intensity drawing her in, until she couldn't bear it any longer, and with a blush she had to look away.*

*So much for avoiding him. Not only had she revealed herself to Adam, he had made it perfectly clear he had seen her too. What wasn't clear was how he felt about her after their last encounter. There had been heat in his gaze, but was it desire? Or disdain?*

*Lily should have escaped while she had the chance, because as soon as the bingo got underway, the noise levels dropped, as concentration reigned, and there was no way she could circumnavigate the hall without interrupting play, at the risk of being lynched. Then, when the first winner exploded out of her seat at the back of the room, Graham instructed the jubilant lady to go and see his 'lovely assistant' Lily, to select her prize. Lily's fate was sealed. She was trapped at the front and had no option but to wait it out.*

*It was a full sixty minutes before there was a lull in proceedings, but even then, Lily was waylaid by Graham, to adjust the depleted prize table to make it look better covered than it actually was. He sorted through what was left.*

*'The second half we're going to have to work harder to hold everyone's attention,' he said. 'They'll have all had a couple more at the bar during the break, and concentration is apt to wander if*

*we're not careful. Next thing you know – bedlam.' He held his hands up, palm out and shook his head.*

*Lily didn't know how to respond, but she needn't have worried.*

*'Here's what I'm suggesting, darling. There are only three more cards in the set, and we've got ample fizz, choccie combo prizes for those, and there's the toiletries and random knick-knacks here for the raffle, but then I've kept back the pieces de resistance.' A wodge of envelopes appeared from his inside pocket. 'A weekend spa break for two, a night in the luxury suite at Ye Olde Grande Hotel, you know the one, down by the park, and a voucher for a full pamper and make over at the boutique on the square. I wouldn't mind that one myself.'*

*'Mmm, lovely,' Lily agreed.*

*'In my opinion, those goodies are far too rich a pot for a raffle at a pound a pop so I'm thinking…' He left a pause to build tension. 'An auction. What do you think?'*

*He obviously found the idea thrilling and Lily couldn't think of any reason to deny him his pleasure. 'It sounds good to me. Perhaps you should just run it past Kiki to be sure there's no reason why we can't do that, but otherwise…'*

*'Marvellous. I'm going to powder my nose and I'll see what young Kiki has to say at the same time.' He pulled a man-bag from under the table and tucked it under his arm. 'As for you, young lady, you're doing a grand job. Take five and I'll see you anon.'*

*Lily watched him leave and decided she should follow suit and visit the bathroom, but whereas Graham crossed the room head held high, meeting and greeting his public as he went, she ducked as low as possible and scampered out, in a desperate bid to avoid a certain handsome man. If she could make it to the loo and back without a confrontation, all her worries for the evening would be over.*

# CHAPTER FORTY

*ALTERNATIVE LILY ARMITAGE - AGED THIRTY*

*Graham was right. The second half of the evening had taken a definitely more raucous turn post break drinks and there were now as many empty glasses littering the tables as there were bingo dabbers and spectacles. Lily was glad to be back in her role of assistant at the prize table, rather than amongst the ribald masses, where she could see Kiki laughing hysterically as she almost slipped off her stool mid-game.*

*When the final card was called, the raffle tickets chosen and all that remained was the auction, she breathed a sigh of relief, considering her work done. There were a couple of spare prizes and, as Graham put on quite a performance talking up the excitement of Ye Grande Olde Hotel, which if she recalled correctly was a rather run-down establishment with a paint-flaked frontage overlooking the bus station, she decided the most useful thing to do was to start packing away.*

*Bids for the prize ricocheted above Lily's head, Graham whipping up quite a frenzy and enjoying every dramatic minute of it. He had borrowed a steak tenderiser from the bar kitchen in lieu of a gavel and was waving it with a flourish as he hollered. 'Going once. Going twice. And sold, to the attractive lady with the red dress and fantastic décolletage. Well done, madam.' It was unclear whether he was congratulating her on the win or on her impressive cleavage. 'Come and claim your prize.'*

*He threw the envelope at Lily who, having not been paying attention, retrieved it from the floor to hand to the flustered lady winner, in exchange for a pile of cash, amid whoops of excitement from her friends.*

*A similar show was put on for the remaining prizes, with each the noise levels increasing and excitement growing almost to fever pitch. The auction idea had certainly gone down exceptionally well and had had an impressive effect on the takings, but Lily was glad the event was now coming to a close, exhausted after her efforts all evening.*

*Graham announced the end of the auction, but the audience wouldn't have it, there had to be more to bid for. Kiki was as vocal as anyone and, before Lily knew what was happening, poor Cosmo had been frogmarched onto the stage like a prize bull, as the next lot for auction. A few sensible men spotted the danger in the situation and made a swift exit, fearing they could be next, but the faces of a number of women in the audience lit up at the prospect of a meal out with this fine specimen of a man.*

*Kiki set the bidding rolling, but when the price increased, she stood down, declaring she could go out with him anytime, so the other ladies were welcome to him in exchange for good, hard cash. Lily continued to tidy, in between checking her watch and yawning.*

*As the hammer came down and a blushing Cosmo was claimed by a little old lady with a fetching blue rinse and obviously a very generous pension, Lily was looking for a suitable place to store the loo brush and stand which, for some reason, hadn't been claimed during the raffle.*

*Caught up in the moment, Graham spotted her and beckoned. 'Ooh, Lily, up here with that, my love.'*

*The sudden attention on her, made her freeze on the spot, but he was not to be ignored. He leaned a hand down to help her up. 'Come on, come on. Up you come.'*

*'Now then, how much will you give me for this fantastic piece of equipment? I mean the brush, of course.'*

*Low level chatter filled the hall as they discussed what the lot actually contained. Graham sensed he was losing them and grabbed Lily by the shoulders.*

*'What I mean is, how much will you give me for an evening with this lovely young lady?*

*'What? No. Wait...'*

*Lily was horrified at the turn of events, but for the life of her, could not make her feet remove her from the stage.*

*'Come, come. There has to be a bid or two for a fine filly such as this.' Graham had passed the point of reason, but he'd misread the crowd, now consisting almost entirely of women.*

*The stretching silence mortified Lily almost as much as being offered up as a lot in the first place. She felt her face flooding redder by the second.*

*Then Adam's voice called out from the rear. 'Five hundred pounds.'*

*A gasp spread across the room at the magnitude of such a sum.*

*'That's more than the spa break!' An unknown figure to the front right was taken aback.*

*'Is she a celeb?' Another whispered loudly.*

*Lily's mouth dropped open. She didn't know how to respond. Her first instinct was to stare at Adam, but after only a few moments Graham gripped her shoulder hard, and she turned towards him.*

*'A popular lot.'*

*Lily didn't much like being referred to as an object, but she didn't have the gumption to complain.*

*'Any advance on five hundred pounds?'*

*An expectant silence reigned, as everyone waited on tenterhooks to see if a bidding war would commence, until a wag in the centre shouted. 'I should bite his hand off in case he changes his mind.'*

*Graham must have seen the sense of the remark, as he immediately slammed down the makeshift gavel and announced. 'Sold to the man with dimples in the corner. Come on, handsome, claim your prize.'*

*Adam meandered to the front and Lily escaped from the glare of centre stage to the footlights. She watched him every step of the way, one ear listening as Graham brought the evening to a close, while the rest of her was completely tuned in to the actions of her purchaser.*

*She didn't know whether to be flattered he'd been prepared to part with such a sum for an evening with her or offended he would see her as a commodity.*

*From midway across the room, he made eye contact with her, as the remaining attendees pulled on coats and gathered belongings, preparing to leave. She wanted to look away, but it was impossible. She was transfixed by him. The confusion about her feelings melted away, as something far more animalistic took over.*

*'Hi.' He halted immediately in front of her.*

*'Hi.' Her lips were dry, and she felt impelled to moisten them.*

*A chair scraped somewhere behind him, and she was suddenly back in the room. 'What were you thinking?' He was so close now he towered over her. 'That's a humungous amount of money.'*

*He shrugged, smiling. It's alright. You don't have to go through with it. I'd decided to donate that amount anyway, but when he put you on the spot like that, I had to step in.'*

*It was an act of pity, or chivalry at best. Her shoulders dropped a little.*

*'Besides, I couldn't take the risk someone else might win you. I never would have forgiven myself for letting the opportunity get away.'*

*Perhaps not pity then. Every cell in her body hollered for her to make use of the get-out clause he had offered, duck out on the date. It wasn't like she had ever agreed to such a thing anyway, but a small voice from goodness knew where inside her somehow made itself heard above the clamour, "go for it", and she listened.*

*'No. That's ok. After all, you've agreed to pay the sum in good faith. It wouldn't feel right to renege on the deal.' She felt this was a way of hedging her bets, make it sound like she wasn't overly keen.*

*The lopsided smile which took over his face suggested he hadn't fallen for it, but he played along. 'That's true. It wouldn't look great for you to back out now.' He coughed to cover a chuckle. 'So, when and where? Sooner rather than later, I think. Tomorrow night?'*

*As soon as that? On second thoughts, so many hours away? But yes, tomorrow would have to do. 'I guess I'll leave the where to you.'*

*'Ok. I'll come up with a plan. Pick you up at seven? If you'll let me have your address.' He handed her his phone to input her details.*

*As she typed, a frown formed on her brow as the circumstances of their previous meeting popped into her mind, and she paused. 'You're sure you want to do this?'*

*The furrow on his brow matched her own as he considered her words. 'I can't think of any reason why I wouldn't.'*

*His adamant response allowed a smile to trickle back onto her face. 'Well, in that case.' She completed her address and handed the phone back. 'Tomorrow at seven.'*

The ombudsman turned to address Lily, only to realise she had vanished from the scene. Removing his headset, he found her sitting on the sofa, gripping the cushions as though afraid she was going to be buckaroo'd off. 'What's up?'

'I've only gone and got me a date with my soulmate.' She slammed a palm to her chest.

'That's a good thing, isn't it?'

'Good? It's colossal! It's fantastic! But is it going to go alright? Will we hit it off? Will we take it to the next level, you know, start a relationship or… I can't believe this. This is just…'

'Hang on, Lily.' She wasn't paying any attention, so he snapped his fingers in front of her face until she focused on him. 'I think you're forgetting one very important factor.'

'What? What have I forgotten?'

'None of this is real.' He shrugged, sorry to burst her bubble. 'It's merely a representation of what might have been, if you'd acted in particular ways throughout your life. It's all made up.'

She took a sharp intake of breath, then slowly slumped back in her seat. 'Yes. Yes, I know that.' Her smile was as fake as the video. 'I guess I got caught up in it, but…' Biting her lips together she thought before continuing. 'Can I still find out what happens next? I mean, it would be good research to find out how I handled the actual date, wouldn't it?'

His eyebrows rose and he bit back a grin. 'Research. Right. You mean you want to know if there was any snogging.'

'What? No!' She tried to feign offence, but knew it was a lost cause. 'Well, yes, a bit. But you can't blame me. I've missed out on so much in real life, it would be nice to know my alternative self at least managed to have some fun.'

The ombudsman rolled his eyes but reached for the headset anyway. 'Everyone's a voyeur. Go on, get yourself goggled up.'

She didn't need telling twice.

# CHAPTER FORTY-ONE

*ALTERNATIVE LILY ARMITAGE - AGED THIRTY*

*Lily had spent the entire night awake, second-guessing Adam's motives for taking her out and debating whether she should risk going or not. The long hours were split between it being a purely charitable act, in supporting the project or saving Lily's face at the auction, and his actually wanting to spend time with her, possibly because he fancied her or, more likely, he wanted to give her a piece of his mind in relation to her comments about her mother. When push came to shove though, she realised that although she'd provided him with her contact details, he hadn't reciprocated, so she had no way of cancelling and she lacked the courage to back out face to face. There was the option of coughing at him on the doorstep, feigning illness, but she wasn't that good an actress. Or simply not answering the door, but she wasn't that rude either. One way or another she had to face up to the reality of going on the date.*

*By the time the doorbell rang, Lily had worked herself into a state of high anxiety and her best hope for the evening was enduring it. She opened the door only wide enough to squeeze out, in an attempt to keep her wayward cat inside, pulling on her jacket as she exited, and avoiding eye contact with Adam. 'Right, let's get this over with.'*

*'Charming!'*

*She marched past him to the car outside her gate and waited for him to unlock. He held up a fob and pressed it, instantly proving she was at the wrong vehicle, and his was further down the road.*

*Harrumphing, she turned and walked the few feet before climbing into the passenger seat, while he traversed the car to the driver's side.*

*He got in and closed the door, fiddling with the keys in his lap. 'We don't have to do this, you know. I did offer to forego if you didn't want to.'*

*She looked out of the side window, unable to meet his gaze. 'No, no. I said I would, so I will. Of course, if you've changed your mind...'*

*Her words hung in the air between them, half statement, half question, while Adam conjured a response. 'Why would I do that?'*

*She shrugged. 'I don't know. All sorts of reasons.'*

*His eyes studied her face, and she felt exposed, but he clearly couldn't read her to his satisfaction. 'Such as?'*

*'I don't know, do I! Who knows what goes through a man's mind? Not me, that's for sure.'*

*Adam sighed. 'Lily, there's obviously something bothering you. For goodness' sake, spit it out so we can get on and enjoy the evening.'*

*Conflicting emotions triggered a wave of chemical reactions within her body, such that it didn't know whether to blush with embarrassment or drain white with the trauma of the situation. 'Honestly, I don't know what...'*

*He was staring right at her and the denial she had intended to muster, died on her lips.*

*She huffed. 'Look, I just don't think you were in your right mind when you bid for me and, if you're regretting it, I wish you'd say so. That's all.'*

*'What? What do you mean?'*

*'Well, alcohol was flowing, and you were surrounded by friends, probably egging you on, but after what I said in the beer garden, I completely understand if you don't want to spend time with me.'*

*A frown had deepened on his brow. 'What are you talking about?'*

*Her eyes widened. Was he really going to make her spell it out? As if it hadn't been shameful enough first time around. 'You know, the thing about ...' She lowered her voice, embarrassed to say it aloud. 'Being better off without my mum?'*

*'What?' His expression suggested he didn't have a clue what she was talking about.*

*'You told me you'd recently lost your mum and then I opened my big gob and said I'd be better off without...' Her words petered out. 'You didn't remember?'*

*He shook his head.*

*'Oh.' She bit her lip, not sure where to go from here. 'But I was so insensitive. You must have thought...'*

*His face was blank.*

*'But you didn't remember, and there was me thinking you'd be thinking I was a right...' She stopped mid-flow again and closed her eyes. 'I am so, so stupid.'*

*With that, Lily got out, fled the car, sprinting all the way back to the comfort of her own house. Unlocking the door, she dived inside and slammed it behind her, naughty Tabitha escaping through it, only missing her tail being caught by a whisker.*

*Lily leaned against the coat stand, tears of humiliation running down her face. Now what? Experience told her if she didn't retrieve the cat immediately it would probably stay out all night, which meant Lily would be awake all night, wondering where it was and imagining it alone, petrified and at the mercy of highway traffic or, worse, the Staffordshire terrier at number fourteen. But there was no way she was re-emerging from her safe place, risking coming face-to-face with Adam again, who must consider her a complete freak by now. He hadn't run after her, she was fairly sure of that, as she hadn't heard his car door open or footsteps behind her, although she had been going like the clappers and her high heels weren't the quietest of footwear. She slipped the shoes off and slumped against the wall.*

*What a dog's dinner she'd made of this evening, and it had shown such promise. She sighed, no it hadn't. It had never shown promise because she hadn't allowed it to. It had been doomed to failure from the moment Adam had bid for her at the auction. No, even before that. It had been doomed from the instant she opened her mouth and garbage came out, but that garbage was the real her, her real self, and therefore the evening had been doomed from the moment her sorry self was born.*

*She spotted her face in the gilt mirror on the wall opposite the bottom of the stairs and glared at it. 'You're a complete waste of space, do you know that?' she yelled at her image.*

*It had the decency to look ashamed.*

*'And so you should,' she retorted.*

*Looking around her house, it felt empty, and she didn't feel the usual sense of well-being from being within its walls. There were some problems even a comfy sofa, squidgy cushions and soft lighting couldn't solve, and this was one of them.*

*The clock in the kitchen clicked loudly as its hands marked the beginning of another hour and Lily realised some considerable time had passed. She was sure Adam would have driven away by now, even if he'd sat and thought about coming after her for a minute or two, though why would he? Sneaking to the window overlooking her front yard, she twitched a curtain and peeked out. She couldn't see his car. Mind you, she wasn't sure she would have been able to from here anyway. She craned her neck and opened the curtain wider. No luck. No sign of the cat either.*

*What was she to do? All she wanted to do was climb into her fluffy pyjamas, down a large glass of Rioja and go to bed, and probably hit the secret supply of chocolate she'd hidden at the back of the bits and bobs drawer. Not that it needed hiding as she was the only person who lived there, but there was always a small chance she'd forget where she'd put it and it would be a nice surprise the next time she had to change a light bulb or put fresh batteries in the doorbell. But even wine and chocolate wouldn't help her relax if she was worrying about the stupid cat. There was nothing for it, she would have to go and find her.*

*With one quick glance over the front yard again, just in case, she approached the door and eased it open a crack so she could see out without anyone seeing her. Except, immediately outside the door was Adam, holding the wayward cat in his arms, a long-suffering half-smile on his face.*

*'Your doorbell needs new batteries,' he said.*

*Lily opened the door wide, as it was clear she'd been busted. 'Does it?' She couldn't face him, instead studying his shoes, butted up against her front step.*

*'As I've been stood here for half an hour wrestling with this little runaway I would say so.'*

*She frowned. 'It hasn't been half an hour.'*

*'No, it probably just feels like it when you've got sharp claws stabbing your shoulder. Do you want him back?'*

*She drew her eyes up from his shoes to the animal and reached out to stroke it under its chin. 'It's a her, not a him.'*

*'Figures.' He handed it over and stood back a step.*

*'Thank you.'*

*Adam shrugged and waited for her to speak further, but, when she didn't, continued. 'I'm going to cancel the restaurant.'*

*'Yes, well...' She didn't know what to say and shook her head rather than finish the sentence.*

*He turned to leave, but paused a couple of steps away, looking back at her. 'Lily, people say stupid things all the time. It doesn't make them bad people; it makes them human. And even if you did mean what you said about your mum, it was a comment based on your life experience, not mine, so it causes me no offence. If anything, it just makes me feel sad for you, that you would feel that way.'*

*'I don't need your pity.' Sympathy made her feel vulnerable rather than supported.*

*'No. I'm sure you don't and that wasn't what I intended.' Putting his hands in his pockets, he kicked at a stone on the path. 'It was more that I had a great relationship with my mum, and I wish everyone could have that in their lives, you included, but I'm aware not everyone does. That's all.'*

*Even with the distance between them she could detect the glisten in his eye as he talked about his mother, and she felt bad for being the source of the reminder of his loss.*

*He walked another step away.*

*'Adam, I'm sorry.'*

*Halting, he turned again to face her. 'You don't need to be sorry.'*

*'Yes, I do. I behaved like an idiot tonight.' She shook her head. 'To be honest, me behaving like an idiot is pretty much par for the course, but tonight was outstanding even for me.' Her shoulders rose and fell in a dramatic shrug. 'I did a stupid thing, said a stupid thing, and felt stupid, and I was too stupid to know how to put it right so I acted completely stupidly. And I'm sorry.'*

*'That's a lot of stupid.' He chuckled.*

*'Tell me about it, but I am sorry and if I could redo the whole thing, I would.'*

*He took a step back towards the house, and her. 'Would you?'*

*She didn't understand. 'Would I what?'*

*'Redo the whole thing because, I mean, we could. Not tonight. There's been more than enough drama for one night, but we could try again, another night?'*

*Lily couldn't believe her ears and, even if the words he said were real, she immediately doubted his sincerity. Why would he want to go out with her after tonight's debacle? 'No, you wouldn't want to...'*

*'I would.' His tone brooked no argument. 'Lily, I don't know if you realise, but I've been wanting to get a date with you since I was eighteen, but something has always got in the way. I'm not about to let a little misunderstanding ruin my chances now, after all this time. Go on, Lily. Say you'll come out with me.'*

*Lily's hand flew to her cheek as she absorbed his words. She absorbed them and believed them. Her mouth opened to reply.*

***

'And that's where we should stop.' The ombudsman removed his headset, leaving Lily watching her other self and Adam on her front doorstep, only a cat and a few centimetres of tension-loaded air between them.

No, he couldn't stop there, her desperation to know what came next would not allow it. She grappled with her headset and found herself back on the sofa. The ombudsman was at the table behind her, pouring a drink.

'Coffee?'

Lily was beside herself. 'No, I don't want coffee. I want to see what happens next. You can't stop there. I need to know.'

He stood up straight, a cup and saucer clutched to his chest. 'Well, you wanted to know how the date went, and there we are. It went. I don't see what else there is to know and, considering your aversion to stressful situations, I would have thought you'd seen quite enough.'

Flinging her arms out, hands palm up, she couldn't believe he wasn't of her opinion. 'But that wasn't the end. There was more to come. Did I accept his offer for another date? Did I chicken out?' Her hands dropped to her lap and her shoulders sagged. 'Did I at least get a little snog out of it?'

His eyebrows raised, he strolled back to his seat at a frustrating speed and rested his cup on the arm of the sofa, sighing deeply. 'No, no snogging. There, that answers your question. Now if you're quite satisfied, I'll give Blessing a buzz and get you heading back. Time's getting on.'

'What? No! I'm absolutely not satisfied. There's so much more I need to know.'

He shrugged. 'Yes, but I think we've got to the point where the benefits of reviewing more of your alternative life are negligible. If what you've seen so far hasn't convinced you of the potential you have to make something of the rest of your life then, to be frank, I don't think anything will.' He took a slurp of his coffee, grimacing at the temperature. 'I've done my best to give you a new outlook. Now it's over to you. I give up.'

'What? No! You can't give up.' Lily's mind was racing. She couldn't let him stop now and had to find the words to make him continue. Standing up, she marched up and down, organising her thoughts. 'I mean, you're so close to changing my mind. I'm so much more positive about the future than I was, but I'm not quite there yet.'

'More positive, you say?' His head tipped to one side as he watched her.

'Definitely.' She repeated the steps, searching for further inspiration. 'To be honest, I think a few more scenes might just do the trick. I can almost see myself ready to go back to my body and start afresh. All it would take would be a little bit more confidence, a little more hope for change.'

The ombudsman's cheeks were sucked in, as if he were trying not to smirk, but his tone was straight. 'You think so?'

'I do, I do. There's definitely a change, subtle, but a change nonetheless.' She sensed she was winning.

'I see. Well, in that case, it would be very remiss of me not to try one last push, wouldn't it?' He picked up the tablet and pressed some buttons, intermittently tapping his lips with his fingertips as he concentrated on what he was reading. 'I think I might have just the thing, if you're sure you won't find it too stressful.'

Her heart fluttered, not knowing what she would be confronted with, but the possibility of witnessing the flourishing of her relationship with Adam was worth it, and she didn't want to jeopardise the opportunity by making the ombudsman aware of her reservations. She spoke through gritted teeth. 'It doesn't matter what it is. If it will help me, I need to see it.'

She reached for her headset and settled it in place, waiting for him to activate the footage. Before he did so, she heard a low guttural chuckle.

'Fair enough,' he said. 'You asked for it.'

# CHAPTER FORTY-TWO

*ALTERNTIVE LILY ARMITAGE - AGED THIRTY*

*She felt rather overdressed for a bus journey in the middle of the day, but Lily was determined to see this through and therefore had needed to get ready hours in advance of her date with Adam. The stop was quite a stretch from the house, but the sun was shining and, provided she took it slow, she should arrive without ruining her feet in the brand-new heels bought for the purpose, and still looking pretty presentable. There was a lot of potential for this to go completely awry, but if Adam was going to be a feature in her life it was imperative that he knew exactly what he was letting himself in for. All she needed was to keep a tight rein on her nerves and it could all come good.*

*The gate squeaked as she swung it inwards, that was new, but everything else was as it had always been, or at least as she remembered it from her childhood. In more recent years, she had kept visits to the absolute minimum. She had enough stress in her life without that, until a couple of weeks ago that was.*

*A couple of weeks ago, she'd had that conversation in the beer garden with Adam, which had wreaked havoc on her life ever since, but the result hadn't just been her aborted date with the man. For a start, her conscience had been mightily pricked. Of course, she felt guilty for saying it in the first place, what with the situation with his own mother, but it also made her think about the state of her relationship with hers. So much so, that on the day of the bingo, she'd travelled across town and paid a long overdue visit. In doing so, she'd misjudged the timing of the journey back and hence arrived late at the bingo, but it had been worth it. Having found Marion in a somewhat subdued and calm state, she and her mother had talked, in a way they never had before. A certain amount of air had been cleared. Of course, today could be a completely different kettle of fish – a calm, subdued mother one day, could be a frantic, frankly mad one the next, and that was something Lily had never got to grips with.*

*The front door was flung open before she reached it, probably due to having informed Marion she would be visiting, and the time of the bus service.*

*'Oh, my darling, you look amazing.' Marion took Lily's hands and moved in to kiss both cheeks then stood back, still holding on, now at arm's length, and took in her appearance. 'That dress is adorable on you. I always told you you could look fantastic if only you made the effort.'*

*Lily smiled; confident Marion was unaware of the veiled insult her words conveyed. 'You did indeed, Mum.'*

*'Right, well, don't just stand there providing eye-candy for the busybodies at their windows, come along inside.' At the same time, Marion craned her neck to see if anyone was actually looking, her voice raised to draw attention if it didn't already exist.*

*Lily was ushered inside with a great deal of bluster and found a small table laid with tea things and what looked suspiciously like a cake hidden under a tea-towel. Clearly, she was guest of honour today, whereas on another occasion she was as likely to be greeted by piles of washing or dishes or overflowing rubbish bins. 'This looks nice.'*

*Her mother clasped her hands together in front of her in delight. 'Nice is such an overused expression, don't you think?'*

*'I suppose so.' Lily bit her tongue. 'This looks marvellous, then. What's under the cloth?'*

*'All in good time. Let me put the kettle on.' Marion rushed away to the kitchen.*

*Lily studied the layout of the chairs, wondering if there was a plan of who should sit where, which had been an issue in the past. 'Where are you sitting, Mum?'*

*Marion's head briefly appeared round the door, and she waved a hand, as if it was a silly question. 'It doesn't matter. Go wherever you like, darling.'*

*It was never that simple on planet Marion and Lily laid a palm on the seat cushions to see which was warmer and most recently occupied. The left was cool, and she settled into it.*

*Her phone buzzed and, when she checked, it was a message from Adam. "Is the plan still as was for tonight? Just wanted to check before setting out."*

*Thank goodness for that. For a moment she thought he was backing out. She quickly typed back. "Still the same. See you soon."*

*Her mother walked in. 'Tsk, tsk. No phones at the tea-table. It ruins conversation.'*

*She slipped it into her handbag and sat back, as her mother arranged a teapot in the centre of the table. Marion picked up a corner of the tea-towel and checked to ensure Lily was watching, then whipped it away with a flourish. 'Ta-dah!'*

*Underneath was a beautiful cake, with a voluptuous topping of swirled buttercream icing, finished off with a wealth of hundreds and thousands.*

*'Wow! Mum, that's ...' She searched for an adjective which could describe the cake and, at the same time, be impressive enough to please her mother. 'What can I say? I'm speechless.'*

*Apparently, that was enough, as Marion's face beamed with delight. 'It is, isn't it? Let me cut you a slice.'*

*'Only a small one, please. I'm going out to dinner this evening and I don't want to ruin my appetite.'*

*Marion dropped the knife. 'I thought you were having tea with me?'*

*'Yes, I am. I'm not rushing off, the table's not booked until seven.' Lily's heart dropped. She recognised the change in her mother's tone, and it wasn't good.*

*'But it's four o'clock now and, if you've got to be home for seven, you'll have to catch the bus again before five. It's hardly worth coming for.' She threw herself back into the armchair.*

*Lily was ready for that. 'Well, that's ok, because I'm not catching the bus back. I'm being picked up here.'*

*Marion grabbed the arms of the chair and sat forward. 'Picked up? Here? By whom?'*

*'He's called Adam.'*

*Before she knew what was happening, Lily was grabbed in a tight embrace, and her mother showed no signs of letting go.*

*Lily muttered into Marion's shoulder. 'What's that all about?'*

*Marion released her and sat down, dabbing a handkerchief at her eyes. 'You've never introduced me to one of your young men before. I'm so… so… happy.'*

*'You met Darren.'*

*'Oh, yes. Darren.' Marion waved a hand as if his existence was irrelevant, which he probably had been to her, Lily mused, as he had maintained a wide berth, only enduring meetings with her when he absolutely had to. 'But tell me about Adam. How long have you been walking out?'*

*Lily smiled at the old-fashioned wording. 'We haven't. This is our first date actually, though I met him years and years ago.'*

*Her mother clasped her hands together in front of her chest, casting her eyes skyward. 'Oh, friends who become lovers. The best kind.'*

*'Hold your horses.' Lily tried to rein her mother's excitement within reasonable grounds. 'We're not anything yet. First date, remember?'*

*'But you will be, I can see it in your eyes. They're sparkling.' Marion winked. 'Anyway, tell me all about him, and don't hold anything back. I want to know every last detail.'*

*As the afternoon wore on, Marion's excitement grew, as did Lily's nerves. An excited Marion was a dangerous one, her mood could change in an instant, but when, finally, a knock came at the door, there was a lull in the chatter, and all fell quiet.*

*Lily looked to Marion. Would it be a lavish show of welcome, fit for royalty, or would first impressions lead her to reject him out of hand? But her mother surprised her in a whole new way.*

*Marion sat forward in her seat, back straight, hands clasped in her lap and closed her eyes, breathing slowly and deeply.*

*Lily observed, suspicious. This was new behaviour.*

*When Marion opened her eyes, she saw Lily watching and a faint dusting of colour reached her cheeks. 'A new technique,' she explained. 'Highly recommended by Hugh at the support group.' She rose to her feet and repeated the deep breathing routine, then glanced over her shoulder at Lily, on her way to the door, taking in her daughter's shocked expression. 'You only get one chance to make a first impression, you know.'*

*If Lily hadn't been caught up with the pressure of the present situation, she would have had a thousand questions, about this support group that she'd never heard of, and about Hugh, who would appear to hold some credence in her mother's opinion. Either way, the fact Marion was even trying to control her reactions was a whole new development, which surely could only be a good thing. Even so, Adam meeting Marion would be enough for today, so she gathered her belongings, ready to join them on the doorstep and head out immediately. She arrived just in time to see the door open and a rather hesitant Adam, shuffling foot to foot outside.*

Marion was at her most gracious. 'Good afternoon, young man. You must be Adam. I've heard a lot about you. Come in, come in.'

'Oh, no. Sorry, mum. There isn't time tonight. We need to get to the restaurant.' Lily attempted to head her off at the pass.

'What? Really, but I was so looking forward to getting to know Adam a little better.'

The potential was there for a massive blow up. Lily should have prepared Marion's expectations better. 'Sorry, but another time.' She was ready to usher him speedily away so he wouldn't have to experience one of her mother's outbursts.

Marion physically bit her lips together to prevent whatever wanted to come out from coming out, before finally releasing them. 'Ok. Well, very nice to meet you, Adam. Another time perhaps.'

Adam glanced from Lily to Marion, then at his watch. 'I think we can spare five minutes, if that's ok with you, Lily?'

Lily met his gaze as a wave of horror washed through her, but he winked and followed an ecstatic Marion into the lounge. Lily hovered by the front door, part of her considering running away rather than face the possibilities this interaction could produce, but the other part held firm. Whatever the outcome, if Adam was to become a feature in her life, he had to know the full truth of what he was dealing with. Better sooner than later when she had become too attached to him. She closed the door, followed her mother's example and took a deep steadying breath and followed them into the lounge.

Against all hope, the five minutes passed without incident and Lily was relieved when Adam tapped his watch and said, 'We'd better make a move.'

Without hesitation Marion rose to her feet and led them to the door. There were no remonstrations, no delaying tactics. She merely took his hand for a moment and smiled. 'Adam, it was truly lovely to meet you. Please do come again.'

*The couple walked away and, as they neared the gate, Adam leaned close to Lily. 'You see? Putty in my hands.'*

*Before Lily could reply, Marion called from inside. 'Oh, Lily, could I have one moment more, please?'*

*Lily and Adam looked at each other and grimaced. Then Lily turned to go back, as instructed. When Lily reached her mother, Marion stared pointedly at Adam.*

*He held up a hand to wave goodbye. 'I'll see you at the car, Lily.'*

*'Ok.' Moment of truth. Clearly, Marion had something to say which she didn't want Adam to witness. 'Yes, Mum?'*

*Marion paused to ensure Adam was out of earshot. 'I like him.' She took Lily's face between both hands and gazed into her eyes. 'I really like him.'*

*'Oh, well, that's good. I quite like him myself.'*

*'And what's more, I know someone else who would like him too.'*

*Lily was confused. 'You do?'*

*'Yes, Ray would love him.'*

*'He would?' Lily was taken aback to hear her mother mention her stepfather's name, it having been taboo since their split.*

*'He would, and it wouldn't do any harm for you to get in touch with him, if you wanted to.' Marion was no longer able to maintain eye contact, instead looking out over the front yard.*

*'Wouldn't it?'*

*'No, it wouldn't.' Marion huffed. 'Hugh says we should let bygones be bygones. Holding on to hurts of the past is no good for anyone. And when all's said and done, he was a good father to you. Better than... Anyway, never mind.'*

*Lily's real father was never mentioned, ever, but now was not the time to pursue the matter. Her mother was compromising enough by suggesting she get back in touch with Ray. 'Are you sure?'*

*Marion shrugged and nodded, grunting a confirmation. 'Go and have a good time with that man of yours.'*

*Demonstrations of affection were rare between them, but Lily felt the urge to kiss her mother's cheek, which she did before turning away. Marion made no objection.*

*In the car, Adam was waiting, the engine running. 'Let's go. I hope she wasn't forbidding you from seeing me again.'*

*'No. She likes you.' Lily pulled the seatbelt around her and slotted it in place. 'Don't get smug though. Next time she might be throwing plates at you.'*

*'Aah.' He pulled into traffic. 'She must come from Brandon's school of anger management. They'd make a right pair. Anyway, let's get to the restaurant before I eat my own arm.'*

*Lily smiled. Perhaps Adam would be up to handling her mother, after all.*

# CHAPTER FORTY-THREE

Lily and the Ombudsman had been observing other Lily and Adam's progress to the restaurant from the vantage point of the back seat of the car. When a strange figure appeared in the path of the car, they both recoiled in their seats, Lily covering her eyes to avoid witnessing the collision, but the impact never happened, and the figure remained static yet somehow constantly ahead of the vehicle.

'I am sorry to interrupt, but it's time to be moving out and Grace'll have my guts for garters if I don't get Lily down to the transfer room sharpish.' It was Blessing, who disappeared as swiftly as she'd appeared, on removing her headset.

Lily turned to the Ombudsman in panic. 'But I haven't seen enough. I want to see what happens between Adam and me next. It's too soon,' she pleaded.

The Ombudsman's face softened as he studied her. 'And I would love to show you, but when Grace says jump, believe me, even I jump.'

She made to argue, but he held up his hand. 'No, Lily. You've seen a great deal. You've seen your potential and anything else we would see is all imagined anyway, not real. It's time to go. Come on.' He whipped off his own headgear, leaving Lily alone in the back of the car.

Taking one last longing look at the pair in the front, Lily sighed deeply, lifted her hand to her head and flipped back to reality. The ombudsman was packing equipment back into boxes, while Blessing hovered by the door, shuffling her feet as she waited.

Knowing the ombudsman would offer no further extension of privileges, Lily applied to Blessing. ‘Blessing, I really neeeed to see a bit more.’ She stretched the vowels to express the importance of her request.

‘It’s not down to me, babe. I just do as I’m told.’ Blessing shrugged. ‘But I do know Grace wouldn’t say it was urgent unless it was. You could miss your chance if you don’t step to it, and that would be a shame.’

The ombudsman stood up and rolled his shoulder muscles, releasing the tension. ‘Yes, it would.’ He met Lily’s gaze head on. ‘Lily, you’ve come such a long way. You’ve seen what your life could be like if you put in the effort, surely you want to go and live it now, rather than simply observing from a distance. Don’t you want a taste of what you know could be?’

‘I do.’ She rubbed the creases on her brow. ‘But I’m also scared.’

The ombudsman rolled his eyes. ‘Of course you are. When have you ever been anything else?’ He tapped his chin with a finger before continuing. ‘But surely now you’ve learned it’s ok to be scared. You just have to push that aside and carry on regardless. The benefits could be enormous. Think of your mum. Think of Kiki and Harriett.’ He lowered his voice. ‘Think of Adam. You could go back and start where you left off. He’s only a few doors away.’

Lily breathed in and out slowly, staring at the carpet, then gradually drew her eyes up to look at her guide. ‘I could, couldn’t I?’

‘I don’t doubt it for a moment.’ A look of pride lodged on the ombudsman’s face. ‘Go on. Go get him.’

She pushed her shoulders back, her neck straight, head aloft. 'Right then, Blessing. Show me the way.'

Blessing winked at the ombudsman. 'Thank the Lord for that. Come on then, babe. Let's do it.'

They both tumbled into the corridor, Blessing setting off at a trot towards double doors at the end.

As they approached the exit the ombudsman's voice called them to a halt. 'By the way, Lily.'

She turned to see what he had to say.

'She's been divorced three times, has a delinquent son and cleans toilets in a working men's club.'

'Sorry?' Lily was confused.

'Marie blinking Wilkie. I thought you'd like to know.' He winked. 'Good luck, Lily. Go get 'em.'

Lily grinned, held a valiant fist aloft, then followed Blessing to her fate.

Grace was pacing with ill-disguised impatience, as Blessing and Lily approached. She tapped her watch. 'There's cutting it fine and there's cutting it fine. There are schedules to be maintained, you know?'

'Sorry, Grace, they were still right in the middle of it. They'd still be there now if I hadn't taken decisive actions.' Despite her words, Blessing was not apologetic in tone or stance.

'Oh, well, no use crying over spilt milk.' The prim middle-aged woman patted Lily's shoulder, then continued to apply pressure to guide her into a room, leaving Blessing to go about her business. 'Let's get this cabaret on the road.'

Lily's courage was already fading, but she gritted her teeth and followed Grace's lead. 'I really do have to do this, don't I?' It was more statement than question.

'You sure do, honey. Sooner the better or, to be frank, we could be too late.'

‘Too late?’ Lily allowed herself to be pushed onto a medical bed, as Grace bustled around, attaching straps and monitoring leads to various parts of Lily’s body. ‘I thought this was all straightforward, that I had no choice but go back, and this was how it had to be done.’

‘Thirty minutes ago, it was all straightforward. Now, not so much.’ Grace was focused on what she was doing, the conversation secondary to her actions.

‘What…’ Lily was struggling to concentrate as she submitted to Grace’s ministrations. ‘What… What do you mean, not so much?’

Grace walked to a computer, set up on the other side of the room, but continued to talk, her back to Lily. ‘What with all this dilly dallying, we’re at the point now where your body is on the cusp, as it were. It could go either way, or rather, you could go either way.’

‘What do you mean? I don’t know if I want to do this anymore.’ She struggled against her restraints, finally drawing Grace’s full attention.

Grace returned to the bed and leaned over Lily’s prone form. ‘Now then. There’s no point getting all hot under the collar, there’s not a thing we can do about it, but you must understand, a body can’t be lying in the street for an indefinite amount of time. Things happen, events take place, people at the scene step up and do what they feel is necessary and that can mean the body is no longer receptive to being reoccupied.’

‘And is my body no longer receptive?’ Lily’s voice was timid as she took it all in.

‘There’s no hundred per cent way of knowing. In all honesty, if it wasn’t for a three-car pile-up on the ring road, a lorry jack-knifed on the dual carriageway and that young missy at number forty-three going into labour ahead of schedule, you would have missed the window of opportunity by a country mile. It’s a good job that little boy was determined to make an entrance whether the world was ready for him or not. When I said time was of the essence, I meant time was of the essence. We can't ever take these things for granted.'

Lily felt her chest tighten as her breathing increased. 'But if my body doesn't want me back, where do I go?'

Grace frowned. 'That's not for me to say…' She rechecked Lily's binds. 'But you sure as squat can't stay here, and the longer we hold back the worse the chances. Now, are you ready?'

Lily's mind flooded with images of Adam and Kiki and Harriett, and poor Tabitha, somewhere out in the wide world at the mercies of the New Year celebrations. She dug deep for the last bit of determination she had. 'Yes. Do it.' She bit her lips together before they could retract the instruction.

Grace winked. 'Good for you, honey.' She marched across the room and put a determined finger to a button. 'You go and have the best life you can, child.'

Everything melted from around Lily, and she felt her body sucked into a vortex of speed, warmth and rushing wind, then everything disappeared.

# CHAPTER FORTY-FOUR

Lily had no clue where she was. It was dark, pitch black in fact, and she was cold, to the point she couldn't tell if it was as a result of the frigid atmosphere seeping into her body or if it was ice in her bones leaking into the air. There was an acrid taste in her mouth, like sulphurous smoke, and it made the breath catch in her throat and there was noise, distant bangs, crashes and whistles and, nearer to her, footsteps and shouting. Nearer still, if she concentrated really hard, there were soft, enquiring voices.

'I think she might be coming round. Bob, did her eyelids move?'

Another voice. 'Don't know.' Slightly less distinct, as if whoever was speaking was facing away. 'Hey, lads, can we get some light in here. Anytime today, Chipper, come on, stop fannying around.'

The darkness faded to light grey and Lily flinched at the sudden change.

'Yeah, there's definitely something going on.' Louder. 'Alright, Lily. Can you open your eyes for us?'

Oh! Her eyes were closed. In the excitement of arriving somewhere, wherever it was, she hadn't given that a thought. It took a moment to remember how to open them, a mechanical action, rather than the usual autonomic response. Light flooded in and she turned her face away, squinting to avoid the full intensity of the rays.

'Chipper, back it up a bit, mate. You're blinding the lass. That's better. Lily, can you see me.'

It took a while to get accustomed to the brightness and then focus on what was in her line of sight. Either side of her head were two rather rugged firemen, leaning over her, complete with square jaws and five o'clock shadow and, beyond that, another two were kneeling either side of her torso.

She gulped. 'I am in heaven, after all.'

The voice attached to the person referred to as Bob, drew closer. 'What did she say?'

'I didn't catch it, but she seems to be regaining consciousness. Get someone she knows in here. Maybe she'll respond to them.'

The four manly faces withdrew and, after a brief hiatus, was replaced by flirty Flick from number eighteen, made-up to the hilt and with more skin exposed than was appropriate for the climate. The taste of smoke was replaced by one of Chanel number five.

'Lily? Lily, it's me, Felicity. Speak to me, Lily.'

Definitely not heaven then. Lily tried to move, but pain shot from the centre of her forehead, through her skull, and she groaned, falling back onto the hard ground. A fireman reappeared, on the opposite side from Felicity, his eyes taking in Lily's discomfort, before being distracted by Felicity's cleavage.

'I don't really like the look of her.'

'No, there's not many can carry off plaid pyjamas, especially not at her age, bless her.' Felicity agreed.

He temporarily pulled himself away from the view, to call over his shoulder. 'Any update on the paramedics?' There was a pause as he listened to an indistinct response. 'Ok, let's have a foil blanket. We can at least keep her warm while we're waiting.' He turned back to Felicity. 'Something tells me you're freezing too. Come with me and I'll find something to wrap around you.'

‘Ooh, how observant of you.’ Felicity breathed an earthy chuckle as she struggled to her feet. ‘My hero. Thank you so much… but should we be leaving…’ She waved a hand over Lily’s prone body.

The fireman looked back and frowned. ‘You’re right. Chipper, get that blanket around the patient and sit with her, while I look after this young lady. We don’t want another casualty, do we?’

Felicity giggled, presumably in response to being described as a young lady.

The couple disappeared, replaced by another pair of hands, struggling to spread the foil sheet and tuck it around Lily’s frame, the wind tugging at the edges.

‘Let me help.’ This was a voice Lily recognised, a calm, steady, comforting voice, which sent shivers down her spine that had nothing to do with the cold.

She opened her eyes and, sure enough, it was Adam, gently slipping the fabric around her neck and under her shoulder.

As he saw her looking at him, his face, pale against the night sky, was transformed by a smile. ‘Hello, you. How are you doing?’

She blinked twice as she conjured words to reply. ‘My head hurts.’

Reaching across, he gently pushed her fringe away from her forehead, revealing an ugly bruise beneath. ‘I bet it does, but help will be here in a minute. They’ll give you something for the pain.’ Adam turned to the firefighter. ‘Any idea how much longer?’

‘They were supposed to be two minutes away. I don’t know what’s taking so long. I guess New Year’s Eve is a busy night for them too.’

Lily was confused. Memories of Limbo were so fresh in her mind, it was the here and now which seemed surreal. ‘A pile-up on the ring-road,’ she whispered.

Adam leaned in to catch her words. ‘She says there’s a pile-up on the ring-road.’

Chipper shrugged. ‘Not that I’ve heard. Hey, Skipper, what’s this about an accident on the ring-road?’

‘Yeah, proper mess, by all accounts. Three cars, so I hear. Green Watch, from the south side, are dealing with that one.’

‘I wonder how she knew about that.’ Adam was studying her face.

‘Must have been on the news.’ Chipper muttered, then shouted across Lily’s body. ‘South side? On the ring-road? That’s our patch. Shouldn’t that have been one of ours?’ His tone suggested he would rather be dealing with a major incident like a road traffic accident than sitting around, waiting for the medical crew.

It took all her strength to muster a murmur. ‘A lorry jack-knifed on the dual carriageway.’

‘An HGV jack-knifed blocking the dual carriageway. It was quicker for south side to get there.’ The skipper yelled back, unaware Lily was ahead of him.

‘That must have been some news report.’ Adam looked at Chipper, eyebrows raised.

‘Social media more like. Half the town knows you’ve farted before you realise yourself these days.’ Chipper struggled to his feet and looked around. ‘It’s a blooming long two minutes. I’ll see if I can find out what’s going on.’

‘A lady at number forty-three has gone into labour.’ Every time she spoke, Lily’s energy levels drained, and her recent memories faded further away.

‘Blimey. That’s impressive, even for social media.’ He continued toward the fire engine and the rest of his crew, leaving Lily alone with Adam.

‘I thought you didn’t do social media.’ He wrapped his arm around her, holding the blanket close to her body. ‘Hey, are you alright? You’re not too cold?’

‘No. I’m alright.’

He withdrew his arm and her body immediately missed it and craved its return, and not merely due to the warmth.

‘No. Leave it. Stay.’ She grasped his arm through the fabric.

A smile softened his face. ‘I’m not going anywhere.’

Regardless she held on to his arm.

‘It seems it’s all happening tonight.’ He settled down, to a more comfortable position next to her. ‘Car crashes, lorries going over, babies being born… you…’ He waved at her head. ‘That.’

‘You don’t know the half of it.’ She sighed, and snuggled closer to him, the bulging bicep she had patted hours earlier surprisingly soft against her cheek.

‘You know, this wouldn’t have happened if you’d come out with me tonight.’ He brushed her hair away from the bruise on her forehead.

‘What? There were no Catherine Wheels at the party?’ Her voice was slow and drowsy. ‘That’s shocking. Who would want to go to a firework party with no Catherine Wheels?’

‘There were plenty of fireworks, and food, and hot chocolate and good company. I could have kept you safe.’

‘And flirty Flick.’

‘Who?’ He looked confused, but then the penny seemed to drop. ‘Ah, yes, well. You see? You could have kept me safe too.’

‘You can look after yourself.’

‘Yeah, but I’d rather somebody else did it for me.’ He conceded with a shrug. ‘Hey, can we make a pact? From now on, I’ll protect you from flying missiles and you protect me from predatory women?’

She chuckled, carefully avoiding moving her head. ‘And how am I supposed to do that?’

‘There are two options, either you could stand beside me with a deadly weapon, ready to ward off aggressors or…’ He paused, maybe gathering up courage. ‘Or you could just lay claim to me and say you’re my girlfriend. That ought to do it.’

‘Girlfriend? I’m thirty-six, you know. Isn’t that a bit old to be somebody’s girlfriend?’

His eyes were only inches away from her own. ‘Girlfriend? Woman friend? Partner? Lover? Take your pick. All job titles are up for grabs…if you’ll take them.’

As her heart beat faster, the bruise on her head throbbed harder, but somehow it didn’t matter. She had returned to her body determined to live a different life, a fuller life, a braver life, and, although her natural instinct was to push him away, this was the first step on the new road, a journey she so longed to be on. ‘That’s a pretty broad range. I might have to think about it.’

‘That’s a start, I suppose.’ A small frown creased his brow, but he made no move to pull away.

Lily recognised the uncertainty on his face, and it softened her heart further. She’d spent too many years unsure of where she stood with people, afraid of saying the wrong thing, doing the wrong thing, being rejected, she didn’t want to make him feel that way. She smiled the widest smile she could manage. ‘I think I could be persuaded. I mean, what’s the benefit package like…?’

Before she could finish the sentence, he closed the gap between them and pressed gentle lips to her own, so whatever she’d been going to say evaporated from her mind in the heat.

A flurry of activity made them draw apart and, when she opened her eyes, she saw the paramedics had arrived, forcing Adam to step away. She allowed them to do what they needed to do, answering their questions, putting on dressings and manhandling her on to a stretcher, but one eye was always on the man waiting patiently on the side-lines.

As they wheeled her away, she grabbed the sleeve of the medic nearest her arm to stall him, calling out. ‘Adam? Are you coming with me?’

He stepped forward. ‘Am I allowed?’

The medic shrugged. ‘There’s room for one more if that’s what the patient wants.’

‘Is that what you want?’ Adam waited for Lily to say it aloud.

‘Yes, please.’

'Right then, I'd better just make a quick call. I said I'd ring my brother at midnight. He'll be worried.'

The paramedic moved off. 'No worries. We need to do paperwork before we go anywhere. We'll be in the back, in the warm. Come along when you're ready.'

Lily turned her head as she was whisked away. 'Oh, Adam. Say "hi" to Brandon from me.'

'I will.' The words had left his lips before it occurred to him to wonder how she knew about his brother. He stared after her, listening to the conversation taking place between Lily and her carers.

'So, how's the pregnant lady on the corner?'

The medic chatted away as he went about his business. 'Fine as far as I know. We left her with another crew so we could come here. I'll check in when we get to the hospital maybe and see if there's any news. You never know, he or she may be the first baby of the New Year.'

The excitement in the man's voice cheered her further. What with crashes and firework accidents and, no doubt, the fallout from New Years' parties, it was nice that what was at the forefront of his mind was the good news of the evening. She smiled. 'Oh, it's a boy.'

'Is that right?' He tipped his head. 'Huh. A boy. Well, that's lovely.'

With Lily safely tucked into the stretcher in the ambulance, the man pulled the door closed.

On the outside, Adam stared at the rear of the vehicle, his phone in his hand, muttering under his breath. 'How on earth does she know this stuff?' He shook the confusion away, put the phone to his ear and waited for his little brother to pick up.

On thc inside, Lily hugged the warmth of the blanket around her as the medication she had been given began to kick in and she realised the New Year had already begun, but for her it wasn't just the turn of a page in a diary, it was the start of a whole new book.

# ABOUT THE AUTHOR

## Sharon Francis

**Born and bred in beautiful North Devon, Sharon is married with two grown up children. She studied creative writing with the Open University, completing her BA in 2017. Her debut novel, Girl Plans, God Laughs, first in the Limbo series, was released in 2020. What Might Have Been is the second in the series.**

**For more information about Sharon, or her books, go to:-**

**Facebook.com/Sharon-Francis-Author-110933057304441/**

**OR**

**www.foursirenspress.co.uk/authors/sharon-francis**

# KEEP UP TO DATE

**If you have enjoyed this book, please remember to leave a review on Amazon, so other readers can have the benefit of your thoughts.**

**You could be the first to know when Sharon's next novel is available to purchase and receive free additional content by signing up for the Four Sirens Press newsletter at -**

**www.foursirenspress.co.uk**

# ACKNOWLEDGEMENT

For years I dreamt of writing a book, but that dream consisted of coming up with a novel idea, creating colourful characters, settings and motivations and putting them all together to create something others would want to read. It turns out that's only the beginning.

The last two years, first in bringing Girl Plans, God Laughs to print and now with What Might Have Been, have been a learning curve. Thankfully, I've had Denise Smith, Sue Hughes and Beverley Carter travelling alongside me up that incline and down the other side. The finished result also relied heavily on the professional editing of Jess Lawrence and the fantastic artwork of Megan Saunders.

Family and friends are the bedrock of everything so thanks to David, Shaun and Beth for keeping me going, and Clare and Christine in particular for their support.

And finally, thanks to all my lovely readers for their messages and encouragement.

Printed in Great Britain
by Amazon

69328544R00170